BOUNTY OF GREED:
THE LINCOLN COUNTY WAR

OTHER FIVE STAR TITLES BY PAUL COLT

Bounty of Greed: The Lincoln County War

Paul Colt

FIVE STAR

A part of Gale, a Cengage Company

Farmington Hills, Mich • San Francisco • New York • Waterville, Maine
Meriden, Conn • Mason, Ohio • Chicago

LIBRARY OF CONGRESS CATALOGING-IN-PUBLICATION DATA

Names: Colt, Paul, author.
Title: Bounty of greed : the Lincoln County war / Paul Colt.
Description: First edition. | Waterville, Maine : Five Star Publishing, a part of Cengage Learning, Inc., [2017] | Description based on print version record and CIP data provided by publisher; resource not viewed.
Identifiers: LCCN 2017007826 (print) | LCCN 2017012658 (ebook) | ISBN 9781432834463 (ebook) | ISBN 1432834460 (ebook) | ISBN 9781432834432 (ebook) | ISBN 1432834436 (ebook) | ISBN 9781432834494 (hardcover) | ISBN 1432834495 (hardcover)
Subjects: | GSAFD: Western stories.
Classification: LCC PS3603.O4673 (ebook) | LCC PS3603.O4673 B67 2017 (print) | DDC 813/.6—dc23
LC record available at https://lccn.loc.gov/2017007826

First Edition. First Printing: July 2017
Find us on Facebook– https://www.facebook.com/FiveStarCengage
Visit our website– http://www.gale.cengage.com/fivestar/
Contact Five Star™ Publishing at FiveStar@cengage.com

Printed in the United States of America
1 2 3 4 5 6 7 21 20 19 18 17

For Dusty

How do you thank someone who made a writer out of a
storyteller? It's a gift bigger than mere words. Dusty
Richards didn't know me from a western writer wannabe
when I finished my first book and contacted him to see if
he had any words of wisdom for an aspiring author. He
asked to read a chapter. "Not ready for prime time," he
said. Dusty critiqued the pages I sent him and told me to
rewrite them. Rewrite them we did, for nearly a year
before the craft of writing entered my head. How do you
thank a man who has become mentor and friend? Dusty
once told me, "There are more western stories than
blades of grass." With his help, I've managed to find a few.
Here's one for you, Pard.

PROLOGUE

Las Vegas, New Mexico
February 14, 2011

Retired police detective Rick Ledger rocked back in his desk chair. Cold gray light filtered through the curtains to his home office from the small pool deck in the backyard. He gazed at the antique tintype in the filigree frame atop his desk. A tall rugged cowboy with a dark rough shave stared back at him. Great-great-grandpa Ty had a story all his own. He was a rancher and deputy US marshal in Lincoln County New Mexico in the 1880s. He was there when they fought the Lincoln County War. He told that story to Rick's Grandpa Brock. Grandpa Brock passed it along to Rick along with a journal kept by Great-great-grandma Lucy. Between that and the history books, Rick grew a boyhood fascination with the exploits of Billy the Kid into a lifelong pursuit of untold facets of the story.

He was often surprised by the intense controversy stirred by events that happened over a hundred and thirty years ago. History, he concluded, affords a cloudy perspective through which we view the past. Legends are fashioned by people. History, it seems, is sometimes written by the devious or uninformed; folks who have an ax to grind and a pen to sharpen it on. Nonetheless, some of it becomes history. When it does, it is accorded the stature of truth, not to be questioned even in the face of uncertainty or contradictory evidence. Rick had seen this during his career as a police officer. Sometimes the law got it wrong.

7

Sometimes Lady Justice could truly be blind. He took the controversy in stride. He felt no need to defend his work. He did wonder what Great-great-grandpa Ty would have thought. He hoped he would have approved. Most likely, though, he'd have been surprised that anyone cared after all these years.

Rick picked up the cracked leather-bound journal he'd found in an old trunk in Grandpa Brock's attic the week after he passed away. Great-great-grandma Lucy set down in her own hand a personal side to the story the writers of history never quite seem to capture. He opened the old volume to the marker he'd left the last time. She'd told the story of how she'd come to Lincoln County in New Mexico Territory. She'd become acquainted with a brash young Englishman with pockets full of money, a soul full of ambition and a head full of big ideas. Stir that into the politics and set way of doing things in Lincoln County, New Mexico, at the time and what you got was a bountiful harvest of greed. All that greed, scrapping over the spoils afforded by Lincoln County in those days and you had a recipe for violence. And not just ordinary violence, you had the makings of a war. It all started shortly before Great-great-grandma Lucy arrived in Lincoln . . .

CHAPTER ONE

Santa Fe
July 1877

A man had to enjoy a good steak. The potatoes were fried crisp in drippings. The wine was decent. The Hotel Santa Fe dining room provided a tasteful setting. He folded the white napkin and eased his chair back from the table. You had to enjoy a meal like that, but eating alone left time to ponder a man's troubles. By rights, Alexander McSween shouldn't have had many. A lawyer with the reputation of an aggressive advocate, McSween specialized in other people's problems. He had a beautiful wife and an established frontier practice in Lincoln. In truth, Lincoln was the problem. It was the county seat and that promised a bright future for an ambitious lawyer when he arrived, but it was also a one-client town.

The onetime partnership of Lawrence Murphy and James "Jimmy" Dolan controlled most of the commercial interests in Lincoln. Murphy's failing health resulted in Dolan buying him out the past spring, but that hadn't changed anything. The House, as its substantial mercantile establishment was known, controlled everything in Lincoln County. If he didn't work for Dolan, all that remained to his practice were small land dealings. He'd gotten on fine with Murphy. Recently, relations with Dolan had become strained over the matter of an insurance claim that hadn't settled to Dolan's satisfaction. Nor should it have. Dolan had no direct interest in the proceeds. The claim

9

had been made for the estate of a local rancher. Dolan's interest arose from his assertion of an unpaid debt levied against the estate. He sought to hold McSween accountable for not settling the debt out of the insurance proceeds. The matter was further complicated by the fact that the deceased's rightful heir had abandoned the ranch holdings and left the county, leaving the estate unsettled. The rightful disposition of all of that would be up to a court. The insurance dispute exposed Dolan's real problem.

He and Murphy were smart businessmen to a point. They reasoned rightly that selling to local landholders and businesses on credit would give them economic and political power. What they hadn't reckoned was the amount of cash it took to sustain such an enterprise. McSween had a way to solve that problem, but he couldn't see wasting it on the arrogant likes of Jimmy Dolan. He hated the thought of pulling up stakes, but unless something changed for the better, things would likely come to that.

He rose from the table. Not quite six feet tall, he wore a dark frock coat with matching trousers. An unruly shock of brown hair fell over his forehead. The quiet hum of conversation coming from the salon invited a drink before turning in. He crossed the polished lobby, his heels tatting staccato echoes. He eyed the dimly lit crowd, searching for a table or a lounge chair. All appeared occupied. He was about to give up when a young man at a table near the door stood.

"I say, I've an empty chair here if you care to join me."

The British accent piqued his curiosity. "That's very kind of you." He extended his hand. "Alexander McSween. May I buy you a drink?"

"John Tunstall. I've just ordered, but kind of you to offer." He signaled the waiter.

McSween appraised the young man as he drew back the offered chair. He affected a serious demeanor with the dignified bearing of British breeding. He had a refined manner, alert brown eyes and a prominent nose that gave his mouth the appearance of being small. He wore his wavy brown hair barbered about his collar and ears. He had a thin mustache and a patch of chin whiskers that might never rise to the stature of a beard. A waiter in a starched white jacket appeared.

"Sir?"

"Whiskey."

"Very good, sir."

"So, Mr. Tunstall you're British I take it."

"I am and please, call me John."

"Then you must call me Alex. You're a long way from home. What brings you to Santa Fe?"

"A bit of business, I hope." The waiter arrived with the drinks. Tunstall lifted his glass. "Cheers."

"Cheers." McSween took a swallow. "May I ask what sort of business you're in?"

"You may. Just now I'm looking for a business to invest in. What do you do, Alex?"

"I have a law practice."

"Ah, a barrister. Here in Santa Fe?"

"No, in Lincoln. About one hundred fifty miles southeast of here."

"Then you, sir, are also a long way from home."

"I suppose I am. Have you found a business that interests you?"

"Not really. I've some thoughts on land speculation, but I've yet to encounter the right piece of property. Santa Fe may be a bit too well established. Tell me about your Lincoln. I've not heard of it before."

"Lincoln is the largest county in New Mexico. The Pecos

River valley makes it prime ranch land. Lincoln is the county seat."

"Those are all ingredients to opportunity."

"You would think they would be. Unfortunately the business community is dominated by a small group that controls everything."

Curiosity pecked at Tunstall. "How do they do that?"

"It starts with the mercantile. They operate the only store in the county. If you need something, you buy from the House at whatever price they think you should pay."

"The House?"

"Locals call Dolan's business the House because the mercantile and offices are the largest building in Lincoln."

"I see. Well that problem seems easily remedied. All you need is another mercantile and a bit of good old-fashioned competition."

"Easier said than done. It takes money to do that."

"Yes, well that is where I might step in. I have capital to invest. I hadn't thought about a mercantile, but this House you describe sounds like an opportunity ripe for the picking. The ranch land in the area may also suit some of my other ideas."

"You're serious, aren't you?"

"Of course I'm serious. I told you I'm looking for a business opportunity."

McSween drained his glass. "In that case, I have another thought for you if you have the time." Tunstall nodded. "Then let me buy that drink I promised." He signaled the waiter. "It will take more than a mercantile to beat Dolan. He sells at exorbitant prices to be sure, but he gets his real power by selling on credit. Everybody owes him money. His problem is that he doesn't take in enough cash. It takes cash to keep the enterprise going."

"Yes, I can see that." The waiter arrived with the drinks.

McSween leaned across the table with a conspiratorial glint in his eye. "I know how to fix that."

Tunstall couldn't disguise his skepticism. "Just how would you go about that?"

McSween smiled. "With a bank."

Tunstall broke into a broad grin. "By jove, that's it, isn't it? A mercantile and a bank, capital idea! I think I shall have to pay your Lincoln a visit. Of course, I shall need legal services for anything I might do."

"When it comes to chartering a bank, you'll need more than legal services."

"Oh, how so?"

McSween sat back. "You're a foreign national and a stranger to the country. You'll need a partner. You'll need a citizen partner people know and trust."

Tunstall pursed his lips and nodded. "I see. Something of a head for business yourself, I see. A partner, you colonials are so quaint. Shall we drink to it then?"

CHAPTER TWO

Lincoln
August 1877

Morning sun streamed through the dusty office window. Alexander McSween examined the deed. He nodded thoughtfully and rocked back in his desk chair, turning to his guest.

"This all appears in order, John. I'll file it with the county clerk's office and you'll have yourself a ranch."

The young Englishman sat back and smiled. "Splendid." John Henry Tunstall arrived in Lincoln early that fall with an abundance of ambition determined to make his fortune. He favored dark suits to affect severity on his boyish appearance, severity in keeping with a ruthless appetite for business.

The mild-mannered, bespectacled McSween had his own ambitions. He and Tunstall had partnered in chartering a bank as part of the Englishman's plan to open a mercantile in competition with Jimmy Dolan's House. Dolan also controlled the most lucrative end of the local cattle business, contracts to supply beef to Fort Stanton and the Mescalero reservation. Dolan controlled his empire with an iron hand by staying on the right side of the Santa Fe Ring, the Republican political machine in the capital that ran New Mexico Territory. McSween pushed a shock of sandy hair off his forehead.

"I'm happy to record the deed for you, John, but I must remind you this property has a history. You're purchasing it from an estate that is the subject of some dispute. The dispute itself wouldn't bother me as your attorney in most cases. We've paid a fair price for the property. What concerns me is the fact the dispute involves Jimmy Dolan."

"Dolan again, is there nothing in this county the man doesn't have his fingers in?"

"I know it seems that way. His claim is on the estate in settlement of some debt. He may try to use that against you for your other business interests. He's tried to force me to pay his alledged debt out of the proceeds of an insurance claim I settled for the estate."

"It would seem to me that is a matter between Dolan and the heir to the estate."

"One would think. Then again this is Jimmy Dolan we are dealing with."

"Fiddlesticks! Record the deed."

"Very well. I'm curious, though. What are you going to do about running the place? You're not cut out for ranching."

He smiled. "No, I'm not. Perhaps I should explain. Since you stand for me at law in these matters, you should have the benefit of the full picture."

McSween removed his spectacles and polished the glass with his handkerchief. "You're right there. I can't represent you effectively unless I know the full extent of your plans."

"You're right, Alex, I don't plan to run the ranch. I have hired Dick Brewer to raise some horses for me. If he manages turnover properly, the ranch should cover itself."

"Turnover?"

"Oh, sorry. British slip, I'm afraid. Profit to you colonials. I plan to use the land in the cattle business."

McSween wrinkled his brow and replaced his glasses. "I'm not sure I understand. If you plan to raise horses, where do cattle come in?"

"Dolan is in the cattle business. He supplies beef to the fort and the reservation. He doesn't own a ranch. He simply takes his profit on the sale. It is a capital idea, don't you think?"

"It's not as easy as it sounds. Dolan holds those contracts because he has political help from Santa Fe and he sells at prices that are well below the market. He buys his stock from small ranchers who are in debt to his store. Rumors say he can do it because the cattle are stolen. That still doesn't explain what you want with the Flying H."

Tunstall smiled as if at some private humor. "Land."

"Land?"

"Yes, land. I was able to acquire the Flying H at something of a distressed price, don't you agree?"

"Well, yes; but if you don't plan to ranch it, I'm afraid I don't see . . ."

"Other small ranchers in Dolan's debt might be similarly distressed. Should they decide to sell out, their land might also be purchased at similarly advantaged prices. One day that land will be worth a fortune."

"And how is it you propose to 'distress' these small ranchers?"

"Winter feed."

"Winter feed? I don't follow."

"It's quite inexpensive early in the year. A clever chap such as myself can buy up the lot of it and put a proper price on it come winter."

"The small ranchers depend on that feed to survive through the winter."

"So I'm told."

"They won't like that."

"I shouldn't imagine they would, but who is to stop it? Once we've recorded our deed, it's all perfectly legal."

"Those already in debt to Dolan may not be able to pay higher prices."

"I rather enjoy the prospect of squeezing Dolan through his suppliers' debt."

"Range wars have started over far less than what you're talking about."

"You mean violence?"

"I do."

"Dick said as much. He suggested we hire some competent men to assist us should the need arise. I take that as prudent advice."

"You seriously mean to force these ranchers to sell out."

Tunstall bobbed his head in animated agreement. "I say, you've come to the same conclusion as I. I expect some of them shall fail. It is the surest way to buy their land at the lowest prices."

McSween blew out a breath. "That could still take a great deal of capital."

"Precisely," Tunstall beamed. "And that is where our bank comes in once again. It can fund more than the mercantile. Mr. Dolan has created quite the opportunity there, don't you think? He's victimized the good people of this county with his store for far too long. It's high time someone gave him a bit of competition. The bank is the key. You said so yourself. The bank and the mercantile bring in money we can loan to a development company, buying up all that lovely ranch land."

"You do think big, John, I'll give you that. I've told you before, though, Dolan won't take this lying down. Your winter feed plan only adds fuel to the fire."

"Dick mentioned that too."

"You'll need more than a few competent men."

"I've considered that. I think we shall have a powerful friend with us."

"Who might that be?"

"John Chisum. He wants Dolan's beef contracts. Without

competition from Dolan's small ranchers, beef prices will rise. Our friend Mr. Dolan won't be able to make a profit on cheap beef. Mr. Chisum will have the opportunity to win those contracts for himself at fair prices."

McSween revised his appraisal of Tunstall. The man was either crazy or a genius. Common sense favored crazy. Then again, you couldn't deny the genius in his plan, ruthless genius, but genius nonetheless. If he pulled it off, he would be the wealthiest man in the territory. Money bought power. Power always needed a good lawyer, in this case, a lawyer with ten percent interest in the bank.

"Are you with me, Alex?"

"We're partners, aren't we? I'm with you." *If you don't get killed first.*

Susan McSween listened to Alex describe his meeting with Tunstall. She had rich auburn hair, an attractive figure and a fresh cream complexion. She cloaked a sharp wit and a sharper still appetite for men she found attractive in the frailty of proper womanhood. Tunstall did not measure up to her taste. She found the self-assured Englishman too smart for his own good. His business ambitions were downright dangerous. Alex may not satisfy her every desire but he did provide a certain social standing she found comfortable. The prospect of his getting killed struck her as inconvenient in the extreme.

"So you are going to go through with this harebrained scheme of his."

McSween pursed his lips defensively. "We've been through this all before, my dear. It is most definitely not a harebrained scheme."

"What else do you call a scheme that is certain to get you killed?"

"Reward comes with risk. In this case, we've a plan to fight fire with fire."

"A plan is it? He who has the most hired guns wins. Is that your plan?"

"Backed up by Chisum, I'd say that would be us. Besides, Tunstall's taking most of the risk. I'm just doing a little lawyering with a modest silent partnership. You do like money, don't you?"

She did, of course, and he knew it. Well, perhaps they could relieve the Englishman of some of that lovely family wealth.

"Has John found a place to locate the bank and the store?"

"He didn't say. Why?"

"The house will be done in a few weeks. You could easily make your office there. This office could be converted to house the bank and the store. John should find these living quarters more than suitable to his needs until his business is established."

"That's an excellent idea, my dear. I shall suggest it to John in the morning."

A little nest egg wouldn't hurt in the event the fool's partnership wasn't silent enough.

CHAPTER THREE

Flying H

Tunstall stuck his head inside the ranch house door and wrinkled his nose. Gray light filtered through dirt-smeared windows did little to brighten the musty smelling, dust-covered interior. A rust-streaked potbellied stove stood in the shadows of one corner, its soot-stained chimney pipe home to a massive spiderweb. The roof sagged noticeably, mindful of a swayback horse. A cracked wooden table boasted two chairs that might be serviceable. The third chair had a broken back with one leg bent at an angle sure to break under the slightest weight. A door frame covered by a dingy torn curtain suggested a sleeping room at the back. He'd not spend any more time here than necessary.

"It don't look like much now, Mr. Tunstall, but me and the boys will have it fixed up in no time."

Brewer might be an expert horseman, but his sense of suitable accommodation stopped well short of even rustic charm. Tunstall calculated he couldn't get back to Lincoln in time to avoid spending the night. "Yes, well, I shall leave the improvements to your discretion, Mr. Brewer."

"Please call me Dick."

Sturdy and rawboned, Brewer had dashing good looks with curly hair and a serious though pleasant disposition. He'd been highly recommended to Tunstall on his arrival in Lincoln as a man who could help him establish an interest in ranch land.

The ranch house and outbuildings might not look like much, but the location of the Flying H suited Tunstall's purposes. If Brewer could raise enough horses to break even on the place, the land could only appreciate in value with the passage of time. Small ranches to the south all the way to Seven Rivers stood ripe for consolidation.

"We'll have time enough to work on the house and corrals over the winter. I'd like to get a start on bringing in some stock before the snow gets bad."

"That's all well and good, Dick. Now, who here about do their business in winter feed?"

"Winter feed? We shouldn't need much of that this year with the size of our herd."

"No, no, not for our consumption. For investment purposes."

"Investment in winter feed?"

"Precisely. It should be quite inexpensive standing in the ground in the spring. A shrewd person might buy it up and hold it until the price rises in fall. In fact if one were to control enough of it, one might actually be in position to set the price."

"You mean higher?"

"Well, of course."

"Folks ain't gonna take kindly to that."

"I have no intention of denying them feed. I only mean to make it available at a fair price."

"Fair to you."

"Indeed."

"Like I've said, Mr. Tunstall, folks won't take kindly to that."

"That's why you are hiring those men we discussed."

"We'll need 'em."

"Business is business. Now, about those winter feed growers . . ."

"Let's see, there's George Peppin and . . ."

★ ★ ★ ★ ★

Brewer stepped out on the porch with his second cup of coffee in hand. His eyes wandered the horizon to the south and west. Something moved in the hills. Two dark shapes resolved into riders approaching at an easy jog. He reached inside the door for the Winchester propped beside it.

"We got company, Mr. Tunstall."

Tunstall emerged from inside, shrugging his shoulders into his coat. "Any idea who it might be?"

"Hard to say. I got the word out, we're lookin' for men. Then again, out here, you never know. You have a gun?"

"Me? Heavens, no."

"Then maybe you best step inside and let me handle this until we know who we're dealin' with."

"I say, do you really think so?"

"I do."

Tunstall stepped back inside.

"Oh, and, Mr. Tunstall, one more thing."

"What's that?"

"With all the business interests you're plannin', you might want to get yourself a gun."

"I say, Dick, I fully intend to abide by the law. I can't imagine any reason I should require a firearm."

"If you don't fancy carrying a gun yourself, I suggest you make it a point to travel with someone who does. This ain't jolly old England. With all you're plannin', some folks is likely to take you for a marked man. Think about it. It's good advice."

"I see. Perhaps so."

The riders drew rein fifty yards out. "Yo the house," one called.

"Yo."

"We heard you're hirin'."

"We are. Ease on in and keep your hands where I can see

'em." Brewer sized them up. The bigger of the two looked like a bare-knuckle prizefighter. He had a handlebar mustache, oiled brown hair under a slouch hat and bright hazel eyes. The other had a wiry, boyish mixed breed look to him, with straight black hair and lean features. "That'll be far enough. Who are you?"

"John Middleton." The big one spoke. "This here's Fred Waite."

"You know what we're lookin' for?"

Middleton drew his coat back behind the butt-forward-rigged Colt on his left hip. "We do. You need proof. Give us a target."

Brewer nodded. "That won't be necessary. Step on down and meet the boss, Mr. Tunstall."

Lincoln

McSween's former office smelled of raw lumber, sawdust and stain. Tunstall stood silhouetted in the sun splash pouring through the front window. Dust mites rose around him as though a sorcerer conjured them up from the darkness below. Lucy Sample followed his expansive gesture in rapt attention.

"That's the teller cage at the end of the counter. The safe behind it is in plain sight to the depositor. Safety, strength and all that, you know." He crossed the floor stepping over and around the skeletal frames for the new shelving. "Soft goods here I should think, don't you? Can't say I've much opinion as to that. Never have been much in the way of a shopper."

Lucy fingered her lower lip in thought. A wisp of a girl, petite, almost childlike, she took her woman's curves from a tiny waist. She had a rich fall of sable hair and creamy complexion barely hardened by the rigors of frontier life. The thing that most set her apart were large dark brown eyes that looked like they came with a story. They did. A story most folks around Lincoln didn't know.

She'd come west with her family as a girl. They'd all been

23

lost crossing the Arkansas, all of them except Lucy. The wagon master took her as far as Dodge. A girl alone, she fell in with the soiled doves and survived the best way she could. Billy Cantrell took her to Denver and on to Cheyenne. She met Belle Bailey on her way to Deadwood. She worked Belle's Red Garter, became part owner and made a little money when she sold her interest back to Belle. She drifted back to Denver and got a job at the Silver Dollar. That's where she had a run-in with the serial killer Patch and that's when Ty Ledger entered her life for the second time.

She'd met him the first time a couple of years before in Dodge. It was a brief encounter, no more than a casual conversation really, yet they both felt a special connection. They'd gone their separate ways. She didn't see him again until that afternoon last year when he strolled into the Silver Dollar with the bounty hunter, Johnny Roth. They were on the trail of the killer who'd attacked her. Roth was after a bounty offered by a banker in Laramie who lost his wife to the killer. A dead wife and unborn child accounted for Ty's stake in the hunt. In the midst of all that grim purpose, something connected between them again. He left Denver following the killer south. She decided to pull up stakes and finish her family's journey down the Santa Fe Trail. She found Ty in Santa Fe and convinced him to take her with him to Lincoln. She'd hoped catching the killer would free him of his grief. Free him to feel something for someone else. It didn't. That's when John Tunstall arrived in Lincoln.

"I say, Lucy, you were about to say something?"

"Oh, sorry. I'd put the soft goods more toward the back. Women will look for that sort of merchandise. Keep the front space for the things people need most."

"Yes, that makes sense. I should have thought of it myself. Have you other suggestions?"

"Hmm, you can store bulk items like coffee and flour in barrels on the end of the shelves."

"Quite so, use all the space we have."

"The shelves behind the counter and the counter should be used for luxury items like candy and cigars. Things people may buy even though they had no intention to."

Tunstall smiled. "You've quite the head for this, Lucy girl. I say you are the very person to run this store!"

She blushed. "A little common sense is all, nothing more."

"I disagree! You are far too modest. I'll hear nothing other than you'll take the job."

"Oh, all right, but only the store, I'll not trust myself with the bank."

"Splendid. The bank won't be necessary. I shall be the president and cashier. I know just the person to manage the teller counter."

"Who might that be?"

"Susan McSween. The two of you can keep one another company while we are making all that lovely money."

Lucy left Tunstall to planning his bank and mercantile. Out on the boardwalk, she pulled her shawl tight around her shoulders against a sharp afternoon breeze. Sun slanted out of the southwest from a vault of bright blue sky. She turned east toward the room she maintained at the widow O'Hara's. The soft clop of a horse sounded behind her. The shadow of its rider crossed her path. She glanced over her shoulder.

"Afternoon, Lucy." Ty touched the brim of his hat. He stepped down in the street beside the boardwalk.

"Good afternoon, Ty." The greeting felt strained. Tall and wiry, he had dark wavy hair and a rough shave in need of a barbering most of the time. Her breath caught in her throat. He had an easy way about him that never failed to have a palpable way with her. Cool gray eyes took her in as though they might swallow her. He'd gone off after his wife's killer the past summer, leaving things unsettled between them. Tunstall had come to town while he was away. Things had grown awkward between them when he came back to find she'd been seeing Tunstall.

"Mind if I walk you home?"

She hesitated. "No, of course not. How have you been?"

He walked along, leading a sturdy steeldust gelding. "Fine. And you?"

"Oh, all right I guess."

"Tunstall fixin' to take over McSween's old office?"

"He is."

"I heard he bought the Flying H. What's he need with an office in town?"

She glanced sidelong at the question. "John's planning to start another business."

"Busy fella. What sort of business?"

She arched a brow, a little uncomfortable with where this question led. "He plans to open a bank and a general store."

"Gonna take Dolan on then. I heard as much." He fell silent for a few paces as if measuring his words. "Be careful, Lucy. Dolan won't cotton to that one bit. He'll play rough. Tunstall has no idea what he's up against. I'd hate to see you in the middle of that kind of trouble."

She stopped and met his eyes. "You say that like you mean it."

He shuffled the toe of his boot in the dirt. "I do."

She held his eyes. "I never know what to make of you, Ty Ledger." She stepped off the boardwalk to cross the street to Mrs. O'Hara's gate. "John's offered me a job clerking in his store."

"You gonna do it?"

"A girl's gotta eat. Besides, it's better than my old life." Ty knew the story most didn't. He'd accepted her for what she was. It didn't seem to matter to him, but maybe that was because he didn't think of her . . . that way. She wondered what John would think if he knew. Ty broke the thought.

"Until lead starts flyin'."

"Lead can fly anywhere." She paused at the gate, searching his eyes for traces of the ghost that haunted him. A familiar flutter inside made her shiver against the afternoon chill. That mysterious connection tugged at her. She drew back. *John's safe.*

"Thank you for walking me home."

He nodded. "You be careful. Hear?"

She nodded. The gate groaned.

Lamplight danced with the shadows on the wall, keeping time to a tune played in silence. The journal lay open on the small writing table, the pen idle beside the ink pot. It felt like she'd faced writing this entry before. It was easier when he wasn't around. John was John. His accent and etiquette amused her. He was safe. He offered a promising, respectable future. If he succeeded in all his business dealings, he was sure to be an important and influential man in the territory. His plans seemed to include her for more than a shopgirl. He had promise. He offered more than she'd ever hoped to aspire to. All she had to do was be there.

Ty.

Just when things seem to be settling in, along he came and unsettled her. Unsettled. That was one way to describe it. She let her eyes drift closed remembering the look of him. Her mind flashed back to the taste of him, the feel of him. He did something to her standing in the street in broad daylight without so much as touching her. How did he do that? How did she do that? All he said was that he worried about her. He meant it. He said so. At some level he cared. Could that be the start of something more? Could it be his wife's ghost might finally leave him in peace? She would if it were her place. Would the woman called Victoria? Only time would tell. How much time? She shook her head. No way to know. She dipped pen in ink.

Ty walked me home from the store today. He's worried Dolan may make trouble for John . . . not really. He's worried I might get caught in the middle of it. I don't know how I feel about that. Yes I do. I just don't know how to admit it.

CHAPTER FOUR

Rio Hondo

They rode north from Seven Rivers, five grim-faced men heavily armed. They crossed Flying H range through hills covered in mesquite and creosote bush under a rumpled woolen sky. Jesse Evans rode the lead followed by Crystobal and his regular Seven Rivers boys. Short of stature and solidly built, Evans had a square jaw, generous mouth and a crooked nose courtesy of a saloon brawl over a soiled dove. Ladies still found the distant look in his eye fetching. He wore a bibbed shirt, bracers and woolen britches with a .44 Colt butt forward on his left hip.

Crystobal rode a spirited black stallion, prancing and tossing his head. He was something of a newcomer to Seven Rivers. A man with a grudge to settle that brought him to Lincoln County. The grudge came courtesy of a gunfight over the favors of a woman Crystobal considered his. He lost. He'd survived out of a lust for vengeance and a mean streak worthy of venom running in his veins. The Chisum man who shot him would pay this time. He'd signed on with Evans to bide his time.

He dressed in black with silver spurs and conchos in his hatband. Pearl-handled revolvers slung at each hip. A pencil-thin black mustache traced the stub of a sometimes-lit cigarillo tucked between thin lips. Hooded dark eyes glittered in a walnut mask. A jagged scar, earned in a knife fight, sliced his left cheek. A shock of coarse black hair fell across his forehead beneath the brim of his black sombrero.

Frank Baker, Buckshot Roberts and Buck Morton made up Evans' regular gang. Baker looked the part of a drifter, with shabby clothes, a rough shadow of dark beard and tobacco-stained teeth. Handy with his gun, he was inclined to shoot first and find a reason why later.

Andrew "Buckshot" Roberts earned his nickname by way of a shotgun wound to his right shoulder. Lean and gnarled as a hickory stick, he wore a wide brimmed slouch hat with a round crown over a shaggy mop of gray hair. He had watery blue eyes shaded by thick bushy brows that met over the bridge of a hawk-like nose. His lean chiseled features were weathered and lined with a heavy drooping mustache tugging the corners of his mouth to a frown.

Billy "Buck" Morton brought up the rear. He had a round moon face. Small blue eyes squinted from fleshy folds that drooped into heavy jowls. Stringy blond hair hung below a battered derby hat. His belly rolled over his gun belt, on spindly legs that gave him the appearance of an overstuffed scarecrow. Morton cooked for the Seven Rivers outfit. He overcame his partners' complaints about the food by serving as his own best customer.

They struck the Rio Hondo northwest of South Spring late afternoon the second day out. Evans drew a halt at the south crest of the river valley wall. The Long Rail herd stretched across the valley floor, browsing winter grass along the river bottom. He cut his eyes east and drifted back along the valley wall across the river. No sign of a watch for this bunch. Dolan needed fifty head for delivery to Fort Stanton. He rocked back in his saddle.

"All right, boys, we'll go in, cut fifty head or so and drive 'em west until dark. Crystobal, you stay here and watch our back trail. If anybody comes along, you know what to do. If nobody shows up before sunset, follow the river west until you catch up with us. We'll cross in the morning, drive 'em north some and change the brands. We should have 'em up to Fort Stanton in a couple of days. Then we'll ride on over to Lincoln and get rid of some trail dust before we ride south."

The boys exchanged grins at the prospect of kicking up a little fun in Lincoln. Crystobal stepped down. He ground tied his horse below the skyline and drew his Winchester from the saddle boot.

"See you tonight." Evans eased his bay down the ridge into the valley.

Crystobal dropped into the tall grass, the Winchester laid across his knees. He wondered if Chisum men would come. Would the one called Roth be with them? The fresh scar on his chest prickled at the thought. He'd been lucky. This time he would not underestimate the gringo. This time his bullet would do the killing.

Clouds drew a thick blanket of felt out of the northwest, scudding across the river valley on a stout breeze. Wade Caneris drew rein on the north valley wall. The wind cut through his coat, the air scented with the threat of snow. The herd knotted along the riverbank. Steel ripples ribboned the surface of the river, reflecting the sky. Caneris made his reputation as a tough, no-nonsense trail boss driving longhorns from Texas to the Kansas railheads in the early seventies. Crews followed him, confident he'd pull them through to payday, no matter what the trail threw at them. Storms, stampedes, river crossings, rustlers, Indians, it didn't matter. Chisum signed him on to ramrod the South Spring cattle operation without a second thought. Caneris earned his complete trust in the years that followed. He eyeballed the herd. An experienced cowman, he didn't need to count them to know they were missing more than the usual strays.

He nudged his chestnut down the ridge to the valley below.

He loped across the grassy flat and splashed the dark gray surface of a creek spilling into the broader river. He circled southeast to west searching for sign. He found it west of the herd and stepped down. Riders had driven fifty or sixty head off to the west. He toed a horse dropping with his boot. Two maybe three days old he judged. He squinted off to the southwest. Not for the first time, he smelled the Seven Rivers boys. Chisum would be righteously pissed. He could send out his gunhands but Caneris knew they were already too late. Those beeves were penned up at Fort Stanton or the reservation wearin' a running iron brand built off the South Spring Long Rail. Standing here he could make out a couple of options the boss had to stop this. He wondered which Chisum might choose, as he stepped into the saddle and squeezed up a lope for home.

South Spring

John Simpson Chisum threw a log on the fire, sending a shower of sparks up the soot-stained stone chimney. The fire crackled, drying the new log with a succession of sharp cracks and pops. Heat spilled into the spacious parlor. Evening chill retreated against the adobe walls in the shadows of firelight. Chisum stood up and turned to his easy chair, ready to rest his frame after a long day. Lean and rangy, he had a bearing about him that made an imposing appearance out of an average frame. He had wavy brown hair gone gray at the temples, neatly trimmed around prominent ears. Intense brown eyes with bushy brows set in lean weathered features. He wore a neatly waxed mustache with a patch of whiskers below his lower lip. He favored plain spun shirts with a black ribbon tie that gave him the look of authority. The clatter of horse hooves caught him up as he reached for the chair. A rider comin' fast usually spelled trouble.

He crossed the parlor to the heavy front door and stepped out into the night chill. Caneris drew rein. His horse snorted clouds of steam as he jumped down.

"What is it, Wade?"

"Rustlers. They hit the Rio Hondo herd two, maybe three days ago."

"How many we lose?"

"Fifty, maybe sixty head. I didn't wait around to make a tally."

"Son of a bitch."

"You want me to post guards on the Pecos and Rio Hondo herds?"

Chisum considered his options. In truth, raids of this size amounted to little more than a bee sting, though every bit as annoying for the principle of the matter. His Long Rail herds, numbering near a hundred thousand head, roamed the free range all along the Pecos River valley. Small ranchers resented it. Jesse Evans and his Seven Rivers boys thought nothing of running off a few head now and again. They had a ready market for stolen stock, courtesy of Jimmy Dolan's contracts to supply beef to Fort Stanton and the Mescalero reservation. "Damned expensive way to swat bees," Chisum mumbled. "We ought to ride down to Seven Rivers and clean that scum bunch out once and for all. I'd do it too, if I could prove it was them."

"What about the guards?"

"When's Dolan's next delivery due? That'd be the time to post a guard."

Caneris shrugged.

"All right, put up your horse. Get Roth and come on back to the house. I'll see if Dawn's got a bite of supper left for you. I got some business to discuss with you and Johnny."

Minutes later, boots scraped the porch outside. Chisum started to rise from his chair by the fire only to pause at the soft pad of moccasins on the dining-room floor. He smiled and sat back.

Nothing like Johnny Roth to bring Dawn Sky running. He rose to greet the boys.

"Let's sit in the dining room. Dawn's got some supper for Wade. Bring us a drink will you, Dawn?"

She nodded. Her eyes never left Roth. She'd become like a daughter to Chisum. Her mother served as his housekeeper for years. Dawn grew up at South Spring. When her mother died, Chisum raised her as if she were his own daughter. She grew to take her mother's place, looking after her benefactor. A willowy young woman she carried the proud bearing of her Navajo people. Her liquid dark eyes might flash like summer lightning or turn soft like a river eddy. She had a short straight nose, high strong cheekbones and full lips drawn taught in a bow. She wore the plain cotton blouse and brightly colored skirt of a peon, though the simple dress gave full measure to the flower of her womanhood. Roth captured her heart the moment his shadow crossed the gate at South Spring the previous fall.

Johnny Roth came to New Mexico with Ty Ledger, following the killer known as Patch. Ledger wanted vengeance. For Roth, the killer meant bounty. He never expected he'd settle down. Then again he'd never expected Dawn Sky. Tall and muscled, he still wore black-leather-rigged, ivory-handled Colts slung on his hips. Old habits died hard. A man didn't wear a rig like, unless he had the talent to use it. He had mountain-ice eyes and a small scar that split his lower lip in a way ladies found fetching. They might still, though to hear Ledger tell it, Johnny Roth had got himself ground tied by a slip of a Navajo girl. Roth didn't argue.

Caneris found his plate at the dining-room table. Chisum took his place at the head. Roth drew a chair across from Caneris. Dawn Sky brought the whiskey bottle and glasses. Chisum poured and passed the glasses around as Caneris dug into his dinner hungrily.

Chisum took his whiskey in a swallow, topped up his glass and looked from Roth to Caneris. "Tunstall's sent word he's ready to open the bank. I'm riding up to Lincoln in the morning. Johnny, I'd like you to ride along."

Roth nodded.

"Wade, I think you're right about posting a guard on the herds. This thing with Dolan is about to come to a head. Tunstall's bought the Flying H. Dick Brewer's hired on as foreman. He's hiring his own crew of gunmen. If this thing with Dolan and the Seven Rivers boys gets ugly, we plan to stand together. I'll be gone a few days. You're in charge here. If anything goes wrong and you need help, send word to Brewer."

Caneris nodded around a mouthful of roast beef.

CHAPTER FIVE

Lincoln

Ty stepped out of the Wortley into a chill winter afternoon sun. He took a breath of fresh air and exhaled a mask of steam. Across the river five horsemen dropped out of the hills to the northwest riding into town. Curious, Ledger lounged in the shadow of the porch covering the boardwalk. He watched the riders splash across the river and jog into town past the hotel. Jesse Evans and his boys took no notice of him. *Crystobal.* He squinted. *At least we know where he's hangin' his hat.*

Evans wheeled to the rail at Dolan's store. The rest rode on to the cantina down the street past Tunstall's new bank and store. They left their horses at the hitch rack and trooped inside. Wonder what that's all about? He decided to pass the news along to Marshal Widenmann.

Widenmann was a deputy US marshal sent down from Santa Fe to look into disputes between Chisum and some of the small ranchers. Territorial Marshal John Sherman had been pressured to do it by Governor Axtell on behalf of Dolan. Dolan complained to his political cronies in Santa Fe when Chisum threatened to take the law into his own hands over the matter of his rustling complaints when Lincoln County's Sheriff Brady refused to do anything about allegations of rustling by the Seven Rivers boys. Dolan owned the sheriff along with most everything else in Lincoln. Chisum suspected Dolan of providing a ready market for the stolen cattle to fulfill his contracts at Fort Stanton and the Mescalaro reservation. Soon after his arrival, Widenmann fairly concluded that Chisum had the right of it. Circumstantial evidence tended to support Chisum's suspicions, though nothing had come of any of it yet. Widenmann had limited jurisdiction in Lincoln, but he was the only law that wasn't in Dolan's pocket.

Ty set off down the boardwalk toward the freshly painted sign hanging over the door to the old McSween place. Widenmann had struck up something of a friendship with the brash Englishman. Ty didn't understand it. A lawman should be able to smell trouble. Tunstall acted like a man with a target painted on his coat just for fun. Get too close and a man might find himself in the line of fire. He read the sign again: Lincoln County Bank. He wondered if Dolan had noticed yet.

Evans strode through the clang of the visitor's bell. The scarecrow clerk blinked owlishly from behind the counter. "Afternoon, Jasper, Dolan in?" The old man bobbed his bald head perched on a spindly neck with a prominent Adam's apple. Evans didn't wait for an answer. He crossed the sun splashed floor and disappeared between the shelves to the office door at the back. He rapped on the frame.

James Dolan looked up from a ledger. Darkly handsome, Dolan projected a confident manner despite his modest stature. Women found him attractive. Others found him cold eyed and ruthless.

"Herd's delivered." Evans pulled the office door closed behind him. He handed Dolan the quartermaster's voucher.

"Any trouble?"

"Nah."

"Good." Dolan opened a lower desk drawer and drew out a strongbox. He counted out two hundred fifty dollars in notes and pushed the stack across the desk.

Evans scooped up the bills and thumbed through them. "Nice arrangement, Dolan. You sit on your ass and make fifteen dollars a head while we do the dirty work for five."

"Damn good money for a couple days' work, Evans. You complainin'? If you are, I can find somebody else to do your part." The muffled sound of the visitor bell echoed the threat.

"Not complainin', just makin' a point. If Chisum puts a guard on them beeves and this turns to gunplay, our price is goin' up."

"If you don't want to get shot at you'll have to be clever. Like I said, I can find somebody else." A soft knock sounded at the door. "Yes?"

Jasper opened the door a crack. "Mr. Dolan, John Chisum's here. I thought you should know."

Dolan scowled. *Speak of the devil.* He glanced at Evans. "You best stay here. No sense givin' Chisum ideas." He followed Jasper back to the store, closing the office door behind him. Chisum stood at the counter with his hired gun, Roth. Dolan forced his best smile. "Afternoon, John, what brings you to town?"

Backlit in window shine, shadow masked Chisum's features. "Dolan, I come in to do a little banking and thought I'd pick up a few supplies."

"Banking? You mean that silly sign the Englishman's put up down the street?"

"Yup."

"That's no bank. He's puttin' shelves in there like he's fixin' to open a store of some kind."

"Oh, it's a bank all right, Lincoln County Bank. I'm sure folks around here will find that real handy. Now, about that order, I guess we'll have to pay your prices one last time."

"What's that supposed to mean?"

"Once Tunstall opens his store, we'll have a little good old-fashioned competition to choose from around here."

Dolan's expression darkened. "Yeah, well, we'll see about that."

"Johnny, what have you got on that list?"

"A dozen boxes of forty-four forties."

Dolan raised an eyebrow. "Kind of a lot of firepower ain't it, John? You expectin' trouble?"

"Already had some. Lost another small herd a few days ago, but then maybe you heard about that."

"No, can't say that I have. Sorry to hear it now, though."

"Sorry. I bet you're sorry. You wouldn't have the slightest idea what became of those cattle."

"You suggesting I know something about your lost cattle, Chisum. Them's strong words unless you can back 'em up."

"I can back 'em up, Dolan. I can back 'em all up. I just can't prove 'em, yet. You just go along and send them boys down my way again. We'll be more than pleased to back up everything we can prove."

"I don't have any idea what you're talking about."

"Oh, I think you do, Dolan. I think you know plenty. You sit up here hidin' out in your office while hired scum do your dirty work for you. They leave tracks, Dolan. We know where those tracks lead. Sooner or later somebody's gonna make a mistake and when they do . . ."

"Don't threaten me, Chisum. You ain't half so big as you think." He turned on his heel and stalked back to the office.

Tunstall leaned on the counter beside the newly constructed teller cage. Widenmann sat on a barrel of nails amid the dust and skeletons of the new store shelves. McSween inspected Tunstall's progress in transforming his former office into a bank and a store. Boots on the boardwalk interrupted the conversation. The men looked to the door as Ty Ledger came in.

Tunstall smiled. "Ty, haven't got a proper bell installed yet. Sorry, old chap."

He nodded. "Rob, Jesse Evans and his boys just hit town. Evans went to see Dolan. The rest of 'em are at the cantina."

"Free country so far, but thanks for lettin' me know."

"I say, who is Jesse Evans?"

McSween wagged his head with a wry smile. "John, if you're goin' to do business in these parts the way you plan, you best figure out who you're up against."

Tunstall bristled. "James Dolan, plainly enough, what is your point?"

"Why do you suppose Brewer has you hiring gunmen?"

"He expects Dolan may take umbrage at my business interests. No surprise there. He seems to think Dolan may not feel bound by the rule of law. He thinks Dolan may become less than civil or even resort to violence."

Widenmann nodded. "Brewer's got the right of it. When Dolan plays rough, Jesse Evans and his gang do the dirty work."

"Oh, dear, you don't suppose he'd start that already?"

"Is the paint on your sign dry?" Ledger said.

Horses sounded in the street. All four men turned to the windows. John Chisum and Johnny Roth stepped down at the rail. They clumped up the steps to the door.

Chisum smiled and shook hands all around. "McSween, Marshal, Ty. You open for business yet, John?"

"I believe the sign says so. Lincoln County Bank is at your service, Mr. Chisum."

"Good. Then I'd like to open an account."

"Splendid. Initial deposit?"

"You'll receive a draft from the Bank of Santa Fe directly."

"I couldn't think of a more lovely form of tender. Step right this way." Tunstall let himself into the teller cage. Chisum stepped up to the counter.

Roth stuck out his hand. "Ty, good to see you're still here."

"Rob needed a little help so I decided to stick around." He tilted his chin toward Tunstall. "Lord knows somebody has to look after the foolish and the innocent."

"The innocent wouldn't be Lucy, would it?"

Ty ignored the question. "Speaking of lookin' after, a friend of yours hit town. He says he's lookin' for you. Your ridin' in saved me a trip to South Spring."

"And who might that be?"

"Crystobal."

Roth puzzled. "You sure? I left that bastard shot good as dead."

"Not quite that good by the look of him. Saw him myself."

"What makes you think he's lookin' for me?"

"I was in the Wortley with Rob last month when he inquired after you. Couldn't believe my eyes, but there he was. You took him once. No tellin' this time if he's after a fair fight or a back shootin'."

"Where is he?"

"It appears he's signed on with Jesse Evans."

"That makes sense. He sent Patch to Evans."

"At the moment he's with Evans' boys over at the Cantina."

Roth's eyes clouded over in thought as they drifted to the window.

"What the hell was that all about?" Evans stepped out from between the store shelves.

Dolan clenched his jaw. "Chisum's throwin' around rustling accusations he can't prove again. He claims he knows where the last herd he lost went."

"One of these times he's gonna get close enough to give us a problem."

"You gettin' cold feet, Jesse?"

"No, I'm just sayin'.'"

"No sense borrowin' trouble. Maybe you best lay low for a spell. Besides I got another problem."

"What's that?"

"The English bastard claims he's opened a bank."

"Don't that take a lot of money?"

"Not as much as you'd think, 'specially if people trust you."

"Who's goin' to trust that popinjay?"

"John Chisum, that's who."

"You think people will follow his lead?"

"Some may. Smart, I'll give him that."

"What do you figure to do about it?"

"I don't know . . . yet."

Evans stepped into the cantina. He let his eyes adjust to the dim light. The boys sat at a back corner table working on a bottle. He pulled up a chair and pulled a wad of bills out of his shirt pocket. He peeled two twenty-dollar gold certificates off the bundle for each man and pocketed the rest. He poured himself a drink and lifted his glass. A familiar silhouette appeared in the doorway beyond the rim. Evans eased the glass back down to the table, suddenly alert.

The boys around the table caught the change. Roberts and Baker cut their eyes to the door. Crystobal tensed unable to see the danger he sensed behind him. Evans lifted his chin toward the door. Crystobal eased his chair back as Roth and Ledger entered the saloon.

"Whiskey," Ledger said. His eyes, shaded under his hat brim, drifted to the men at the corner table. The tall one with silver conchos on his hatband rose and turned toward the bar. His mouth twisted in a cruel sneer at the sight of Roth.

"Well, if it isn't Crystobal's old amigo. I'm surprised you came out from behind your woman's skirts."

Roth stepped back from the bar. "I heard you was in town, Crys. I'm surprised you didn't come lookin' for me. Had enough the last time maybe?" He laughed. Crystobal started forward. Roth leveled his guns in a blink. "Best stop there, friend, before I finish the job I should have the last time."

Evans started to rise.

Ledger cocked his .44 and dropped it on a firing line. "Go ahead, Evans. Give me an excuse."

Roth looked past Crystobal's shoulder. "What brings you to town? You ride over from Fort Stanton to settle up with Dolan for fifty or so head of Long Rail cattle?"

"I don't know what you're talkin' about, Roth. Now, you and your boy put your guns up and get the hell out of here while me and the boys still got our good humor. You got no chance against all of us." Baker, Roberts and Morton slid their chairs back.

"Any of you sons a bitches so much as shoo a fly, you're dead." Widenmann stepped out of the back room behind the corner table, cocking both barrels of a sawed-off shotgun to make his point. "Your play, Johnny."

Roth holstered his guns. "All right, Crys. This is what you want. Only this time you know what you're up against." His voice barely carried above a rattler's hiss coiled to strike. "Last time you made a stupid mistake. I almost killed you. Sloppy of me I'm sorry to say. I guess I owe you. You know, make it right this time. Com'on have a go at it. I'll make it up to you."

Crystobal's hands hung at his sides his fingers flexed. Roth read his eyes. Beads of sweat gathered at the bridge of his nose. "You talk a good game with all these guns at your back, Roth. Talk is cheap. We shall have our day soon, amigo, one day very soon. One day when it's just the two of us." He strode past Roth, his spurs ringing in the stillness.

"Com'on, boys." Evans started to leave.

Chisum stepped out from behind Widenmann unarmed.

"Next time you come callin' on one of my herds, Evans, I'll see you dance on the end of a rope."

"I don't know what your talkin' about, Chisum, but any rustler worth his salt would shoot your sorry ass to hell before he'd let himself get caught by an old man like you."

"Like your Mex friend says, Jesse, 'Talk is cheap.' "

CHAPTER SIX

George Peppin's ranch house sat on a low rise near the center of a broad valley surrounded by lush fields of winter hay turned golden in the slanting afternoon sun. At one time he ran a small cattle operation until his age and the pressures of the big producers convinced him he could feed the small ranchers' herds at considerably less effort with only a small loss in income. As it turned out this year, he'd earned more than he ever had running his own herd.

A slope shouldered man in his middle fifties, Peppin had a wiry build, white hair, bushy mustache and an explosion of eyebrows, giving his watery blue eyes the look of perpetual surprise. The sun burned his fair cheeks red where the brim of his battered hat gave up its shade. He wore a rough spun shirt and a well-worn vest. He'd carved his ranch out of the Pecos valley at a time when a man had to hold it against roving bands of Comanche and the rustlers and outlaws thrown off in the wake of the war. It accounted for a raw grit those who knew him came to admire.

He stood by the potbellied stove in the sparsely furnished ranch house, pouring a cup of coffee. Movement beyond the window caught the corner of his eye. Past waving hay and running clouds not much moved out here most of the time. The dark silhouette of a rider stood out on the landscape. Without thinking, he checked the Winchester leaning against the wall beside the door. He watched the rider come into view and relaxed. Jesse Evans, one of his regular buyers, come for his winter feed. This year he'd come too late.

Peppin waited until Evans drew rein in the yard before stepping out to the porch. "Afternoon, Jesse."

"Afternoon, George. Fine day for November ain't it?"

"Good as it gets this time of year. Com'on in. I just brewed a fresh pot of Arbuckle's."

"That sounds mighty good after a long ride."

"Thought it might." Peppin led the way into the house. A rough cut wooden table with a pair of worn barrel-back chairs stood beside the stove. "Have a seat and take the chill off." He gestured to the table and poured Evans a cup of coffee.

Evans warmed his hands on the tin cup, savoring the smell. "Crop looks real good, George. 'Bout ready for cuttin' I'd say."

"I got a couple boys comin' in to help with the cuttin' next week."

"Guess I'm right on time then. I'll take the same order as last year."

"Sorry, Jess, the crop's all sold."

"Sold?"

"Every last bale."

"To who?"

"John Tunstall."

"Tunstall! What the hell does he want with that much feed? He don't even run cattle."

"Said somethin' about goin' into the feed business. Bought my whole crop with options to buy the whole lot for the next two years."

"So what am I supposed to do for winter feed?"

Peppin shrugged. "I'd say talk to Tunstall."

"Son of a bitch."

"Sorry I cain't help you, Jess. It's a little late. You care to stay the night?"

"Thanks anyway, George. I gotta ride into Lincoln."

South Spring

She smiled that inward smile of hers. The sound of the horses told her all she needed. He was back. She'd baked the pie, knowing it would be today. The smell of warm apples and cinnamon filled the house. She took the pan from the oven and set it on the sideboard to cool, glancing out the kitchen window toward the corral. Johnny stepped down beside Señor John. Soon they would see Padre Bernardino. It made her warm inside. She left the kitchen, crossed the dining room and opened the front door. The little warmth given by the winter sun disappeared quickly with the coming of sunset. She pulled a shawl around her shoulders against the chill breeze as she stood in the shadow of the front porch, waiting for Johnny and Señor John to reach the house. He waved as they crunched up the path.

Chisum smiled at Dawn Sky as he passed into the house, leaving the young ones to their greeting. They were in love. Nothing he could do for it, other than worry. The run-in with Crystobal confirmed his concern for Dawn. Roth might be a fine young man with all the best intentions toward her, but he was a man with a past, a past that spelled trouble.

Johnny slipped his arms around Dawn and she lifted her lips to his. The sweet scent of cinnamon said he was home. They followed Chisum into the house.

"Supper will be ready soon."

Roth furrowed his brow with question. "How did you know we'd be home?"

Her eyes smiled.

Roth glanced at Chisum.

He shrugged. "I can't explain it. Never could. You get used to it. How about a drink?"

"Sounds good."

Chisum led the way into the parlor. Roth hung his guns on a peg beside the door and followed. He dropped into a chair across from the big stone hearth. Chisum threw a log on the fire and stirred it to light. The fire cracked and popped, giving off a light scent of mesquite. He brought a bottle and two glasses to the side table and poured. He handed Roth his glass and took his seat.

"How much trouble is this Crystobal likely to be?"

Roth cocked an eye. "You seen him. He went packin' without much trouble." Chisum accepted the answer. Johnny sensed more to the question. "Look, John, I know you're worried about Dawn and me. You know I wouldn't hurt her for the world."

"Not you I worry about, Johnny. I worry about Dawn gettin' widowed young. How many more skunks like that one are there to come after you?"

"I can handle myself."

"I'm sure you can, lessen some of 'em turn out to be back shooters."

"What do you want me to do?"

"If you love her, think about what's best for her."

"Johnny best for Dawn Sky."

Chisum winced. She stood in the doorway behind them.

"Dawn Sky sees the spirits. She knows." She returned to the kitchen as though nothing more need be said.

Roth picked up the bottle and poured Chisum a fresh drink. "I'm told you get used to it."

Chisum shot him a look.

"I hear you, John."

Flying H

Tunstall rode down to the ranch, his face wrapped in a muffler against an icy blast of winter that escaped the mountains with a suddenness particular to mountain winter weather. Snowflakes swirled in the gray sky making it seem that much colder. Big Jim French and Henry Brown accompanied him. He admitted he knew nothing about gunmen, but he'd asked around. Both men appeared to have the requisite credentials. Of course, he'd made it clear to both of them that Dick Brewer had the final say.

French was a bear of a man with powerful shoulders and a thick barrel chest. He had dark swarthy features and black eyes, possibly owing to some mixed breeding of indistinct lineage. Greasy black hair hung to his shoulders.

Brown was a lanky angular man with cropped brown hair, drooping mustache and eyes so dark they might be taken for black. A long neck, prominent Adam's apple and gawky appearance gave him the look of a schoolmaster, made the more so for an ill-fitting black frock coat.

You could see Brewer's hand at work before they even reached the ranch house. A sizable horse herd dotted the hills and meadows leading onto the rise west of Rainbow Creek. They came across Brewer and a couple of the boys checking for strays as they rode in.

"Afternoon, boss." Brewer smiled through a cloud of steam.

"I say, things seem to be moving right along, Dick."

"We got a fine start on a first-class remuda."

Tunstall puzzled. "Re-mu-da?"

Brewer chuckled. "Horse herd."

"Yes, quite so," Tunstall covered.

"I see you brought company with you."

"These men are interested in employment. This gentleman is Big Jim French. The other is Henry Brown. Gentlemen this is Mr. Brewer. He will make the final decision on your employment."

Brewer nodded to the new men. "We can settle all that down

at the house where it's a little warmer." He wheeled away at a lope.

Tunstall, Brewer and the boys arrived at the ranch. They drew rein at the corral and dismounted. Brewer took Tunstall's horse and led the boys to the corral gate.

Henry Brown spotted him. "Rider comin'."

Brewer followed Brown's eyes. "You expectin' more company, Mr. Tunstall?"

"Company? None invited."

Brewer slipped the hammer thong on his gun, watching the rider come. "Hell, it's only Frank Coe."

"How do you know?" Tunstall asked.

"I recognize the mule. I expect I know what he wants."

"You do?"

"Sure. Coe gets his winter feed from Oscar Tanner."

"Splendid! Our first customer."

"Big Jim, Henry, spread out. This here's your on-the-job trial."

French and Brown spread out left and right flanking Tunstall and Brewer. Coe drew the mule to a stop.

"Afternoon, Frank. What can we do for you?"

"What the hell you doin' here, Brewer?"

"I'm foremen at the Flying H now."

"Then I suppose you know somethin' about Oscar Tanner's winter feed crop. I heard the fop who owns this place bought it."

"That 'fop' as you say would be me. John Tunstall at your service."

Coe narrowed a squint. "I need winter feed."

"Splendid. We shall be more than pleased to accommodate you. How much will you require?"

"How much you charge?"

"Ten cents a bale."

"Ten cents! Oscar charged three on account of the haul."

"So he did. But that was last season. I do see your point about the trouble with drayage. I'm a fair man. I shall make an exception in a gesture of good will, and let you have it for eight cents a bale."

"Eight cents ain't good will. It's robbery."

"Robbery? Heavens no, my good man, merely the economics of supply and demand."

"What the hell is he talkin' about, Brewer?"

"Price of winter feed, I think."

"We'll see about that." Coe reached for his old army Colt. Three guns cocked in rapid succession before he could clear leather. He looked from Brown to Brewer to French and back to Tunstall. "So that's how you want to play it."

"Eight cents a bale is more than fair. It is simply a matter of business. No reason for you to threaten violence."

"This ain't a game, Tunstall. Out here winter feed is life and death. It don't get played like a business, yours or anybody else's. You best understand that."

"Oh, but I do. You see, I own the crop. I make the rules."

"We'll see about that." Coe wheeled his mule and spurred up a lope.

Brewer cut his eyes to Tunstall. "I didn't expect your little feed business to go over real well."

"Oh, it will go over all right. As soon as his cattle get hungry enough. Mr. Coe will pay. Either that or we shall buy up his ranch sooner rather than later. And at the right price to be sure. By the by, I thought the two new men played their parts quite nicely, didn't you?"

"You're hired, boys."

CHAPTER SEVEN

Lincoln

Cold light spilled through the dusty window. Lucy swept a pile of sawdust between the finished shelves. The first of three freight wagons worth of inventory were parked out back, waiting to unload. Tunstall bustled about tallying the shipment against the bill of lading. The store was days away from opening and they had a thousand things left to do. The door opened. Still no bell, she added to her mental list.

"Good morning, Lucy."

"Marshal Widenmann."

"Please, call me Rob. Everyone else here does. The place is really shaping up."

She paused, broom in hand and sighed. "I suppose it is." She glanced around at the neat rows of freshly stained shelves ready to receive merchandise, the completed counter and the paint pots ready to create a window sign. "It's just that we have so much left to do before we open. I'm afraid all I see is what is left to be done."

Tunstall came in through the back door, checking off the last items on the bill. "I sent the driver off to have his lunch. We shall unload the wagon this afternoon. Oh, Rob, I didn't see you there. Good morning."

"Good Morning, John. I was just telling Lucy how nice the place looks."

Tunstall set his papers on the counter and looked around. "It is beginning to look like a proper store, isn't it? I expect we shall be ready for business by the first of next week."

"There's already a little buzz around town. People are anxious to see how your prices compare with Dolan's. How's business been on the bank side of things?"

"Quite steady, actually. Word is spreading. John Chisum opening an account produced just the vote of confidence I anticipated."

Boots clumped the boardwalk. The door swung open. Jesse Evans filled the door frame followed by Buckshot Roberts. "Which one of you is Tunstall?"

"I'm John Tunstall. To whom do I have the pleasure of speaking?"

"Jesse Evans. We'll see if it's a pleasure. George Peppin tells me you bought up his winter hay."

"Why, yes, as a matter of fact I did."

"I buy my winter feed from George. He said I'd have to come and see you."

"Quite so, well I shall be pleased to sell you all the winter feed you might need."

"How much?"

"Ten cents the bale."

"Ten! George charged five."

Tunstall shrugged.

"Hell, I'd sooner buy from Oscar Tanner and haul it halfway across the county than pay you ten cents. It's damn near robbery."

"Yes, Mr. Evans, I'm told you may know something about that. But let me save you the journey. Mr. Tanner's hay costs ten cents this year too."

"What do you mean?"

"I mean I purchased Mr. Tanner's crop also."

Evans did a slow burn. "We'll see, Tunstall. We'll just see."

"It seems there is quite a lot of that going around these days. Do come back when you change your mind then, Mr. Evans. Good day."

Evans slammed the door and stomped down the street toward Dolan's store.

Lucy pulled a worried face. "Perhaps you've set the price too high, John. What good does it do if people won't pay it?"

"Oh, they'll pay it, my dear. Either that, or their cattle will starve this winter."

"Some of the small ranchers may be forced to sell out."

"So they may."

Widenmann furrowed his brow. "Lucy has a point, John. You may not want to make an enemy of Evans. You've already stirred up Dolan and you haven't even got the store open yet."

"Oh, please, I don't understand all the nattering. It's only business."

Ty stepped out of the Wortley. It was one of those winter days when the chill in the air softened to the touch of bright sunshine. You couldn't call it warm, but somehow it felt good to be outside. He took a seat on the hotel porch bench, stretched his legs and crossed his boots at the ankle.

He'd decided to have lunch rather than go down to Tunstall's store with Widenmann. Lucy'd be there and the less he saw of her with the Englishman, the better. Funny he felt that way. He had no claim on her. He guessed he could have if he'd tried. Part of him wanted to, but that part couldn't get past the part that still mourned Victoria. He had an empty place inside scarred by the bloody corpse, fresh graves and burned-out home he'd left behind. He'd resigned himself to the fact that Victoria's memory would always be part of him. He was also slowly coming to understand that life held more than memories. Maybe that's what Lucy meant when she said not to let too much of it slip away with his grieving. It was probably good, well-meant advice. But that was before John Tunstall came along.

He couldn't blame her for takin' up with the newcomer. Lord knows he'd been no prospect in his condition. Tunstall had prospects, ambition and money. He had a ranch, a bank, and now a store. Ty had none of it. Then again, he hadn't made any enemies yet, either. Tunstall sure as hell had him there. The way he did business, folks was linin' up fast in the enemies department. You was either for him or agin' him. Most folks had no use for Jimmy Dolan. Tunstall knew how to take advantage of that. Dolan knew how to play rough. He doubted Tunstall knew how to deal with that. That's the part that made him fearful for Lucy. Maybe it wasn't so bad Widenmann befriended the Englishman. Somebody needed to look after the fool greenhorn.

He shook himself out of his reverie. All such hard thinkin' did nothing for his digestion. He glanced down the street to see a lone rider on a good-looking roan high stepping his way. *Good-lookin' horse and a bad-lookin' rider.* The shabbily dressed hombre in a battered sombrero eased the roan over to the Wortley hitch rack as if he'd overheard Ty's unspoken opinion.

He stepped down and threw a rein over the rail. The rest of his rig didn't look any better than the hat. He wore a plain spun shirt, stained canvas vest and wool britches that hung baggy on his slight frame. Underneath the hat a rather pleasant, boyish young man women might fancy to mother looked him over. He had sandy brown hair, a gap tooth buck grin, cherub cheeks and a glint in his eye somewhere between good-natured mischief and murder. He sported an attempt at a mustache and beard. Together they amounted to patches of fuzz on his lip and chin.

"Howdy." He smiled.

"Afternoon. New in town?" He had to be. Ty had never seen him before.

The kid nodded. "Sure am. William Bonney's the name."

"Ty Ledger."

"Pleased to meet you. Say that looks like Marshal Ledger, don't it?"

Ty nodded. "What brings you to Lincoln, William?"

"That an official question, or just passin' the time of day?"

"Just passin'."

"Then call me Billy. All my friends do."

"Fair enough, Billy. My friends call me Ty."

He smiled again. "I hear folks is hirin' around here. I come to see about a job."

"What kind of work you favor?"

A vacant chill crossed his eyes like a curtain. He drew his vest back over the butt of a .41 Colt Thunderer holstered on his right hip with a half smile.

"I see. Well I hear John Chisum's hirin' down at South Spring on the Pecos. Dick Brewer's hirin' for Tunstall at the Flyin' H. Jesse Evans has some boys work for Dolan from time to time. I suppose you could take your pick."

"Hell that sounds like a war."

"Not yet."

"Which side you figure to win?"

"Hard to say."

"Hmm, maybe I'll just hang around a spell. See which way the wind blows before I sign on."

"Might be smart that way."

"Much obliged, Ty."

"Good luck, Billy."

"The son of a bitch bought up every last speck of winter feed in the county."

Dolan listened to Evans fume, amused. "What do you want me to do about it?"

"Well I figure you might do somethin'. He's robbin' us blind for winter feed; and he's about to put a hole in your store. That damn Englishman ain't good for nobody's business but his."

Dolan stroked his chin between thumb and forefinger. "These things have a way of working themselves out."

"Without winter feed, my cattle have a way of starvin'."

"So buy the damn feed."

"I ain't payin' that bastard his price."

"Why not?"

"The hell, Dolan, you gone soft in the head? I don't make enough money as it is without payin' twice the price for feed."

Dolan shook his head. "Jesse, Jesse, Jesse, you're not listening. I'm sayin' buy the feed with Tunstall's money."

Evans wrinkled his brow. "You're talkin' in riddles."

"Fort Stanton's got a requisition out for fifty head of remounts. Tunstall's boys just rounded up a herd at the Flying H. So run off a few, fill the army requisition and pay Tunstall for his feed with his own money."

A slow smile played at the corners of Evans' mouth. "Now you're talkin' sense."

"Of course I am. Tunstall will get his. I'll let you know when it's time."

Evans took his leave. Dolan rubbed his chin in thought. Tunstall bought the Flying H from that estate that owed him money. McSween must have sold it to him. First, the insurance settlement, now this. McSween is near as much trouble as the Englishman. Something has to be done about both of them.

Lucy pulled her shawl around her shoulders, preparing to leave the store at the end of the day. The encounter with Evans still bothered her. The man had a reputation. He could be dangerous. John didn't understand that. He assumed civility. He respected the rule of law and expected others would abide by it too. A blind spot like that could prove dangerous.

"John, maybe you should pay more attention to Marshal Widenmann's advice. He knows what men like Evans are capable of."

Tunstall straightened up from the bank's daily ledger. He came around from behind the counter and went to her side. "Now, now, my dear, there's no need to worry. It is only business after all. I assure you it is all quite legal and proper. You are far too pretty to bother yourself over such ominous thinking." He lifted her chin and kissed her tenderly. "I should much prefer to have you join me for dinner at the Wortley this evening."

Tepid and safe, she sighed. "That would be lovely, John." Candlelight flickered over the journal vellum.

Jesse Evans came to the store today. He tried to buy winter feed from John. He left hopping mad when he found John's price and the fact that he bought up all the feed in the county. John doesn't understand men like Jesse Evans and James Dolan. He thinks "it's just business." He thinks that as long as his business dealings are legal, he has nothing to fear. I've tried to warn him. So has Marshal Widenmann. He doesn't listen. Not really. Dick Brewer convinced him to hire some gunmen, but that only means gunplay will end in more gunplay. He's a sweet man really, very smart, brilliant in some ways. How is it that someone so smart has no common sense?

Wind howled out of the northwest, whining through the store rafters and rattling the office window. Gusts lashed sheets of dust and sand into a dun fog. Dolan seemed not to notice. The ranch suited his purpose. He had his claim on the Fritz estate. Tunstall now owned a ranch that made up a substantial portion of that estate. He could assert his claim with a lien easily enough given a little help from his friends at court in Santa Fe. Yes, a simple lien on the stock should do it. Who would object? Tunstall was a long way from Santa Fe. He had no standing there even if he did object. No, this was Jimmy Dolan's word and no one in authority in Santa Fe would question it. A lien didn't mean much in the grand scheme of things. It was more about serving it. The action was sure to irritate Tunstall, maybe enough for him to do something stupid. All Sheriff Brady needed was an excuse. Hmm, no, not Brady, he'd have to give that some thought. None of that would matter to Santa Fe, of course. He put pen to paper.

Hon. T. B. Catron
US Attorney, New Mexico Territory

Tunstall stepped off the boardwalk a few paces into the street clotted in stiff ruts and patches of brown slushy snow. He admired the storefront. The new finely lettered sign in the window proclaimed J. H. Tunstall & Co. Mercantile. He nodded approval. The shelves were stocked, the prices fair enough to undercut Dolan. The bank attracted new accounts at a steady rate. Customers who came into the store would soon add to the bank numbers. He rested his hands on his hips and smiled to himself. It was only a matter of time until Dolan felt the squeeze like the ranchers who paid him for feed. His eyes swept the street up one side and down the other. He didn't own Lincoln County yet, but the commercial tentacles of that ownership stretched out all around him.

He strolled back to the boardwalk and scraped the mud and snow from his boots before turning to the store entrance. He smiled greetings to passersby and welcome to those who stepped inside to shop or browse. Lucy stood at the counter assisting customers. She made a nice improvement over that old fossil, Jasper, Dolan had collecting his outrageous prices. Susan Mc-Sween sat behind the teller cage, serving the needs of his banking customers. It truly was a powerful combination of services he'd hit upon. Dolan had made so many enemies along the way, he'd opened the door to his own destruction. The only thing missing was a competitor with the vision to seize the opportunity. Tunstall had that vision and more. His ranching foray in feed would yield a land empire beyond Dolan's imagining. One day he might even lease grazing rights to the likes of John Chisum. By then, he expected to be the richest man in the territory, soon to be one of the richest men in America when statehood inevitably came to New Mexico.

Tunstall half smiled, congratulating himself as a gap-toothed young man in a battered sombrero and baggy clothes ambled down the boardwalk trailed by a roan horse. The horse followed along in the street, trailing his master like a dog. The picture amused him. The kid smiled a crooked greeting.

"Afternoon. You the storekeeper?"

"I am the owner. John Tunstall at your service, young man."

"William Bonney."

"How may we be of service, Mr. Bonney?"

"I'm needful of some supplies and hopeful your prices is better than that bandit down the street." He tossed a thumb over his shoulder in the direction of Dolan's store.

"I am quite sure we can accommodate you, Mr. Bonney. I think you'll find the prices at J. H. Tunstall and Company Mercantile far more palatable than those of our worthy competitor."

The kid's eyes drew blank. "Worthy comp . . . Say, you ain't from around these parts, are you?"

Tunstall chuckled. "No, I'm afraid you've found me out. I'm from England, actually."

"Never been there. I ain't from around here, either."

"Then it seems we have something in common." Tunstall beamed. "Come in and let's see about those supply needs of yours." He stepped back with a half bow and followed the kid into the store.

Dolan stood in the shade of his storefront down the street. He drew a cheroot from his coat pocket, bit the tip and spat it into the street. He fished in his vest pocket for a lucifer and scratched it to light on the door frame. He puffed a cloud of blue smoke and steam into the chill air, watching the Englishman inspect his store and greet his customers. *Son of a bitch, I ought'a burn the damn place down.* Frustration did no good. Time would take care of things. The bastard would play himself out. He needed patience. Let the law do it, or at least some convenient version of the law. He'd get the lien from Catron. He'd get Brady to deputize some of Evans' boys to serve it all legal like. Evans was already pissed at Tunstall over his winter feed. It wouldn't take much irritation from the persnickety Englishman to light Jesse's fuse, not much at all. He pitched his cheroot into a muddy rut and retreated to the warmth of his office.

CHAPTER EIGHT

Flying H

Evans rode into lengthening purple shadows in an arroyo southwest of the Flying H. A brilliant ball of winter sun painted the mountaintops crimson in the west throwing a pink blush on the cobalt-blue sky above. Morton, Baker, Roberts and Crystobal waited with their horses. Evans stepped down.

"They couldn't set it up for us no better if we'd asked 'em." The boys gathered round. "The stallion's penned up. They got a herd of fifty head or so pastured below the ranch house. Real neighborly of 'em to do most of the hard work for us. They must be fixin' to run 'em up to Fort Stanton for a quick sale. I guess we'll just have to save 'em the trouble." The boys laughed. "We'll hit 'em when things is all settled down for the night. Crystobal, you can have a little target practice, keepin' Brewer and his men pinned down in the house while me and the boys run off the herd. You can slip away once we got 'em good and gone."

Crystobal nodded with a glint in his eye.

Give the man a target and he knew what to do with it. "Might as well try to get some rest now, boys. We got a full night's work ahead of us."

"What about a fire?" Morton was always one to worry after his comforts.

"No fire. We ain't givin' them boys no smoke sign we're here."

"It's gonna get damn cold, Jesse."

"You got a blanket. Use it."

Brewer woke to the stallion's whicker. What's got him riled up? He put it down to a varmint and tugged the blanket a little tighter. Hopefully the soft snores and heavy breathing of the men would put him back to sleep. The stallion trumpeted again, more loudly this time. Hooves prancing nervously in the corral accompanied the sound. He threw back his blanket. *Son of a bitch,* whatever it is, best not ignore it. He heard horses moving. Not just the stallion, likely the herd down in the pasture. He grabbed the Winchester beside his bunk.

"Boys, we got trouble." He crossed to the door followed by grunts and mumbled curses. He opened the door and stepped onto the porch. Bright moonlight flooded the corral and meadow beyond. The stallion had his ears pinned back and his nostrils flared to the night breeze as he danced back and forth across the corral, momentarily distracting Brewer. Dark shadowed riders moved among the herd in the pasture below. He levered a round into the Winchester.

"Rustlers, boys! Get your asses out of bed and saddle up!" A muzzle flashed off to the southwest. The bullet bit the porch railing punctuated by the rifle report. Brewer dropped to a knee and squeezed off a round in the direction of the flash. Off to the left more shots flashed and popped, driving the herd northwest across the ranch yard. Dust billowed gray plumes in the moonlight, obscuring horses and riders.

One by one the men tumbled out the door, struggling with britches, boots and gun belts. Big Jim led the way down the porch followed by Waite. Somewhere beyond the dust cloud another shooter lit up the men running for the corral. They dove for cover, firing wildly in the general direction of the shooter.

Brewer fired at the phantom behind the muzzle flash. "Get

back inside! We're like ducks on a damn pond in this light." The men scrambled back inside the ranch house. Big Jim and Waite each took a window. Brewer held the door. The shooting fell silent. The only sounds that remained were the herd galloping away to the hoots of the rustlers driving them.

"Henry," Brewer hissed. "You and John, see if you can slip out the back. Saddle a couple of horses and at least trail the sons a bitches until we can figure a way out of here." Brown and Middleton scrambled through the darkness to the back door. Brown cracked it open. Two quick shots greeted him for his trouble. "Looks like they got us covered back here too."

"How the hell many of 'em is there?"

Crystobal laughed as he circled his horse back to the east. He had a good look at the back corral where the men's mounts were stabled. As luck would have it, whoever built the place hadn't bothered with windows on the north side. He could sit off at a distance with his rifle and keep them away from their horses, covering both the front and back doors by riding a narrow circuit. To the men trapped inside he might be many men. A shadow moved in the front doorway. He squeezed off a shot and nudged his horse west away from the futile return fire.

An hour passed, then two. The moon waned in the west draping the front of the house in shadow. That tilted advantage, though slight, to Brewer and his men. Crystobal judged Evans and the boys' getaway safe enough. He eased his mount off to the northeast, reckoning Brewer and his men would go after the horses once they discovered they were no longer pinned down.

Lincoln

Brewer galloped up the town's only street, coat flapping in the wind, his horse throwing clods of mud amid a swirl of wet snow. His gray mount blew clouds of steam little distinguished from the dim cloud-filtered light. It gave horse and rider the spectral appearance of some ghostly mythical manbeast. He slid the gray to a rutted stop in front of the Tunstall store and leaped down.

He stamped up the boardwalk and burst through the door, sounding an alarm announced by the newly installed visitor bell. The entrance startled Lucy and Susan McSween. Tunstall ducked out from the back storeroom, sensing something amiss. Marshal Widenmann followed behind.

"What is it, Dick?"

"Rustlers hit us night before last. Ran off the herd we had rounded up for Fort Stanton."

Tunstall exchanged glances with Widenmann. "Rustlers, do you know who is responsible?"

"It was dark. They were too far away to make out who they were. I got my suspicions, but I can't prove nothin'."

"Well, horse theft is unacceptable. What do you suggest we do, Marshal?"

"Horse theft is Sheriff Brady's jurisdiction."

"We shall report this to the sheriff straight away then." Tunstall pulled off his apron and threw on his frock coat.

Brewer looked at his boss in disbelief. Sometimes, he just didn't understand the man. "You're goin' to report this to Sheriff Brady?"

"Of course, he has the responsible jurisdiction, does he not?"

"Well, yes, but . . ."

"But nothing. He is responsible to bring these miscreants to justice. It's the law. Civil society demands nothing less. Come along, Dick." He stomped out the door and down the street to the sheriff's office, trailing steam like a runaway train.

Brewer gaped after him. He glanced from Widenmann to Lucy to Susan, shrugged his shoulders and set off after the boss. He hurried to catch up.

"You know Brady's not likely to do anything about this."

Tunstall scowled. "Why ever not? It's his duty."

"Likely as not this is some of Jesse Evans' work. The Seven Rivers boys usually deal in cattle, but whatever they do, Dolan protects them."

"If they've broken the law, they should be brought to justice. What can that possibly have to do with James Dolan?"

"Dolan owns Brady."

"Dolan can't own the law."

"I didn't say he owned the law. I said he owns Brady. It amounts to the same thing."

"You are talking in riddles, Dick. I shall simply demand that Sheriff Brady do his duty."

"Suit yourself."

They swung into the sheriff's office. Brady looked up in surprise.

"Mr. Tunstall, Brewer, good afternoon. What can I do for you?"

"We should like to report a rustling, Sheriff."

"A rustling." Brady lifted his eyebrows to Brewer.

"Hit us night before last. Got away with fifty head of horses."

"I see. Any idea who it might have been?"

"Nothing I can prove. We got a trail. My men are following it. Looked like they were headed toward the Rio Hondo, I'm guessing that's where they'll lose it."

"Hmm. Not much to go on, is it?"

Tunstall drew himself up to a righteous stature. "So, Sheriff, what is to be done about this outrage?"

Brady could scarcely conceal his amusement.

"How soon can you organize, I believe you refer to it as a posse, to recover my property?"

"I'm busy with other things at the moment, Mr. Tunstall. Let's see what your men come up with. If they find a solid lead, I'll get right on it."

"So, for the moment you propose to do nothing."

"I said let's see what your men can find."

"Sheriff, I've been robbed. Is this how you protect the citizens of this community?"

"Mr. Tunstall, I'm the sheriff in Lincoln County. I'm elected to protect the county. That doesn't mean dropping everything I'm doing every time a new complaint arrives."

Tunstall leaned across the desk. "Sheriff, I'm afraid I must insist. That trail is getting cold as we speak here. It is your duty to recover my property. Unless I get your cooperation I shall be forced to write a most strongly worded letter of complaint to the editors of every newspaper in the territory. The electorate has every right to know precisely the sort of lackadaisical law enforcement on which the safety and security of their lives and property depend."

Brady sat back. "Lacka-what?"

"Lackadaisical, my good man and if you don't like the fit of that term, you've only to force me to write the rest of that letter."

He threw up his hands. "All right, all right. I'll get up some men and have a look in the morning."

"Very well then, I shall expect the recovery of my property forthwith."

CHAPTER NINE

Fort Stanton

It started with a bottle of good whiskey. Well actually there was more to it than that. The whiskey was a thank-you. The friendship came with it. The thank-you involved a tight spot Ty and Roth got into trying to bring the killer Patch to justice. It seems quite a few people wanted a piece of that hombre, including a renegade Comanche by the name of Chero and about twenty of his warriors. Ty and Roth sort of snatched the killer out from under Chero's nose. The renegade didn't appreciate it. The Comanche came after them hard. They ran Ty and Roth to ground with their prisoner. They got pinned down bad enough for a man to think about saving that last bullet for himself. The things Comanche did with a skinning knife made the bullet a preferable choice. Right about then, along come Lieutenant Colonel Nathan Augustus Monroe Dudley with a cavalry troop out of Fort Stanton. Nate, as Ty had come to call him, and his men turned up just in time to run off the renegades before the boys started dealing in last bullets. First chance he got, Ty bought that bottle of whiskey and rode out to the fort. By the time he and Nate found the bottom of the bottle, they'd struck up a friendship. After that, every couple of weeks, Ty would ride out to the fort or Nate would come into town. They'd have a good meal and a couple of drinks, usually not the whole bottle, and enjoy one another's company.

Fort Stanton sat in a shallow valley in the foothills of the

White Mountains west of Lincoln. Ty rode out of the hills and jogged west toward the fort with its central quadrangle laid out in neat military precision. Off to the south he noticed a dust cloud. He hoped it didn't spell trouble. It'd be a shame to have a sociable evening interrupted by some business Nate might have to attend to. As he approached the perimeter sentry station, he made out a herd of horses being driven to the fort. It looked like a delivery of remounts and nothing more exciting than that. Good.

The sentry stepped out from behind his guard post. "Halt. State your business."

"Deputy Marshal Ledger to see Colonel Dudley." It might not be official business, but the badge made things easier when dealin' with folks like sentries. The trooper waved him in without a second thought. He jogged across the parade ground to the post commander's office, drew rein and stepped down. He looped a rein over the hitch rack and climbed the step to the office door. Inside a crusty sergeant major sat at a cluttered desk in the cramped outer office. "Sir?"

"Marshal Ledger. Colonel Dudley is expecting me."

"Ty." Dudley filled his office door with a broad smile. Tall and a touch on the portly side, Dudley still managed a soldierly presence. He wore his wavy brown hair neatly trimmed, though a slightly receding hairline gave him the appearance of a long face with a prominent nose and bushy mustache. A strict disciplinarian, he could be pompous at times. His men thought his temper stormy, but none questioned his competence in the field. He put all of that aside for his visits with the unlikely Texan.

"Nate, good to see you."

"Come in, come in."

He crossed the office and shook Dudley's hand.

"Sergeant Caleb, notify the mess. We'll need steaks for supper."

"Yes, sir."

With that the office door swung open. A corporal came to attention and threw up a salute. "Sir, Captain Purington sends his compliments. A prospective remount herd has arrived on post. Do you wish to inspect them?"

Dudley scowled. "Sorry for the interruption, Ty, but I really should take a look before we spend this kind of money."

"Do whatever you need to, Nate. Mind if I tag along?"

"Feel free. Your opinion on horseflesh is probably every bit as good as mine."

He followed Dudley out of the office and across the quadrangle to a corral steaming a thin veil of dust raised by fifty head of horses circling, prancing and snorting at their new confinement. Dudley made a slow circuit around the corral, inspecting the herd. Ty followed along absorbed in the herd. A ramrod-straight officer wearing captain's bars met them at the gate with a salute. A familiar figure stood beside him.

"Sir, may I present Jesse Evans. Mr. Evans is offering this herd against our current requisition."

Ty waited for Evans to notice him. Dudley extended his hand. Evans shook Dudley's hand.

"Mr. Evans. May I present my friend, Ty Ledger."

Evans looked past the colonel with a scowl. "Ledger."

"Jesse."

"Then you two know one another?"

Ty nodded. "We've met. I didn't know you were in the horse business, Jesse."

"Had to find some way to pay the cost of feed this winter."

"You got a bill of sale for them horses?"

"Range stock? Hell, no."

"Whose range they come off?"

Evans' anger flared. "Ain't none of 'em wearin' a brand."

"No, I suppose not."

Evans dropped his hand to his hip. "You got somethin' to say, Ledger, spit it out."

"Kind of testy over a couple of simple questions, aren't you, Jesse?"

Evans turned to Dudley. "You lookin' for horses, Colonel, or not?"

Dudley glanced at Ty. He had nothing more to say. "Carry on, Captain." He started back across the quad. Ty swung in beside him. "You think the horses are stolen?"

Ty shrugged. "Nothin' I could prove. When it comes to rustlin',' Evans has a knack for showin' up nearby."

Rio Hondo

Brady had little appetite for getting off his ass to go chasing around the Pecos valley looking for Tunstall's rustlers. He counted on Dolan's patronage and the usual privilege of tax collection to pad his income, but at the end of his term he still had to face the voters. The Democrats never mounted much of a challenge, but give them the kind of bad publicity Tunstall threatened and even that bunch of buffoons might come up with a candidate. He appreciated Dolan's support, but the man didn't have many friends in Lincoln County. Given the chance, he had no doubt the voters would be pleased to throw him out of office. He had to at least give Tunstall a show. So, on a cold winter morning covered in fresh snow, he rode south out of town with deputies George Hindman and Billy Mathews.

Hindman was like an old habit. His best qualification for keeping his job was fawning over Brady while doing his bidding. He clung to the ragged end of his middle years with a bushy mop of hair shot through with gray. He wore a baggy canvas vest long past the time when it buttoned over his paunch. These days it provided a place to pin his badge and a pocket for his makin's. The battered .44 riding butt forward on his hip posed little threat he might actually use it.

Mathews was another story. He had a foul temper and a hair trigger you couldn't hide behind a badge. He had vacant eyes, a bunched brow and a twisted scowl that gave the unsuspecting as much warning as a snake's rattle. He wore a plain spun gray shirt, wool pants and a gray hat with silver conchos in the band. Double-rigged Colts slung on his hips. Mathews gave Brady a ready answer when the situation called for a violent conclusion.

The morning wore into midday when Brady drew a halt. He eased down from the saddle, ground tied his horse and stretched out the aches in his frame. "George, fix us a fire and put on some coffee. I got a hankerin' for something warm to wash down a little hardtack." Hindman ambled off to gather firewood.

Mathews brushed the snow off a flat rock and sat down. "How long you figure to stay out here on this wild-goose chase?"

Brady smoothed the corners of his mustache, chewing over the question. Billy had a point.

"You know we ain't gonna find any rustlers lessen we go on down to Seven Rivers."

"Now, Billy, you mind yourself. You're a peace officer. You can't just go off and make wild accusations you can't prove."

"Wild accusations, yeah right. So how long do you figure to keep this up?"

"Long enough to make that fool Englishman believe we tried."

"Long enough to freeze our sore asses you mean. Look up yonder." He tossed his head to the north. "Them look like snow clouds buildin' in again."

"Quit bitchin'. It ain't no help."

Hindman struck a match to a clump of dry tinder and blew a small campfire to light. He scooped coffee into a pot and added water from his canteen. He set the pot beside the fire to heat.

Smoke sign promised warmth against a threatening cold sky.

As Hindman filled their cups, a lone rider appeared in the distance. "Looks like we might have company." He pointed with his chin. Brady and Mathews followed his line of sight to the approaching rider. He wore a battered sombrero and sat a sturdy roan. He drew rein and favored them with a gap-toothed grin.

"Thought I smelled coffee."

"Step on down," Brady offered. "I expect we got a cup left."

"Much obliged." He glanced at Brady. "Sheriff."

Brady rose. "William Brady, out of Lincoln." He extended his hand.

"I reckon I can remember that, William Bonney's the name." He took the sheriff's hand.

"These are my deputies, George Hindman and Billy Mathews."

Bonney nodded at the two men and accepted a cup from Hindman.

Mathews eased himself up. "Bonney, Bonney, somehow you look kind of familiar."

"Can't say you do. Must be I got a common face."

"Nope, not that common."

By the time Bonney realized what was happening, Mathews had both guns cocked and leveled at his gut.

"Get his gun, Sheriff." Brady lifted the Colt from Bonney's holster. "The last time I saw you was Silver City three years ago. The name was Henry Antrim then. I helped Sheriff Whitehall bring you in for horse stealin'. Looks like we got us our rustler, Sheriff. No need gettin' our asses froze off any worse than they already is."

CHAPTER TEN

Lincoln

Snow billowed out of a rumpled gray sky, swirling in sheets on a howling wind. The door clanged open to the visitor bell. A chill blast followed Jesse Evans' bundled figure.

"Where's Tunstall?"

Lucy blinked. "In the back, I'll get him."

"No need of that, my dear." He stepped out of the back room into the store. "Mr. Evans, isn't it, I believe. How may I be of service?"

"I need twenty hundred-weight bales of winter feed."

"Splendid! I shall be pleased to take care of that for you straight away." He stepped around behind the counter and scratched out his ciphers. "That comes to one hundred dollars." Evans tossed five twenty-dollar gold pieces on the counter. Tunstall scooped up the coins and slid a receipt across the counter. "Simply show this receipt to George Peppin and he'll be pleased to show you where you can load your feed."

Evans' jaw muscles bunched. "Double the price and you don't even touch the stuff. It's robbery I tell you, nothin' but black-hearted robbery."

"It's business, Mr. Evans. If you don't like my price, you're more than free to obtain your feed elsewhere."

"You know damn good and well you bought up all the feed in the county. You double your money and ranchers like me, haul it away for you."

Tunstall smiled. "Lovely little business, don't you think, Mr. Evans? Nearly as lucrative as rustling, but that of course is robbery."

Evans glared. *Not now. Not yet.*

Santa Fe

The US attorney for New Mexico Territory, T. B. Catron, scanned Dolan's letter by the light of a desk lamp. The dim light of late winter afternoon filled the corners of his spare office with shadows. Darkly handsome with lively brown eyes, Catron had lean, hawk-like features. His lanky frame folded in his desk chair as though confined to enforced inactivity. Ordinarily this sort of thing wouldn't merit his attention. He'd pass the request to an underling or disregard it altogether. In the case of Jimmy Dolan he knew better. Dolan had strong connections to Governor Axtell and even more importantly to the real power in the territory, Stephen Elkins. The Santa Fe Ring took care of its own. A debtor's lien on the livestock of an immigrant nobody ever heard of was a simple matter. No need to bother the higher-ups as long as he took care of it. If Dolan didn't get what he wanted, he'd go up the line and before you knew it, the damn thing would roll back downhill with a full head of steam. Who needed headaches like that for some no-account named Tunstall?

Lincoln

Ty lost a day to the storm getting back to town. The storm cleared out leaving the air sharp and bitter. The steeldust kicked up glittering puffs of snow as it jogged into a sun-washed Lincoln. He spotted Widenmann's horse at the Wortley hitch rack and checked his stomach, time for lunch. He wheeled his horse to the rail and swung down. Inside, the Wortley dining felt warm and smelled of fresh baked biscuits. Widenmann sat at a corner table. He glanced up and smiled.

"Grab a chair. The beef stew's hot and tasty."

"That sounds mighty good." He waved to the waiter. "I'll have some of that stew and coffee."

"Anything new over at Fort Stanton?"

"Just snow. Anything new around here?" The waiter arrived with a steaming bowl of stew and a cup of hot coffee before Widenmann could answer. "That looks damn good. I might just stick my fingers and toes in it till I can feel 'em again." He picked up his spoon. Widenmann picked up the conversation.

"Somebody hit the Flying H for fifty head of horses a few days ago."

Ty stopped a spoonful of stew halfway to his mouth. "That explains it."

"Explains what?"

"While I was at the fort, Jesse Evans and his boys come in with a herd of horses the army was lookin' to buy. Struck me as odd. I never knew Evans to deal in horses. Must have been near fifty head as I think about it."

"Sounds like too much to credit coincidence, don't you think?"

"Way too much where Evans is concerned. I was with the colonel when he checked 'em out. No brands, so anything we got is circumstantial."

"Still, it'd be worth reporting to Sheriff Brady. He's got an outstanding complaint from Tunstall."

"A lot of good that will do."

"Think of it as entertainment. Will Brady ride down to Seven Rivers to check it out or not?"

"You couldn't find anybody fool enough to take that bet."

"We know Brady's in Dolan's pocket. Evans is just speculation. If Brady don't check out the lead, it's one more brick on the side of Evans and Dolan bein' in cahoots."

"How many bricks you figure you need to prove the obvious?"

A draft of cold air from the office door announced visitors. Brady rocked back to a groan from his barrel-backed desk chair. Widenmann filled the door followed by Ledger. *Now what?* "Afternoon, Marshal. To what do I owe the pleasure?"

"Afternoon, Sheriff. Deputy Ledger has something for you on the Flying H horse theft."

"I see. Well, let's hear it, Ledger."

"I saw a herd of about the size reported stolen bein' delivered for sale at Fort Stanton two days ago."

"What makes you think those horses belong to the Flying H herd?"

"Fifty head is a good-sized herd. It don't hide easy. It'd be a lot to put down to coincidence, don't you think? It's at least worth askin' the man who brought 'em in where he came by 'em."

"And who might that be?"

"Jesse Evans."

Brady furrowed bushy brows. He shrugged. "Chasing all the way down to Seven Rivers in the dead of winter over a range herd of mustangs don't make no sense. Besides, we already got the Flying H rustler in custody."

Widenmann raised his brows. "Really? And who might that be?"

"He goes by the name William Bonney these days, though we got a witness who knows him as Henry Antrim from his horse thievin' days up to Silver City."

"You have a witness to the Flying H theft?"

"No, I said we got a witness that knows him for a horse thief."

William Bonney, Ty remembered the good-humored young man he'd met on the street. "You mind if we have a word with the suspect?"

"Be my guest. He'll deny it, but that's for a court to decide. He's back in cell two. You'll have to leave your weapons here." Brady rose and crossed the office to the jail door. "You got visitors, Bonney."

Ty and Widenmann dropped their gun belts on the desk and crossed the office.

Widenmann lowered his voice as they stepped inside the small cell block. "What do you hope to gain by talking to the suspect?"

"The truth."

"What makes you think he'll tell the truth."

"I've met the young man. I want to look him in the eye and ask him if he did it."

"Marshal Ledger, isn't it?" The kid blinked.

"It is, William. This here's Marshal Widenmann."

"Pleased to meet you." He gapped a smile at Widenmann and turned to Ty. "Marshal, I don't give a damn what the sheriff or that deputy Mathews says, I didn't steal no horses. Hell, all I done was ride into their campfire lookin' for a cup of coffee. Next thing you know I'm locked up on the say-so of that deputy."

"I believe you, William. We think we know who stole those horses."

"Then you think you can get me out of here?"

"We'll try."

Ty and Widenmann jogged their horses down the street to Tunstall's store as the late afternoon sun beat a hasty retreat into the mountains west of town. Whatever feeling of warmth the day might have offered disappeared quickly with the arrival of evening.

"You're sure about him?" Widenmann's words hung in steam. A light white frost tipped his mustache.

"The kid is tellin' the truth, Rob. You don't run off fifty head of horses single-handed. Evans had three men helpin' him with that herd."

"Seems like you're basin' a lot on circumstances."

Ty cut his eyes to the marshal. "Where there's that much smoke, somethin's burnin'. Evans is guilty sure as I'm standin' here."

"I don't know how you're gonna prove anything, but I'll talk to Tunstall." They drew rein in front of the store and stepped down, just as Lucy came out bundled in her shawl for the walk home."

"Marshal, Ty." She smiled.

Widenmann tipped his hat. "Miss Lucy."

"You go along, Rob. I'd like to walk Lucy home. I'll meet you later for supper."

He gave Ty a knowing nod and crossed the boardwalk to the greeting of the visitor bell.

"Mind if I walk you home?"

She hesitated a moment and smiled. "Kind of like old times." She started down the walk. He trailed along in the street, leading the steeldust.

"How is the store doing?"

She tilted her chin with a half smile. "Business couldn't be better. Murphy and Dolan really did have a stranglehold on this county. John has changed that. People come to the store to shop at better prices. Then they trust their money to the bank. The bank and the store get stronger together."

"How much longer does he think Dolan will take all this lying down?"

She knit her brows in thought. "John doesn't believe Dolan can do anything about it. He could lower his prices, but it wouldn't make that much difference. People resent him for all the years he and Murphy took advantage of them."

"Tunstall is wrong about that."

"About people resenting Dolan?"

"No. About Dolan not being able to do anything to stop him."

She took his warning with a worried set to her jaw as they reached the widow O'Hara's front gate. She tugged her shawl tight around her shoulders. "It's cold, Ty. Would you like to come in?"

"Would you like me to?"

Her eyes found his. "Yes, yes I'd like that."

Ty looped the steeldust's rein over the picket fence and opened the gate to a familiar squeal. He followed Lucy up the walk to the green door. She let them inside and hung her shawl on a peg by the door. She took Ty's hat and hung it on the peg over her shawl.

"Lucy, dear," Mrs. O'Hara called from the kitchen. "Dinner won't be ready for a few minutes." She appeared in the dimly lit hallway. "Oh, Marshal Ledger." She smiled. "So nice to see you again. It's been ever so long. Will you be staying for supper?"

"No, thank you, Mrs. O'Hara. I have to meet Marshal Widenmann."

"Perhaps another time then."

She still liked him. He could tell.

"Do come in and sit for a minute." Lucy led the way to the parlor. She took her place on the settee. Ty took a seat beside her.

"Thanks for walking me home."

He folded his hands in his lap. "I wanted to talk to you. I think Tunstall underestimates Dolan. The situation is dangerous. I don't want to see you get caught in the middle of that kind of trouble."

"A girl's got to take care of herself."

"She—" he started to object. "Look, it's not my place.

Trouble is coming. I can smell it. I can't help but worry."

Her eyes softened. The old connection was still there. She felt it.

He met her eyes and felt it too.

"It's sweet of you to care."

He looked away suddenly uncomfortable with what more to say. He felt that special something. He didn't trust himself with it. "You probably don't even carry that pepperbox anymore."

She smiled, a wistful warmth in her eye.

"I best be goin'." He rose.

Lucy followed him to the parlor and retrieved his hat from the peg. "Thanks for walking me home, Ty. And thanks again for caring." She pulled herself up on her toes and kissed his cheek.

The air between them grew soft and warm. He touched her cheek, and let himself out into the cold.

CHAPTER ELEVEN

Tunstall sat behind the counter balancing the bank ledger for the day's transactions. He set his pencil aside at the sound of the visitor's bell. He greeted Widenmann with a smile.

"Good evening, Rob. We were just closing up. Is there something you need?"

"Just stopped by for a talk."

"Always good to see you for that. What's on your mind?"

"Ty got back from Fort Stanton this afternoon. Jesse Evans delivered fifty head of horses there two days ago."

"My horses. That would explain where he got the money to pay for his winter feed. The scoundrel bought the feed with the proceeds from the sale of my stolen property." He shucked his apron. "We must notify Sheriff Brady at once."

"We already did. Brady's got a man in jail charged with stealin' your herd."

"Then it would appear he has the wrong man. He should release him straight away and go after Evans."

"That's not likely to happen, John. Evans is Dolan's man and so is Brady."

"You can't possibly mean the sheriff would permit such a miscarriage of justice."

"That's exactly what I mean."

"Well we shall see about that. I've made my intentions quite clear to the sheriff. If he fails to do his duty in the recovery of my horses, I shall be forced to expose him to every newspaper in the territory."

"Dolan wouldn't like that. Dolan's friends in Santa Fe wouldn't like it, either. You're already a burr under Dolan's saddle, John, what with the store and the bank. You haven't made any friends with the small ranchers, either, over your feed business. It won't take much encouragement for Dolan or one of his friends to decide you've become a problem that needs takin' care of."

"Are you implying Dolan might resort to violence?"

"I'm not implyin'. I'm promisin'."

"I've done nothing illegal. Dolan isn't free to violate the law at his whim and pleasure."

"Dolan is the law in Lincoln County."

"So what's to be done about it?"

"You didn't hear this from me, but if I was you, I'd have Brewer and your boys ride down to Seven Rivers to see what they can find out."

"Take the law into our own hands, you mean. I don't like the sound of that. It makes us no better than Dolan. Perhaps you could deputize my men. At that, we'd be carrying out the law, where the sheriff refuses."

He smoothed his mustache. "I suppose I could do that. We'd have to come up with some reason to raise a posse under federal jurisdiction."

"Splendid. Then we've only to go down to that jail and obtain the release of that innocent man."

Ty walked me home from the store again tonight. He warned me about John underestimating Dolan. He's right, of course. He says he doesn't want to see me caught in the middle of that kind of trouble. I think he means it. I asked him in. He asked me if I meant it. I did. He didn't stay long, but it was long enough for one thing. That old something, it's still there. I kissed him good-bye. I probably shouldn't have, but I did. Wish I knew what to make of this.

She set her pen aside and blew on the page. She closed the journal and stretched. Her chair scraped back. Her silhouette bent to huff out the lamp. She felt her way to the bed. The springs gave a comforting groan. She stared into the darkness. He appeared, tall and rugged. She felt his strength and something more. The vision faded.

John. He had that suave manner, so certain, yet so unaware in so many ways. He wore his feelings on the sleeve of a brown coat. Could a man like that beat Jimmy Dolan? He thought so. Ty doubted it. She doubted it. Mrs. O'Hara doubted it first. He had John Chisum's support. What did that really count for? South Spring was a long way off. Still she had a decent job and the prospect of more financial security than she might ever have imagined. What was a girl to do?

Ty . . . she drifted off to sleep.

Morning sun rode high in a bright blue sky with enough warmth to thaw street ruts to a sticky slur. The air smelled of mud and horse droppings, making a hint of spring out of the familiar scent of snow. Tunstall crossed the street to the sheriff's office ankle deep in the sucking sounds of false promise. He climbed the steps, anxious to be about his business and get back to the store.

Sheriff Brady blinked behind smudged spectacles, his immediate reaction irritation. "Good morning, Tunstall. What's on your mind?"

"I understand you are holding a suspect in the matter of my stolen horses."

Brady nodded.

"I'd like to see the prisoner."

"I can't imagine what for."

"They are my horses, Sheriff."

"Suit yourself. Follow me." He rose, took the keys from a peg beside the door and led the way into the jail. Gray light spilled out of two small windows, barely banishing night chill on solid adobe walls. They found the kid lying on his bunk, wrapped in a thin blanket, staring at the ceiling.

"There he is, Tunstall. Calls himself William Bonney, though there's some dispute about the claim."

"I've had the pleasure of meeting Mr. Bonney."

"Pleasure to meet a horse thief, you do beat all, Englishman. I don't suppose you have any need to get in there with him."

"Of course not. Don't be ridiculous."

"Let yourself out then when you're done." He ambled back to the office, his boot heels clicking the floorboards, keys jangling softly.

The kid sat up on the bunk. "Mr. Tunstall, what brings you to see me?"

"Very direct, I like that. The horses you are accused of stealing are mine. I want to know what became of them."

"I already told the sheriff. I have no idea. I didn't steal your horses or anybody else's. I rode into the sheriff's cook fire lookin' for a cup of coffee. Deputy Mathews claims to know me from Silver City. He accused me of stealin' your horses on account of that. So they arrested me. I didn't do it, Mr. Tunstall. I swear I didn't. Besides ain't no man alive can herd fifty head of horses to no useful purpose by his-self. Run 'em off maybe, but that's about it."

Tunstall pursed his lips and nodded. "I may not be an accomplished horseman, but I see the logic in that. I believe you, William."

The kid's jaw dropped. "You do?"

"I do. Now we shall see what is to be done about getting you out of here."

Footfalls announced Tunstall as he strode purposefully into

Brady's office. "Sheriff, I insist you release that young man at once."

"What?"

"He is clearly innocent of the charges you have placed against him."

"What?"

"You've made no attempt to investigate a most incriminating set of circumstances surrounding the recent delivery of a herd of horses to Fort Stanton."

"You've been talkin' to Ledger and Widenmann."

"So have you. Still you've made no effort to investigate an event too curious to credit to coincidence."

"Ledger can't prove a thing."

"And neither can you with respect to Mr. Bonney. His arrest is little more than a ruse to cover the likelihood of Jesse Evans' guilt."

"Little more than a what?"

"I insist you release Mr. Bonney at once."

"Who the hell do you think you are?"

"The plaintiff. And since it is clear you have no intention of pursuing the matter, I'm dropping the charges."

"You're what?"

"You heard me. I thought the statement quite clear. I'm dropping the charges. Now release the young man at once."

"You're crazy."

Tunstall rested his hands on the sheriff's desk and leaned across to the bridge of his nose. "We'll see who is deranged, Sheriff. The citizens of this county deserve law and order and that means vigorous law enforcement. I intend to do somewhat more than write that letter to all the newspapers in the territory. I believe there is feeble Democrat opposition to you and your fellow Republicans. The citizens of this county are clearly benefiting from a little competition directed at your Mr. Dolan.

Well it's high time law enforcement around here benefited from a little competition. I intend to make it my business, not only to expose you, but to find a suitable candidate for the Democrats to run against you. I intend to see to it that you are run out of office. Your Mr. Dolan's days of running this county like his own private fiefdom are over. Now release Mr. Bonney this instant."

Brady rocked back in his chair. He leveled a venomous glare at the Englishman over the rim of his glasses. "You have no idea what you're gettin' yourself into, Tunstall. No idea."

"Is that a threat, Sheriff?"

"Take it any way you like. I'd call it good advice."

Brady clumped back to the jail. Moments later he returned with a grinning William Bonney. He opened the bottom drawer of his desk and handed the kid his gun belt. The kid strapped it on and checked the loads.

"Come along, William. It's a bit stuffy in here."

The kid tapped the brim of his hat to Brady and sauntered out the door behind Tunstall. Outside he took a deep breath of free air. "Thanks, Mr. Tunstall. I appreciate you stickin' up for me like that."

"The least I could do, William. What will you do now?"

He scratched the stubble on his chin. "I was on my way down to South Spring to see if Chisum was still hirin' men when the sheriff arrested me. S'pose I'll head that way again."

"I've got a better idea. Come along to the store with me. I'll write a recommendation to Dick Brewer, my foreman on the Flying H with instructions to hire you on as one of our men."

"Why that's the nicest thing anybody's ever done for me."

Tunstall studied him for a moment. "You mean that don't you, William."

The kid nodded.

"Very well then, you can save me a trip in the bargain. I want Dick to look into the matter of those stolen horses. I have reason to believe Jesse Evans and his Seven Rivers boys may have had a hand in it."

"Glad to do it, Mr. Tunstall."

"Splendid. Then come along, William. We shall get you started in our employ straight away."

"Much obliged, Mr. Tunstall. And please, call me Billy."

December 1877

Dolan spilled the contents of the canvas bag on his desk. Dull gray light seeped through the window seeming to shrink the small pile of currency and coin. He scowled and counted. He went to the office door.

"Jasper, where the hell did today's receipts go?"

"Those are today's receipts."

Dolan returned to his desk. He counted the cash, opened a ledger and entered the figures. He scanned the column. *The son of a bitch is killing me.* He stood and paced to the window. Light snow swirled in the gathering gloom. He clasped his hands behind his back. He needed cash to keep the store stocked. Cash had gone short since Tunstall opened his store. On paper, he held substantial assets in the form of the credit balances owed by his customers. That was on paper. The immediate problem was the cash he needed to meet his own obligations. The question was where to get it?

Then there was the problem of what to do about Tunstall. He'd had more than enough of the tight-assed Englishman. Following Chisum's lead, customers walked down the street to buy their supplies at lower prices. He'd lowered his prices only to have Tunstall match them. Given the choice of trading with Tunstall or the House at even pricing, people were choosing the Englishman. Tunstall offended a few small ranchers by cornering the market for winter feed. Between Chisum and Tunstall they'd recruited a small army of gunmen. Evans was already whining about the difficulty of obtaining stock for him. If he had to buy cattle to fill his next delivery for the reservation, he'd lose money on that too. It took cash to buy cattle, completing the circle back to the problem at hand. A rap at the door frame sounded behind him.

"Dolan, I thought you'd best hear about this."

Dolan glanced over his shoulder. Brady stood in the doorway. *Now what?*

"What is it, Sheriff?"

Brady stepped in and closed the door. "I had to let Bonney go."

"What the hell for?"

"Tunstall dropped the charges."

Dolan reddened. *Tunstall again.* "Did he find his horses?"

"In a manner of speakin'. Ty Ledger seen Jesse Evans deliver a herd to Fort Stanton. Tunstall figures that proves the kid didn't do it."

"What are you going to do about it?"

"You know me, Dolan. I don't plan to do a damn thing about it."

"So what's the problem?"

"Tunstall. He says he'll write letters to the editors of every newspaper in the territory complaining about the lack of law enforcement in Lincoln County."

"Big deal. People write to the newspapers all the time."

"That's just the beginning. He says he's going to make certain the Democrats have a competent candidate to run against me in the fall. He says the good citizens of this county benefited from a little competition in the mercantile business. Now it's time for them to benefit from competent law enforcement. He said I should be sure to pass that along to you."

"Hmm, it seems our Mr. Tunstall is getting far too big for his britches. A man best be careful when that happens. He could choke on his necktie or suffer somethin' even more unfortunate. You leave Mr. Tunstall to me, Sheriff. Now, let me ask you another question. Where do you stand with your tax collections?"

Brady shrugged. "I'm about to send the year-end receipts to Santa Fe."

"How much?"

"Three thousand or there about, why?"

"I'm in need of a temporary loan."

"A loan of territorial taxes? I never heard of such a thing. What will Santa Fe say?"

"You leave Santa Fe to me. Now go along back to your office. Pack up those tax receipts and bring them to me."

"You sure, Mr. Dolan?"

"Sure as hell, Sheriff. Now get to it."

Brady let himself out.

Dolan turned back to the window. *Go on and write your letter, you scrawny little bastard. You want to play rough, I'll show you rough. I'll show you a damn war.*

CHAPTER TWELVE

South Spring

Roth tugged the cinch finger-snug. The black snorted twin clouds of steam that let him know he had the saddle secured. He eased the stirrup fender off the saddle and gathered the rein at the corral rail. He felt her presence. She made no sound. He turned to her and smiled. She smiled weakly, a trace of something uncertain in her dark eyes. "I'm just ridin' down to check the river valley herd. I'll be back by suppertime."

She knew all this. It seemed not to matter when he discussed it with Señor John at supper last night. But that was before her dream. It woke her just before dawn, a dark presence. Señor John spoke of such men, one of those from his past. One of those was coming. She drew her shawl around her shoulders.

Bounty hunters had to read the men they were after. Their lives depended on it. He could read Dawn sometimes, but like most women, not always. He read her now. Something troubled her. He didn't know what. "What's wrong?"

"Dawn Sky had a dream."

"About?"

"A man."

She could be short on words sometimes. "What sort of man?"

"A man with a gun."

"Lots of men have guns."

"Not men who try to kill you."

He put an arm around her, as much for the cold as her fear.

"Look, I'm goin' down to check the river valley herd. I'll be back for supper. There ain't nothin' between here and the Rio Pecos but coyotes and maybe a deer or two." He kissed her hard. She held him to her soft warmth. "Now, don't fret. I'll be back before you know it."

She lifted her chin, her eyes still veiled in uncertainty. He stepped into the saddle with a smile and wheeled away at an easy jog. She knit her brow, dissatisfied. *Men.* He did not listen.

She turned away, determined. Her moccasins padded the hard ground along the corral fence to the stable. She stepped into dim light, the sweet smell of hay pungent with horse scent and a hint of warmth coming from the stalls. Horses made soft sounds quietly munching their morning feed. She heard the big black man in the loft, pitching hay to the stalls below. She climbed the ladder. He turned to greet her as she made her way along the loft among piles of fodder.

"Mornin', Miss Dawn." He smiled, his teeth bright white in the shadowy light. A light sheen of sweat glistened on his broad dark features in spite of the cold. "What brings you climbin' up here to see Ol' Deac."

Deacon Swain came to South Spring with Wade Caneris. He was a big powerful man. A former slave in South Carolina he ran away early in the war and fought for the Union serving with distinction. He drifted west after the war, caught on with the cattle trade moving herds north from Texas to the railheads. He'd worked several drives for Caneris who respected the quiet competence of the dark giant. Dawn Sky quickly came to trust the man's simple honesty. He accepted her dreams and visions without the questions that seemed to trouble so many whites.

She returned his smile, sobered and held his eyes.

"Ah, must be somethin' a troublin' you now." He set the pitchfork aside. "What is it, Miss Dawn?"

"Johnny gone to check the river valley herd."

"Someone do that most every day. I don't see no trouble with that."

"Bad man comes to look for him."

"Bad man?"

She nodded. "Bad man with gun."

"I 'spect this be one of them dreams of yours."

She nodded again.

"Did you tell Mr. John?"

She shook her head. "Señor John is afraid for Dawn Sky to marry Johnny because of the bad men who follow him." Her eyes filled with appeal.

"So you want Ol' Deac to follow along and keep an eye on him."

She nodded.

"Who's goin' look after feedin' these horses here then?"

She smiled and picked up the pitchfork.

Pecos River Valley

Crystobal drew rein. The sun climbed the morning sky, bright with a false promise of warmth. At least it did not snow. He reached under his serape and withdrew a cigarillo from his shirt pocket. He scratched a lucifer to light on the broad pommel of his Mexican saddle. He blew a mask of blue smoke and steam, savoring the harsh tobacco burn. He took warmth from hatred where his serape gave way to chill. He swept his eyes across the surrounding high desert hills, studded in snow-frosted juniper. His horse dropped its nose to sniff the frozen ground in search of something to browse. It could not be much farther to the Long Rail hacienda. With luck he would find him. He picked up the horse's head. His ears pricked up. He picked up his prance, anxious to be away. Crystobal eased him forward, weaving his way through the hills to avoid the skyline.

Two hours later a lone rider jogged out of the hills to the

north angling southeast to the river. Crystobal eased his horse into the shade beside a stand of juniper and watched the rider. A small smile creased his thin lips. He couldn't believe his good fortune. *The gringo rides alone.* With fortune such as this, he may have the pleasure of giving him a slow death. He swung onto Roth's back trail, keeping one eye on his prey while he searched for a place to ambush him.

The sun climbed high toward midday, burning off the morning chill with too little warmth to make up for a cutting wind. Something didn't feel right. Maybe it was Dawn and her dream. Roth had seen enough of her knowings and visions over the past year so as not to dismiss them out of hand. She had a knack for something she couldn't explain. He didn't understand it and neither did Chisum who had years of trying. This morning he had a strong feelin' he was bein' followed. He'd had that feeling before. He remembered the day a year ago. He'd checked his back trail all the long day before the night the Comanche captured him. He didn't like the feeling. He checked his back trail for the third time. Nothing.

Midday wore into early afternoon. The trail mounted the crest of a ridge and fell away in an easy dun-gray meander to the river valley below. The herd sprawled along the grassy riverbank, peacefully grazing and watering just like it should. No trouble here. He'd catch a bite of lunch and ride home. Routine, just like it should be. Things should have eased his mind for the thought. They didn't.

Crystobal followed the river below the rim of the valley wall to avoid painting his presence on the skyline. He drew rein and stepped down. He climbed to the crest and dropped to a knee. A half mile below, Roth's pony picked its way down the slope. He studied the valley wall to the south. A quarter mile further on another dry wash dropped through the hills, out of sight along the line Roth would follow. He smiled, returned to his horse and picked up a lope tracking his prey at a pace sufficient to overtake him.

Near the valley floor Roth felt it again. *Son of a bitch,* he just couldn't shake it. He checked his back trail one more time. Dust sign this time sure as hell. He checked the trail ahead. A rockfall piled around a narrow wash spilling in from the west. He could fort up there and wait to see who was on his trail. Dawn may have had the right of it after all. He eased the black on down to the wash and nosed him around a large boulder.

A shot rang out. The bullet bit the boulder behind his head, singing its death song in a shower of stone chips. Roth dropped from the saddle and scrambled into the rocks.

That was close. He peered through a crevice between two boulders. The shot came from somewhere up the trail he'd been riding. Slightly below him he guessed from the angle, somewhere below the south wall of the wash. The decision to pull off the trail likely messed up the shooter's ambush and saved his life in the bargain. Saved it, for now at least.

"You are one lucky hombre, gringo."

The voice echoed across the wash. *Crystobal.* "And you're one lousy back shooter, Crys. Can't draw, can't shoot and that's before the ladies speak up." Roth ducked. Wild rifle fire showered him in rock chips. "Why don't you throw that rifle where I can see it and com'on out so we can settle this like men?"

"You're a dead man, gringo."

"And you'd sooner piss your pants than face me."

Two more shots exploded and whined. "Waste of good ammunition, dumb ass."

The throaty report of a heavy-caliber rifle echoed down the

wash from above. Two quick shots answered. Powder smoke gave up Crystobal's position.

"Looks like we got company, Crys. Company that plays on my side."

"You all right, Mr. Johnny?"

Roth smiled. He recognized the voice and had a pretty good idea of how it got there. "I'm fine, Deac. Keep the son of a bitch pinned down with your Henry. Since he won't face me, I'm just gonna have to kill him."

The west side of the wash opened fire from above and below. Swain and Crystobal traded rounds fast and furious. Roth drew his guns and eased down to the base of the rockfall that covered him. He crouched low and dashed across the trail to the far wall. He worked his way down the slope judging the distance to the Mexican pistolero's position. He moved on a few yards to an opening where he judged he could come around behind the man. The shooting fell silent. Time to reload, he guessed. That made it time to move. He slowly climbed the wash wall where it grew shallow near the valley floor.

The flashy black burst from the rocks before he reached the crest. Crystobal lay on the horse's neck, trailing covering gunfire as he galloped away. Roth rose up and fired to no effect as his assailant disappeared around a nearby outcropping and hightailed away. *He'll be back. Count on it.*

Moments later Swain eased a sturdy bay down the trail. Roth climbed down from the rocks.

"Sorry I didn't get him, Mr. Johnny. He got his-self up and run 'afore I could reload."

"Don't give it another thought, Deac. I was mighty pleased to see you and Mr. Henry there come along when you did."

"Don't thank me. You best thank Miss Dawn. She know'd you be in trouble. She made Ol' Deac come after you."

"I figured as much. Let's grab us a bite to eat and go on

home. I figure we've seen the last of that one for a spell."

They ground tied their horses in the wash near the crest of the ridge. Roth didn't expect the Mexican pistolero would come back so soon, but holding the high ground with cover never hurt. Deac boiled up a pot of coffee to take the chill off and wash down a hardtack trail lunch. They settled across the fire to eat.

"How does she do it?" Roth said almost to himself.

Swain shook his massive head. "No way to tell, but she sure 'nuf do it. I seen it with that Patch man you tracked last year. Now this."

"She warned me. I guess I should have listened. Even more so when I got the feelin' I was bein' followed."

"Maybe next time you come to learn some."

"So how'd she happen to convince you to follow me?"

He chuckled deep in his belly. "Miss Dawn, she got her ways. She can make Ol' Deac do most whatever she please."

"She can be single-minded when she fixes to. What did John say?"

"She don't tell Mr. John. She done my chores so's I could go without gettin' in no trouble. She's fixin' to marry you, you know."

He laughed. "So I'm told."

"A man couldn't do no better than Miss Dawn. Best be good to her."

Roth rode with his thoughts on the trail back to South Spring. Swain's curiosity got the better of him as the sun descended into the west.

"Why was that Mex shootin' at you, Mr. Johnny?"

Roth nodded. He didn't much want to talk about it. Then again, he owed Deac and talking might help his current troubles some. "Name's Crystobal. He's a gun for hire. Works for Evans down here. I crossed him in Santa Fe last year. He called me out for crowdin' in on a woman he figured belonged to him. He lost. I thought I finished him. Turns out I didn't. Now he's come lookin' for me."

"A woman, that must a been before Miss Dawn."

Roth cocked an eye and smiled. "It was."

"So what you fixin' to do about this Crystobal? He run off, but he'll be back."

"I'll have to face him sooner or later."

"Ain't none of Ol' Deac's business, but if I was you I'd make it sooner before later. Miss Dawn says he's a trouble to Mr. John. You don't want a go frettin' Mr. John none."

"I know. Trouble is, Deac, I got a past. Crystobal may not be the last one to come gunnin' for me. John worries about Dawn Sky like she was his daughter. Can't say I blame him. Not much I can do about the past. For now, I'll just have to deal with Crystobal and do it soon."

CHAPTER THIRTEEN

South Spring

Winter sun set early. Temperatures dropped fast when it did. Horses and riders huffed clouds of steam in the glimmer of starlight as Roth and Swain jogged through the gate. Lamplight set the hacienda and bunkhouse aglow with warm welcome. They turned their horses toward the barn, drew rein and stepped down.

Swain smiled bright in the fading light. "Let me put up these horses," he said, taking Roth's rein. "You best get on up to the house." He lifted his chin to a figure, standing in the porch shadow, her breath haloed in the first pale glow of moonlight. "Someone's waitin' on you."

Roth passed him the rein with a grateful nod. "Thanks, Deac. Thanks for everything."

His old slouch hat bobbed. "You go along now and take good care of that little girl."

Little girl. Roth crunched across the yard. He bounced up the steps and swept her up in his arms. She shivered against him, her arms fierce with possession. Cinnamon in her hair mingled with the scent of new snow. She lifted her chin, her eyes in his.

"He came?"

"He did. Deac ran him off. Thank you for sending him."

"I was afraid."

"Did you tell John?"

She shook her head. "Señor John does not want Dawn Sky to

99

love you. He is afraid bad men will hurt her."

"Are you afraid?"

"Only if you are hurt."

He took her lips in his. Time slowed. He gave her warmth in the cold.

She sighed and rested her head against his chest. "Come in. Supper is ready."

It felt good to be home.

Flying H

The kid arrived with a break in the weather. With spring still a long way off, even a little warm-up thawed the hard edges. Brewer sat at the table and read Tunstall's letter by the sooty light of the kitchen window. "Well, it appears you're hired, Bonney." He turned to Middleton. "John, show William here where to stow his gear. Then gather up the boys. The boss has a job for us."

"William is it." Middleton looked amused.

"Aw shucks, call me Billy. All my friends do."

"All right, kid. Com'on. Bunks are in back."

Tunstall's Regulators gathered in the Flying H parlor. Brewer checked the room. Middleton, Big Jim French, Henry Brown, Fred Waite and the new kid, everyone accounted for.

"Boys, it seems the boss has run out of patience with Brady. Jesse Evans delivered fifty head of horses to Fort Stanton last week. To me that sounds like proof of what we smelled. Brady won't do nothin' about it."

The men exchanged looks.

"The boss thinks maybe we should take a ride down to Seven Rivers and have a talk with Evans. See if we can get to the truth of it or at least let the son of a bitch know we ain't fooled."

The men brightened at the prospect of a little action.

"I'll ride on over to South Spring to see if Chisum wants some of his boys in on the action. I'll be back day after tomorrow. We'll sort out a plan then."

South Spring

Swain paused, a forkful of hay poised over the stall below. A black spec moving through the hills caught his eye. He squinted against the slanting afternoon sun. "Rider a-comin'."

Caneris ambled over to the barn door. His eyes swept the hills south of the gate. Dust sign marked a lone rider. He waited and watched. These days in the Pecos valley a man never knew. The man drew closer and wheeled through the gate at an easy lope. He recognized Dick Brewer. Instinctive tension eased. Brewer pulled up and slipped down.

"Good day, Wade."

"Dick, it's been a while. What brings you up here?"

"A bit of business for Tunstall. Probably best if I chew it once. Is Chisum around?"

"Up to the house. Come along, maybe he'll find us a cup of coffee."

"That'd go good about now."

They trudged up to the house. Caneris knocked on the door. "Comin' " came with muffled footsteps within. Chisum opened the door.

"Hello, Dick. You lookin' for strays?"

"After a fashion."

"Com'on in. You too, Wade. Me and Johnny was just havin' a cup of coffee. Care to join us."

"I was hopin' you'd ask," Brewer said.

Roth stood to greet the new arrival as the men trooped into the dining room. They pulled chairs around the table. Dawn Sky appeared with fresh cups and the coffeepot. Chisum took his seat at the head of the table. "What's up, Dick?"

"I 'spect you heard we lost some horses a couple of weeks back."

"We did."

"It'll come as no surprise then that Brady ain't done shit about it. He made a show of arresting an innocent man. Tunstall dropped the charges against him."

"What makes you so sure he was innocent?"

"Two things. First, he says he didn't do it."

They laughed.

Brewer sobered. "Second, Jesse Evans sold fifty head of horses to the army at Fort Stanton three days after our herd was stolen."

Chisum clenched his jaw. "Now that sounds more like evidence. We've knowed Evans for a rustler for some time now, but this is the closest anyone's ever come to provin' it."

"Well it ain't proof enough for Brady to so much as get up off his ass and go ask a few questions."

"Likely he and Dolan know the answers already and ain't interested in anybody else findin' out what they are."

"That's pretty much the way we see it, John. Mr. Tunstall asked me and the boys to ride down to Seven Rivers and poke around to see if we can find out anything or at least let Evans know we're on to him. I thought you might want to have a hand in it."

"I'm all for sending Evans a message. Far as I'm concerned, he or any of his boys so much as leave a horse droppin' on South Spring, I'll be pleased to stretch his neck from the nearest tree."

"My men and I are ridin' day after tomorrow. Anyone you want to ride with us is welcome to stay the night at the Flyin' H tomorrow."

Roth turned to Chisum. "I'd like to ride along, John."

Chisum took his interest with a nod. "Take Frank and Tom with you."

"I expect you'll want to start back in the morning, Dick."

Brewer nodded.

"Good, then you'll join us for supper. Johnny will fix you up with a place to bed down in the bunkhouse."

Roth eased his chair back. "I'll tell the boys to get ready."

Chapter Fourteen

Seven Rivers

Brewer threw up a hand and brought the band down to a walk. The horses needed a blow from the brisk pace he'd pushed on the ride down to Seven Rivers. Roth and Chisum's man, Frank McNab, flanked Brewer at his stirrups. They had a warm day by January standards, which meant the cold wasn't bad enough to numb a man's fingers. The sun dodged in and out of puffy gray clouds, muting the warmth with gusts of chill and a threat of snow if the clouds were to get organized.

"How much farther?" At six feet tall with broad shoulders, square jaw and clear blue eyes, McNab made a commanding presence. He exuded a quiet confidence that usually placed him in a leadership position when gunmen gathered. In this case, Brewer had that job courtesy of the paymaster.

Brewer cocked an eye to the sun. "An hour or so, if we keep up the pace."

Further back a ruddy young Irishman eased his horse up beside the kid. He had an unruly shock of red hair peeking out from under his hat brim, a splash of freckles across the bridge of his nose and a mischievous glint in his eye.

"So, how long you been workin' for Tunstall?"

Billy measured his questioner. "Who's askin'?"

"Tom O'Folliard." He flashed a ready smile.

The kid caught the mischievous schoolboy look in his eye, somewhat out of place among the hardened gunfighters that made up this bunch. He had one too. "William Bonney." He extended a hand across his saddle. "My friends call me Billy."

O'Folliard took his hand. "Pleased to meet you, Billy."

"I signed on with Mr. Tunstall a couple weeks back."

"I thought Brewer did all the hirin' for that outfit."

"Mostly he does." The kid straightened in his saddle. "He hired me on Mr. Tunstall's say so."

"Handpicked by the man himself." O'Folliard looked impressed.

"S'pose you could say that. I'm mighty grateful to him for springin' me out of the Lincoln jail the way he done."

"Jail, how'd he do that?"

"That son of a bitch Brady locked me up for stealin' some of Mr. Tunstall's horses. I didn't do it. Mr. Tunstall believed me. He dropped the charges and got me out. We're on our way down to Seven Rivers to find the man who truly took them horses."

"That part I knew. This Tunstall must be a stand-up hombre."

The kid nodded. "Mr. Tunstall is the only man ever treated me like I was free-born white."

Brewer turned in his saddle. "We'll be crossin' into Seven Rivers range pretty soon now. Be on the lookout for range stock." He squeezed up a lope.

Brewer drew rein at the crest of the valley wall. The men fanned out in a line to his left and right. A ramshackle ranch house and outbuildings nestled in the shallow valley below. A broken-down corral stood empty beside a barn with a sagging roof. They found no sign of Flying H stock on the ride down. A wisp of smoke from the ranch house stovepipe gave the only sign of life below.

McNab scanned the horizon. "Looks like they've cut and run

or gone off somewhere."

Brewer eased forward in his saddle. "You're sure no one's down there. How can you tell from here?"

"Fire's dyin'. They ain't been gone long, but they're gone."

Roth had his doubts. "Let's ride on in. Maybe we get lucky and pick up a trail or find somebody who'll tell us where they've gone."

McNab glanced at Roth. "Tell us?"

Roth shrugged. "Might take a little encouraging."

"Just might. Spread out men. Don't give 'em no bunched-up targets."

A search of the house and barn turned up the embers of a dying fire. They found fresh horse sign around the corral, but no more trail than one rider gone here and another there. McNab waited on the ranch house porch with Roth while Brewer and the rest of the men finished their search. Brewer was the last to return. He looked from man to man with little to show other than a head shake, a shrug or the occasional grunt.

"Nothin'. It's like they knew we was comin'."

McNab shifted a match stick from one side of his mouth to the other. "Sure looks that way, don't it."

Brewer spat. "Hell of a long ride for nothin'."

CHAPTER FIFTEEN

Lincoln

He'd done it. The prissy little shit had gone and done it. Brady tossed the *New Mexican* editorial page aside. *"A man of competent credentials," to run against me; who might that be?* Hell, it could be anybody. The question was what's to be done about it? Dolan wouldn't like it. He already had it in for Tunstall, plenty. He could count on Dolan. Unless Dolan decided he might lose. Then what? Play the game, do what you're told and this is the thanks you get.

The dinner crowd at the Wortley dining room mostly catered to drummers. This night James Dolan and George Peppin had a back corner table. Dolan pushed last week's issue of the *Santa Fe New Mexican* across the table.

"Read this." He swirled the whiskey in his glass and took a swallow.

Peppin picked up the paper. He drew a pair of smudged spectacles from his inside vest pocket and fitted the wires over his ears.

Dear Editor,

    As a businessman recently arrived in New Mexico, I have quickly embraced territorial aspirations to statehood. It is widely understood that the establishment of law and order is essential to winning admission to the Union. It is with grave concern then that I must report the shoddy record of performance in that duty by William Brady, the current sheriff of Lincoln County.

Recently, a small ranch holding of mine was victimized by a murderous band of cutthroat horse thieves. Fully fifty horses were stolen in the dark of night at considerable risk to the lives of my foreman and ranch hands. Sheriff Brady made no effort to investigate the crime until extreme pressure was applied on my own behalf as plaintiff. Only then did he arrest a man whose innocence was later established. An eyewitness reported the sale of fifty horses to the army post at Fort Stanton by credible suspects in the matter a mere three days following my loss. To this writing, Sheriff Brady has refused to investigate this report, raising questions concerning his own complicity.

Sheriff Brady, a Republican, must stand for reelection this fall. I call on the law-abiding citizens of Lincoln County and all New Mexicans concerned for admission to statehood to apply their energies and support to defeat Sheriff Brady and root out corruption in Lincoln County law enforcement. I shall do all in my power to see that a man of competent credentials is selected to oppose him.

Sincerely,
John H. Tunstall

Peppin passed the paper back across the table. "Kind of highfalutin', ain't he?"

"That letter has run in every newspaper in the territory. Brady isn't popular to start with. We've mostly kept him in office by seeing to it he runs unopposed. Up to now the Democrats haven't been able to find their ass with either hand in a well-lighted room. Tunstall means to change that. He's already caused plenty of trouble with his business dealings. We can't afford to let him do any more damage to our little arrangement here, now, can we?"

"What's it to me, Dolan? I kind of like his little winter feed business. I grow it, cut it and his customers come pick it up. Pretty easy."

"At twice the price you get."

Peppin shrugged.

"I'm not here to talk about hay, George. Though, if you like the arrangement, I'll be more than happy to take over the contract should Tunstall, shall we say, default for any reason."

Peppin read the threat in Dolan's expression. "If we're not here to talk hay then, what do you want with me?"

"I want you to run for sheriff in the fall."

"What about Brady?"

"If you run, he'll lose Republican backing. With it, you'll beat whoever Tunstall and the Democrats come up with."

"Hedgin' your bets already? Tunstall's really got your number, don't he?"

Dolan scowled.

"Why don't you call out the son of a bitch and shoot him. It'd be quicker and a damn sight cheaper." He glanced over Dolan's shoulder at the door. "Speak of the devil, here he comes now."

Dolan followed Peppin's gaze. Tunstall stood just inside the door with Lucy Sample and the McSweens. The waiter showed them to a table not far from the door.

"Let's get out of here. The air in here has got foul. We can continue our discussion over a drink at the cantina." Dolan scraped his chair.

Peppin led the way past the Tunstall-McSween table.

"I say, George, good to see you." Tunstall stood with a smile and offered Peppin his hand. He didn't notice Dolan following along. "I didn't know you were in town. I believe we've sold most of your cuttings from last fall."

"Pretty near."

Dolan stopped behind Peppin.

"Ah, sorry, old man, I didn't know you were, ah busy. Dolan." A curt nod passed for greeting.

"Com'on, George. Like I told you, the air in here has gone foul."

Tunstall chuckled. He nodded to the paper tucked under Dolan's arm. "I see you've read my letter. It's been in all the papers."

"So I hear. If you're planning on running for sheriff, Tunstall, you best start carrying a gun."

"Oh, my heavens no, you flatter me. I shan't run myself." He sobered. "I merely mean to see to it that a competent man opposes your lackey."

"You best be careful, Tunstall, before that mouth of yours gets you killed."

"I believe that sounds like a threat, Dolan."

"No threat, just neighborly advice." He eased his coat back, exposing the butt of a gun resting in a shoulder holster. "Though I'd be more than happy to oblige if you ever have the guts to strap on a gun."

Tunstall laughed. "You can't be serious; a duel? Dueling went out with powdered wigs."

"Not out here."

"Yes, I suppose I should have expected something like that of a hinterland colonial. You see that's the problem with you, Dolan. You're old school. It is precisely that sort of thinking that denies New Mexico's aspiration to statehood. The voters of Lincoln County understand that. You'll soon learn it too, come the next election. The noted English playwright, Edward Bulwer-Lytton said it best when he wrote, 'The pen is mightier than the sword.' "

Dolan clenched his jaw. "We'll see, Tunstall. Nobody ever got lead poisoning from a pot of ink." Dolan turned on his heel and stalked out the door, trailing Peppin.

Tunstall took his seat, making a show of arranging his napkin on his lap.

"You know you really shouldn't goad him like that, John."

He cocked an amused eye at McSween. "He makes it so deliciously easy."

"I'm telling you as a friend and your attorney. If Dolan decides to play rough, it will be his game and his rules. You won't like either of them."

"He doesn't frighten me. He threatened me in front of witnesses. Should anything untoward happen, he would be first to come under suspicion."

"A lot of good that will do if you're dead. Ask yourself, who's going to satisfy your corpse by enforcing the law?"

Tunstall leaned forward as if to object. Lucy cut him off.

"Alex is right, John. Men out here don't do things the way they are done back in England."

"Yes, well it's high time New Mexico got around to civil society."

Dolan's head hurt. Cold morning sun streaming through the dusty office window did nothing for it. He'd let the damn Englishman get under his skin. He tried to put the anger out with whiskey and now he had to pay the price for that too. He should have shot the son of a bitch where he stood. Humiliate him like that in front of folks with his high-minded airs. Out here men died for less than that. Well, John Tunstall was as good as dead. He didn't know where and he didn't know when, but the man wouldn't live to see election results. There, at least his anger felt some better.

Two Weeks Later

McSween sat at his desk sipping his morning coffee. Bright sunlight reflected off a fresh snowfall filled the room with a cool white light. A rap at the door summoned his attention. He went to the door. The Englishman's familiar silhouette stood on the porch beyond the lace-curtained window. He opened the door.

"Good morning, John. What brings you by so early?"

"Just this." He drew a folded copy of the *New Mexican* from under his arm and held it up.

"Come in. I expect this means we've something to discuss."

"I should think." He shrugged out of his heavy coat. McSween took it and hung it on the coat tree beside the door.

"Come into the office." He led the way. "Care for a cup of coffee?"

"Thank you, no. I can't make a taste for it. I've just had a cup of tea with my breakfast."

McSween took his seat, gesturing to a visitor chair across from the desk. "Now, what's on your mind?"

"This." He unfolded the newspaper and laid it on the desk.

McSween glanced at the banner. The paper was a week old. Tunstall pointed to a schedule of tax receipts printed in conjunction with the governor's annual report to the territorial legislature.

"What am I looking for?"

"Lincoln County tax receipts."

McSween traced a finger down the column. "Zero?"

"Zero. I do recall you paying your taxes as well as remitting mine for me."

"What happened to them?"

"My question exactly."

"You don't suppose . . ."

"Quite possibly. We do know our Mr. Dolan is, shall we say, pinched for cash."

"I find that hard to believe even of Jimmy Dolan."

"You may if you wish. As a taxpayer, I wish to know what became of my tax money. How do you suggest we proceed?"

McSween paused. "I'll wire the governor's office and ask for an explanation."

Two Days Later

Tunstall hunched over the bank ledger card when the visitor bell rang. McSween came through the door and glanced around the store. Tunstall waved from behind the teller cage. The lawyer crossed to the desk holding a sheet of yellow foolscap. He met Tunstall's gaze.

"You were right." He slid the telegram across the teller counter.

Tunstall read. The reply to McSween's telegram to the governor's office came from the US attorney's office. It stated that proceeds of the Lincoln County tax receipts for the past year had been extended as a loan to the firm of J. J. Dolan with the approval of the appropriate authorities. The telegram was signed T. B. Catron. Tunstall slid the telegram back across the counter.

"I suspected as much, but suspicion makes the admission no less outrageous."

"It is outrageous. Some might suggest criminal, but I'm sure no charge of that will ever be brought. Undoubtedly those responsible will have adequately covered their tracks for that."

"So you're saying nothing can be done about this?"

McSween shrugged. "I'm afraid that's the case."

Tunstall pounded a fist in the palm of his hand. "Damn it! There must be something." He lifted his gaze to the ceiling in thought. "I have it. The law may not be offended, but any man with a sense of fair play will be. We've caught the bloody bastard with his hand in the taxpayer's cookie jar. We can expose that even if the law fails to do so."

"What are you thinking, John?"

"Another exposé in the territorial newspapers seems appropriate."

"John, you don't want to do that."

"Oh, but I do."

"You saw how Dolan reacted to the Brady letter. You do it again and that gun of his won't stay in the holster."

"You say. I say Dolan is nothing but a blowhard and a dishonest one at that."

"Dishonest maybe, but don't bet he won't use that gun."

"We shall see."

"If you write that letter, my advice is get yourself a gun and learn to use it."

February 6th

The visitor bell clanged loud enough for a fire alarm. Jasper blinked behind his spectacles. The sheriff stomped off to Dolan's office without so much as a good afternoon.

Dolan was in a foul mood courtesy of another imbalance between his obligations coming due and cash on hand. The commotion coming from the store added to his irritation. Brady filled the door frame.

"Have you seen this?" He tossed a paper on the desk and closed the door.

Dolan picked up the *New Mexican*. This wasn't a letter to the editor. This was a news story, but there could be little doubt of the origin. The Englishman was quoted as though the reporter had interviewed him. Not likely. They'd tried to talk to the governor's office. That attempt had been passed to the US attorney's office. T. B. Catron did his best to dismiss the suggestion of impropriety, but the facts at hand were presented as clearly irregular. All of it was laid at the doorstep of J. J. Dolan and Sheriff William Brady. They even went back to repeat the charges leveled against the sheriff in Tunstall's earlier letter.

Finished, he tossed the paper back at Brady.

"I thought you said you'd take care of Santa Fe?"

"I did, you idiot. You're not under arrest, are you?"

"No, but this ain't gonna help if they find a Democrat to run in the fall."

"Fall's a long way off. If we don't find a way to stop that scrawny little English bastard, the election ain't gonna matter. Now get out of here and let me think." He massaged his temples, another damned headache. The answer was plain enough. The pompous little Englishman just signed his own death warrant.

Jasper tapped at the office door. "This letter come in from Santa Fe. Looks kind of official." He handed a thick envelope across the desk.

Dolan fumbled with his fine print reading spectacles and tore the envelope open.

By order of the US District Court, New Mexico Territory . . .

He refolded the order. T. B. Catron came through. He tapped the folded papers on his palm. He had a lien on Tunstall's stock. It wasn't a big thing when you considered the whole of the Englishman's business interests, but that wasn't the point. The point was what the righteous bastard might try to do about it. Dolan smiled. His head did feel some better.

The office door swung open to a chill blast. Dolan stepped inside.

"Sheriff."

"Afternoon, Mr. Dolan. What can I do for you?"

He pulled up a chair beside the desk and took a seat. He stretched his legs and crossed his boots at the ankle. He folded his hands across his belly. He looked too smug for the roil in

Brady's gut. He had somethin' on his mind or maybe up his sleeve.

He glanced at the paper on Brady's desk. "Kind of thrown down the gauntlet there, hasn't he?"

Years of dealin' with the unruly had taught him when in doubt, bluster. "Talk's cheap."

"Oh, that ain't talk, Sheriff. The man's dead serious. Told me so himself. I told him he might catch a case of lead poison if he didn't watch himself. It appears he don't listen too good."

Brady smoothed his mustache in the web of his thumb and forefinger. "So what are we goin' to do about it?"

Dolan lowered his voice. "Not we, Sheriff. You."

"All right then, what am I goin' to do about it?"

"Serve this." Dolan tossed a packet of papers across the desk.

Brady picked it up and read. He shrugged. "So you got a lien on his stock. He won't like it. So what?"

Dolan wagged a finger as though instructing a slow-witted child. "It's all in how you serve the order, Sheriff."

"Are we gonna sit here all day with me guessin' what the hell you want or are you gonna spit it out plain?"

"Do I have to spell out everything for you?" He sighed in disgust. "All right, shut up and listen. You go on down to Tunstall's store. You show him the court order. You tell him your men will be down to the Flying H to impound the stock next week. You get up a posse to do that. You put Billy Mathews in charge. If Tunstall objects, well, you know we can count on Billy to do the right thing."

Brady rocked back and smiled, remembering the Englishman's letter. *Yup, them's competent credentials all right.*

CHAPTER SIXTEEN

February 11ᵗʰ

The visitor bell split the morning stillness like a gunshot. Lucy jumped. Sheriff Brady stood in the doorway silhouetted in bright sunlight.

"Tunstall here?"

The abrupt question sounded official. "He's in back. I'll get him." She hurried around from behind the counter and made her way through the shelves to the back of the store. She found Tunstall deep in a corner of the dimly lit stockroom.

"Sheriff Brady is here to see you."

"Brady? Whatever might he want?" He wiped his hands on his apron and followed Lucy back to the store.

"Good morning, Sheriff. Don't tell me you've managed to apprehend those responsible for stealing my horses. No, I suppose not. That would be far too much to ask."

"Save your attitude, Tunstall. I'm here to serve a court-ordered lien on your Flying H stock."

"You'll have to pardon me, I'm afraid. For a moment there I thought you said someone's placed a lien on what's left of my herd."

"That's exactly what I said." He handed over the court order.

Tunstall scanned the document. "This is preposterous. The obligation is clearly that of the previous owner. I have no part in this."

"That's not how the court sees it."

117

"Well, the court has misjudged the matter."

"That's between you and the judge."

"Curious the alleged debt should be owed to James Dolan. This has the distinct odor of his Santa Fe friends about it."

"All I know is that my men will be down to the Flying H next week. Your boys best have them horses rounded up and ready to surrender."

"Mr. Dolan may be disappointed in the value of the remaining stock. You know we've suffered some recent losses to rustling. Oh, that's right, you do know."

"That'll be enough out of you. Just have those horses ready for my officers when they arrive."

"We shall see about that."

McSween read the complaint seated at his desk in the bookshelf-lined study that served as his home office. Midday sun filtered through lace curtains, bathing the room in a warm glow. Tunstall paced the pegged floor, barely able to curb his anger.

"Dolan is a rogue and a scoundrel. I don't doubt for a moment that he's trumped up this whole allegation simply to vex us."

"Hmm." McSween set the order aside. "That may be so, but we'll have to go to Santa Fe to fight it."

"I can't be bothered by such a frightful waste of time."

"The only alternative is to pay off the lien."

"That is robbery."

"I agree; but you don't have much choice in the matter."

"I shan't be bullied."

"What do you propose to do about it?"

"I'll not surrender my horses for one thing."

"Then you'll be found in contempt of court and thrown in jail. Look, John, the horses are small potatoes among the rest of your business interests. Surrender the horses and we'll go up to

Santa Fe and fight this thing."

"What makes you think we shall get a fair hearing, standing before a kangaroo court that makes its business the bidding of Dolan and his political cronies? I say we do every bit as well standing here defending our rights."

"You're the one who's always preaching law and order. How is it you can defy a court order when it inconveniences you?"

"Fighting is a civic duty when the order is unjust."

"Agreed. And that's why we need to go to Santa Fe to fight this according to the law."

"You fight it your way and I'll fight it mine."

"I can just picture it. Your Honor, my client is unable to dispute the merits of the matter before this court as he is presently incarcerated in the Lincoln County jail held in contempt of your order. Now there's a winning argument if I ever heard one."

"I see your point. You shall need a better argument then."

February 15th

The Colt .44 revolver action worked smoothly. Tunstall hefted the weapon, extended his arm and sighted it through the storefront window on a water barrel across the street. Oil mingled with the scent of metal and polished wood. He'd prefer a shotgun. He had some experience hunting doves with those. Strictly a gentlemen's outing, mind you, but firearm experience nonetheless. This weapon offered far less margin for error. Still he could take some comfort from the fact of having it. He thumbed the hammer and dry fired the gun. The sound reassured him.

Lucy peeked out of the fabric shelves drawn to the sound. Her eyes widened at the sight of the gun. "What are you planning to do with that?"

"Protect myself if need be. All you alarmists have convinced me I should arm myself."

"Have you any idea what to do with that?"

"I've some experience with firearms."

"Enough to get yourself killed most likely. If you're worried about needing protection, why don't you send for a couple of the boys? You're paying them to protect things. No reason that can't start with you."

"Hmm, your usual practical thought, leave it to the professionals. I shall have someone come along with me when I return. No time for that now, though. I shall see for myself until then."

"Where are you going?"

"I must ride down to the ranch to discuss the business of this court order with Dick."

"What is there to discuss?"

"Lucy, my dear, you don't suppose I'll allow Dolan to bully me, do you?"

"It's like Alex says, right or wrong, he's got the law on his side."

"There is no right to it in this case. The law is wrong. I can't stop Brady from trying to serve his writ, but we don't have to gift wrap my herd for him, either. If he wants them, he can round them up himself. I should think that by the time we are done, that will be no small undertaking. Put this pistol on my account, along with a box of cartridges and a holster."

She shook her head. *You'll get yourself killed.* "At least see if Rob Widenmann will ride down there with you."

Flying H
February 16th

"Riders coming." Fred Waite pointed off to the northwest. Brewer let down the fore hoof he'd been fitting for a shoe. He straightened up and followed the jut of Waite's chin across the bay's withers. The horse stamped as if protesting the interruption.

"We expectin' company?"

"None I know of," Brewer said.

"Looks like Mr. Tunstall," the kid called from the loft.

Brewer squinted. It did: *hawk-eyed pup, that one.*

Tunstall and Widenmann rode in at an easy jog. The kid scrambled down from the loft and waited at the corral to take their horses. They drew rein and stepped down.

"Here, Mr. Tunstall, let me take them horses for you. I'll cool them down proper and turn 'em out."

"Why, thank you, Billy. You're most kind."

Brewer stepped around the bay's rump, wiping his hands on a rag. He extended a hand. "Mr. Tunstall, Marshal, what brings you all the way down here?"

"We have a situation to discuss, Dick. May we go up to the house?"

"You're the boss."

Tunstall hunched his shoulders and set off for the house on a purposeful stride, trailing Widenmann behind. Brewer and Waite exchanged glances. The ramrod shrugged and hurried after his boss. Inside he pulled a couple of chairs up to the table.

"Coffee?"

Tunstall wrinkled his nose. "No thank you."

"I'd have a cup, Dick," Widenmann said.

Brewer poured two cups and settled in a chair. "What's on your mind?"

"Dolan has trumped up some unpaid debt against the ranch. He got a court in Santa Fe to issue a lien against the stock. The sheriff will be along in the next few days to take possession of the horses."

"You want us to round 'em up?"

"I do. Round them up and hide them."

121

Brewer smiled. "Gonna call their bluff?"

"No. I simply refuse to be bullied. Dolan has no claim on those horses. His only claim is on the jurisdiction of a corrupt court. Until such time as we have honest law enforcement in this county, it shall be our civic obligation to resist."

"Me and the boys will take care of it in the morning. Will you be ridin' back to Lincoln with Marshal Widenmann?"

"Not straight away. I believe I shall accompany you when you disperse the herd into hiding. I shall ride back to Lincoln from there. One more thing, I plan to take young Bonney back to Lincoln with me if that won't be too inconvenient."

Brewer shrugged. "Sure, no problem. Why?"

"Lucy and Alex are forever warning me about Dolan turning to violence over our business competitions. I'm sure their concerns are wholly overdone, but he did challenge me to one of your western gun duels last month. Rob was kind enough to accompany me down here on the chance of such an eventuality. I've also taken the precaution of acquiring a gun myself, but Lucy reminds me that since I've hired professionals for the purpose of protecting things, I should let them take care of that sort of thing."

"Sounds like good advice." He eyed the Colt on Tunstall's hip. "You know how to use that thing?"

"I've a rudimentary familiarity with a shotgun and doves."

"That hog leg matched against a man who knows how to use one is a far cry from bird huntin'."

"I thought as much."

"Let me and the boys round up the horses tomorrow. We'll leave Bonney behind to give you some shooting lessons. We'll go off and hide the herd day after tomorrow."

★   ★   ★   ★   ★

Lincoln

February 17ᵗʰ

By the time you allowed for a desk and a potbellied stove, the posse filled the sheriff's office and cell block with a few men spilled out on the boardwalk. Brady mulled the problem. You had to have someplace to take the horses once you had them. He smiled to himself. What could be better than Jesse Evans' neighboring ranch? That would sure as hell stick in Tunstall's craw. You could count on it. Maybe even goad the son of a bitch into doing something stupid. Evans brought Frank Baker and Buckshot Roberts along to help out. That pair would shoot first and ask questions later. Dolan would approve. Hell, knowing Dolan, he likely put Evans up to it. With Mathews in charge, this posse had the feel of dynamite on a short fuse.

"Swear in your men, Billy."

"Raise your right hands. Do you swear to uphold the law?"

They nodded.

Mathews handed out badges.

"All right, men." Brady looked from one to the next. "Billy, you got the court order?"

Mathews nodded.

"Good. Billy's in charge. Jesse, you and your men follow his lead."

Evans and the boys nodded.

"Once Brewer surrenders the horses, you drive 'em down to Seven Rivers for safekeepin'. You remember now, Mr. Dolan's got a lien on 'em. You'll be paid for their keep, but you best be sure nothin' happens to 'em."

Evans scowled. "Yeah, yeah, Brady, we understand."

"Good. See you don't forget it."

Mathews turned. "All right, boys, mount up."

They trooped out of the office.

Flying H

Bonney led the way down to the corral. He carried a stack of empty tomato cans he set in a line along the top rail.

"How much experience have you got with a gun, Mr. Tunstall?"

"To be honest, precious little I'm afraid, William. I've some experience hunting doves with a shotgun."

"Then you know enough not to point a gun at anything unless you mean to shoot it."

He nodded.

The kid shrugged. "That's a start. Doves is small and quick. A shotgun will forgive you a near miss. Men is bigger and slower. An armed man won't forgive you a near miss. You'd best hit him if you intend on using your gun. If you decide to use your gun, hit him first. He's less likely to hit you if you do."

"I see. Well that seems plain enough."

"Let's start about twelve paces." He led the way.

"This seems rather close. Not terribly sporting, I should think."

The kid knit his brow. "Nothin' sporting about a gunfight, Mr. Tunstall, it's life or death mostly. Now, let's see you shoot that can on the left."

He drew his gun, thumbed the hammer and extended his aim in the posture of a gentleman raising a dueling pistol. The .44 bucked a cloud of blue smoke. The can stood untouched.

"I say, that has quite a kick. Not as easy as it looks."

"High right."

"High right?"

"You missed, high and right."

"How do you know?"

"I saw it."

124

"You saw it?"

"I did. Try again."

He tightened his grip prepared for the concussion. He cocked the gun and fired. The shot bit the rail low left. The can stood its ground.

"Again."

He fired.

"Left. Again."

He fired.

"High."

"I'm beginning to see the wisdom of Lucy's advice."

"What's that?"

"She said let the professionals look after the gun work."

The kid nodded. "Here's why." In a blink he drew and fired five times in rapid succession. The cans danced off the rail, the last in the air before the first hit the ground.

"Oh, my. Is James Dolan that good?"

"No. But he's good enough."

"I'm hopeless then."

"Not hopeless, Mr. Tunstall, we've just got more work to do. Let me put those cans back up on the rail."

CHAPTER SEVENTEEN

Ruidoso Valley
February 18th

Late afternoon sun lingered, warming a mild winter afternoon. Brewer, Waite, and Tunstall pushed a small horse herd up a rise. Brewer had the left swing with Tunstall on the right. Waite held drag. The juniper-dotted rise descended into a narrow rock-strewn canyon bordered on both sides by broad sloping walls studded in patches of mesquite and creosote. The canyon fell away, spilling into the broader valley beyond.

Brewer had come up with the plan to hide the herd southwest of Lincoln, more or less under Brady's nose. Tunstall thought the idea amusing. He pictured the sheriff's posse miles to the south, searching trackless ranch land for a phantom herd. Brewer had Bonney and Middleton cover their back trail to provide warning of anyone attempting to follow. Now, descending the canyon with their destination in sight, all the precaution seemed needless.

The herd trailed down the canyon floor raising a light mist of dust. The occasional sound of a hoof striking rock punctuated their progress. As the canyon floor leveled out to a gentle descent, a flock of turkeys exploded from a creosote patch in a rush of wings and alarmed gabble.

"A couple of those would go good in the cook pot, Dick," Waite said.

Brewer nodded, drawing his Winchester. Waite drew his and

held it to Tunstall.

"Have a go at a hunt, Mr. Tunstall?"

"You go along, Fred. You're much better with that rifle than I. I'll push these horses along whilst you have your sport."

Brewer and Waite peeled away and loped up the hillside on the turkeys' line of flight. The flock settled somewhere up the hill, having taken sufficient flight to allay their alarm. Tunstall slipped back to drag, relying on the terrain to channel the herd along the way to the valley. Satisfied he had the situation in hand, he turned his attention to the turkey hunters.

Bonney and Middleton crested the rise. The canyon stretched out before them. A single rider pushed the herd dust cloud.

"Where is everybody?" Middleton said.

"There." Bonney pointed to the hillside west of the road.

"What the hell are they up to?"

As if to answer the question, the hunters jumped a turkey. One charged a puff of smoke, followed by a rifle report. The bird dropped. A second flushed to the second hunter's shot.

"So we've turned this drive into a turkey shoot."

The kid smiled. "Looks like fun. Com'on." He squeezed his roan into a lope down the hill.

"Hey, what about our back trail?"

"What back trail? We're about done."

Middleton followed the kid down to the canyon floor and jogged along toward the retreating herd and the hunters.

Tunstall took the first shot for another turkey then realized it came from behind. He turned in his saddle. He saw Bonney and Middleton similarly turned in their saddles fixed on a large band of riders cresting the rise at the south end of the canyon. More shots followed. Bonney broke west and spurred his big roan up the canyon floor toward a wooded thicket on the hillside. Middleton wheeled his horse and galloped toward Tunstall. Farther up the canyon hillside, Brewer and Waite were drawn to the volley of gunshots ringing off the canyon walls. They too galloped back toward cover of the wooded thicket on the hillside.

Tunstall circled his skittish mount trying to decide his best option as the posse thundered down to the canyon floor. Middleton waved his arm and shouted incomprehensibly as he raced up the canyon hillside to the east. The posse, perhaps twenty in number, divided. The main body raced to the west slope intent on assaulting the men taking cover in the thicket there. A smaller band appeared to pursue Middleton who, it seemed, would easily outdistance them until they turned toward Tunstall cutting him off from any run to safety. Unable to avoid confronting the sheriff's erstwhile deputies Tunstall settled his horse and stepped down. He expected the shooting on the west slope to stop as soon as he made it clear he did not mean to resist. It did not.

The riders drew closer. Badges confirmed these men for Brady's officers. He took some comfort. *They must be bound by the law they stand for.* Comfort withered with recognition. *Jesse Evans, what the hell was he doing wearing a badge?*

The leader drew rein. The posse men stepped down. Evans, Baker and Roberts spread out. "Tunstall, Deputy Sheriff Billy Mathews." He held up the court order. "We come for your horses."

"There they are. Now call off those men shooting over there. There is no need to attack my men."

"They seem to be resisting an officer in the performance of his duties."

"Resisting nonsense! You and your men opened fire on them. Now cease it at once!"

"You ain't givin' the orders here, Tunstall. I am. Now where are the rest of them horses?"

"That's all that remain after my rustling losses." He glared at Evans. "Now call off your men before someone gets hurt."

Evans stepped up next to Mathews. "Are we gonna stand here all day jawin' with the son of a bitch?" He jacked a round into his Winchester and leveled it at the Englishman. "Tunstall, you got ten seconds to tell us where to find the rest of them horses or I'm gonna shoot you for resisting arrest."

"You've an order to impound my horses. That is hardly an arrest warrant."

"You and your men will be under arrest for interferin' with an officer in the performance of his duties if you don't hand over them horses. Now where are they?"

"Sorry, old chap, I'm afraid I can't help you. You might be best to answer your own question. I suggest you start at Fort Stanton."

Evans' rifle bloomed muzzle flash and smoke. Tunstall staggered back. He grasped his side. Bright blood oozed between his fingers. He looked up in disbelief.

"I say, you've shot me. I'll see you hang for attempted murder."

Mathews drew his gun and thumbed the hammer. "You ain't seen nothin' yet, Tunstall. There's no attempt to it. You just ain't been shot good enough yet." The gun exploded. The back of Tunstall's head burst like a ripe mellon, his lifeless body slammed back against his horse and slumped to the ground. Evans stepped forward, straddling the body. He slammed his rifle butt across the bridge of the dead man's nose, flattening it between sightless eyes. "How's that for dead, you stinking son of a bitch?" He drew Tunstall's gun, fired it twice and dropped it beside the body.

"Com'on, Billy, let's get the hell out of here."

★ ★ ★ ★ ★

Lincoln
February 19th

Nature draped the sky in somber gray crape for the ride up to Lincoln. Brewer took the lead. The kid followed behind, leading Tunstall's gray with the body slung over the saddle. Middleton and Waite brought up the rear.

"Kid sure took it bad," Waite said.

Middleton nodded. "He told me once, Tunstall treated him like the father he never had."

"Didn't know him all that long, did he?"

"Nope. Then how long's long enough? The kid figures he'd have done hard time on that rustlin' charge if Tunstall hadn't sprung him. A man gets that personal with the idea of bein' behind bars for a spell, he can be damn appreciative of the man that gets him off."

"Why'd John do it?"

"The kid claimed he didn't do it. Tunstall believed him."

"How many times do you know that ever worked?"

Middleton spat a stream of tobacco juice. "Never."

"That about says it, don't it."

"Them fellers we run off the other day might have got clear of us, but I s'pect they ain't got clear of that kid. You can see it in his eyes."

"This thing between Dolan and Tunstall ain't over. Dolan may think it is, but he's wrong." He spat again. "That lawyer fella, McSween, had an interest in Tunstall's business. He's likely to take over the rest of it and he ain't goin' away."

"Chisum's got a stake in this too. Those boys weren't all Brady's regular deputies. I recognized some of Jesse Evans' Seven Rivers boys. If Evans had a hand in this, you can bet Chisum will take an interest in stringin' up them's responsible."

"We'll know soon enough. There's Lincoln up yonder."

Dolan stood at the window, hands clasped behind his back. Thick lacy snowflakes spread a light mantle over the somber procession making its way up the street. Brewer led the way followed by the Bonney kid leading Tunstall's horse with a blanket-covered body slung across the saddle. Two of the Englishmen's hired guns trailed behind. A lot of good they'd done him. The whole thing played out about as well as he could have planned it. He figured they'd put up more of a fight. Finding Tunstall alone made it easier than he could have imagined. By not turning over the horses, the arrogant fool's final act played right into his hands.

The stock he had left didn't cover the lien. He'd refile it against the ranch and get the whole shebang for the price of a bookkeeping transaction. With the Englishman out of the way, the future of the store and the bank were up in the air. The next order of business would be to offer McSween the chance to sell his interest. With Tunstall's businesses out of the way, it would be back to business as usual. Well, not quite usual, the bank provided cash and the river of profits that went with it. The Englishman had been smart about that, too smart for his own good. He'd gotten exactly what he deserved.

"Oh, no! Susan!" Lucy's hands shot to her mouth. Realization hit her in the chest and slowly sank to her stomach in a sour ball.

Susan left the teller's cage and ran to the window. She put a comforting arm around Lucy, who sobbed against her breast.

"I was afraid of this. He was too righteous for his own good. He had no idea what he was up against. I tried to tell him."

Susan could sympathize with the girl. They both knew what a man should expect going up against the likes of Jimmy Dolan.

131

She stroked Lucy's hair. "We all did, dear. Sometimes you just can't make a man listen." Somehow those words sounded more prophetic than profound. She dismissed the thought. Alex could take care of himself.

Lucy blinked at her tears and wiped her eyes on her sleeve. She sniffed. "Com'on. They're taking him to the sheriff's office. Let's go see what happened."

She started for the door. Susan grabbed her shawl from the peg beside the door. She took Lucy's too and hurried out the door, running after her over frozen muddy ruts. Snowflakes swirled in the air, melting against her cheeks.

Brewer and the boys stepped down. He looped a rein over the hitch rack as Lucy ran up to him.

"What happened, Dick?"

"Brady's posse hit us in the canyon south of the Ruidoso Valley. I figure they planned to serve the lien on our stock, but that was no more than an excuse. They opened fire before they even got to us. Most of us took cover in the hills to shoot it out. Mr. Tunstall got cut off. John Middleton tried to lead him to safety but he didn't follow. He may not have thought he was in danger. You know how he was about law and order."

"Why would they shoot him over such a thing?"

He shrugged. "We're here to report the killin'. We'll see what Brady has to say for himself. Fred you stay with the body. Com'on, kid."

Billy squared his shoulders and followed Brewer up the boardwalk. Brown and the women fell in behind. They crowded into the sheriff's office, finding Brady, as usual, at his desk.

"What do you want, Brewer?"

"You know damn good and well what we want. We brought in John Tunstall's body. He's been murdered."

"Murder's a reckless charge, Brewer. Tunstall was shot resisting arrest."

"Arrest on what charge?"

"Obstruction of a peace officer in the performance of his duty."

"That a shootin' offense?"

"The man was armed. He fired on my men."

"That cut and dried, is it?"

"That's how the law sees it."

"Then how come your men run off once they killed him?"

"You mean when you and Tunstall's hired guns fired on them."

"Bullshit, Brady! Pardon me, ladies. We both know John Tunstall was murdered sure as we're standin' here. Once he was dead, your boys did what murderers do. They ran."

"You got no proof, Brewer. I got the sworn statements of four duly authorized deputies. Now get the hell out of my office."

Brewer leaned across the desk. "You ain't heard the last of this, Brady."

"No, I s'pose not. Now you gonna take the body to the undertaker or should I."

The kid stepped up beside Brewer. "I'll take care of Mr. Tunstall, Sheriff. Like Dick said, you ain't heard the last of this. I'll see to that personal. You and every one of the stinkin' sons a bitches what killt John Tunstall is gonna hear from Billy Bonney. Count on it." He turned on his heel and led the way out of the office.

Chapter Eighteen

February 19th

The Regulators gathered in the Tunstall store with Widenmann and McSween. The kid stood at the window, watching the street.

"Mathews and Brady is up at the House," he said. He opened the gate and spun the cylinder of his Colt checking the loads. He holstered the gun and started for the door.

"Where are you going?" Brewer said.

"I'm gonna kill 'em."

"Look, kid, I want those responsible for Mr. Tunstall's death as bad as you do, but we have to figure a legal way to make them pay."

"Legal? Hell, Brady's the law. He's the one ordered the killin'."

"You don't know that. We know who done it. We need to get the law on 'em."

"They was Brady's men. Brady's the law. He won't do nothin'. So that leaves me to do the killin'."

"Now hold on. Mr. McSween, you're a lawyer. What should we do?"

McSween scratched his chin. "Rob is a deputy US marshal, but that's federal jurisdiction. Maybe you could stretch the fact that John was a foreign national, but even at that, he'd need authorization. It's best if we handle it as a local matter."

"So we're back to Brady."

"Not necessarily. Maybe we can get the justice of the peace

to issue warrants and appoint a constable to serve them. Dick, are you and Billy willing to swear out complaints that name the killers?"

Brewer looked to the kid. He nodded. Brewer nodded.

"Then we kill them," the kid said.

February 20th

McSween, Widenmann, Brewer and Bonney stood before Justice of the Peace John Wilson. He read the list of those named in the affidavit sworn by Brewer and Bonney. The attestees identified William Mathews, Jesse Evans, William "Buck" Morton, Frank Baker, George Hindman and Andrew "Buckshot" Roberts. Unnamed others were also implicated. He peeled off his spectacles and massaged the bridge of his nose between thumb and forefinger.

"That's quite a list. How'd you manage to leave Sheriff Brady off?"

"He'd a had to get off his butt to make the list," Brewer said.

Wilson chuckled. "Quite a few of Jimmy Dolan's boys too."

"If Brady planned it, Dolan ordered it," McSween said.

"Can you prove it?"

"No."

"Then this is about as good as we can do. I can issue warrants, but who is going to serve them?"

"You can appoint a constable," McSween said.

"That'll take some balls. You got anyone in mind?"

"Dick here will do it."

Wilson glanced at Brewer. He nodded.

"Raise your right hand."

The House

Brewer mounted the boardwalk fronting the Dolan store. The kid and Fred Waite followed. The visitor bell announced their arrival. Billy Mathews and Jesse Evans stood at the counter with Jimmy Dolan. Brewer and his men drew their guns.

"Billy Mathews, Jesse Evans, you're under arrest for the murder of John Tunstall."

"Says who?" Mathews snarled.

"Says these warrants. Get their guns, Fred."

Waite stepped forward to claim the guns. Dolan cut his eyes to Jasper, the clerk, and tossed his head to the back of the store. The clerk disappeared. Dolan turned to Brewer.

"What the hell do you think you're doing, Brewer?"

"I'm arresting these men for murder."

"On whose authority?"

"Justice Wilson issued the warrants. I'm his appointed constable and these are my deputies."

"Wilson knows very well we have a county sheriff."

"A sheriff most of whose men are implicated in the murder charges."

"What you call murder was a simple case of resisting arrest."

"That's for a court to decide." He waved his gun at the door. "Come along, boys."

Brady and Hindeman appeared in the doorway, guns drawn. "Not so fast, Brewer."

Baker, Morton and Roberts emerged from the back of the store, guns leveled.

"Now let's see who's under arrest. Get their guns."

Mathews and Evans retrieved their guns and relieved Brewer, Waite and the kid of theirs.

"Under arrest on what charge?" Brewer said.

"Impersonating a peace officer."

"Lock 'em up, Sheriff," Dolan said.

Dolan watched Brady march his prisoners down the street to the jail. Wilson stepping into local law enforcement added to the overall problem. Wilson had made up a legal jurisdiction to interfere with Brady's control over law and order. He'd need Governor Axtell to fix this little problem. He sent a telegram to Santa Fe that afternoon.

Tunstall Store

"He what?" McSween said.

"He locked 'em up," Widenmann said.

"On what charge?"

"Impersonating a peace officer."

"We'll see about that. Justice Wilson can straighten Brady out."

"Maybe he can legally, Alex, but that isn't likely to change anything. Brady's version of the law ain't interested in what's right and what's not. This is going to get ugly."

"I'm afraid you're right. Once we get Dick and the boys out of jail, we've still got conflicting jurisdictions respecting John's murderers. Maybe we should try to get federal jurisdiction based on the fact John was a foreign national."

"How do we go about doing that?"

"Normally you could petition the US attorney. In this case, that's T. B. Catron. That makes it a waste of time. Ask Marshal Sherman to ask Washington."

"That will take time."

"Can't be helped. In the meantime there is one thing we could try."

"What's that?"

"Brady doesn't know you need specific authority to assert jurisdiction."

"You saying I should bluff?"

"I'm saying you could try."

★　★　★　★　★

February 21ˢᵗ

Blue sky and morning sun colored the chill winter air with the illusion of warmth. The potbellied stove flavored the smell of fresh coffee with a hint of mesquite. Brady poured a fresh cup as the door swung open to a blast of cold air.

"Morning, Sheriff."

"Widenmann. What do you want?"

"I want you to release Brewer, Bonney and Waite."

"On whose authority?"

"Justice Wilson has the legal authority to issue those warrants and appoint constables. Those men were duly authorized officers of the law and you know it. If anything, you and your men obstructed those officers in the performance of their duties."

"What's that to you? You got no jurisdiction here?"

"Don't be too sure. John Tunstall was a foreign national."

"So?"

"So I'm looking into his murder. Those men are material witnesses. I want them released so that I may use them in the pursuit of my investigation. Now, are you going to release them or do I have to arrest you for obstructing a federal officer? If I have to, I'll lock you up at Fort Stanton and be very careless with the key."

"You . . ."

Widenmann brushed his coat back and rested his hands on the butts of his guns.

Brady set his cup on the desk and removed a ring of keys from a peg on the wall.

February 22ⁿᵈ

One of those spring-promise thaws showed up for the funeral. Frozen ruts turned to mud. A light cold rain added misery to the mourners gathered at the freshly dug grave beyond the corral in back of the store. Ty stood beside Lucy. She held a parasol over their heads. The McSweens stood on the other side along with Widenmann, Brewer, Bonney and a few of the men.

Reverend Dr. Ealy, the Presbyterian minister, officiated as he regularly did for the deceased, regardless of religious preference. He bowed his head, his somber black suit dampened by the rain.

"The Lord is my shepherd; I shall not want. He maketh me to lie down in green pastures . . ."

The kid listened. He hadn't heard the familiar words in some time. He didn't hold much with religion. His mother had done the prayin' in the family. It wouldn't do Mr. Tunstall's memory no good. He wouldn't rest until the men responsible got what they deserved. He let the minister's words come to him.

"Thy rod and thy staff they comfort me . . ."

Rod and staff, he fingered his gun butt. He remembered another passage, something about an eye for an eye. He bowed his head about as close to prayer as he could come.

The reverend doctor passed a shovel to Alex McSween. He handed it across to Lucy. She took the shovel and stepped it into the dirt mounded beside the freshly dug grave. She lifted a small shovelful and poured it onto the coffin lid. The clods of wet dirt thumped hollow on the raw pine. She handed the shovel back and buried her face in Ty's chest.

"Earth to earth, dust to dust, into Thy hands we commend this spirit."

The small crowd drifted away in silence. The kid stood beside the grave. Brewer, Brown and Waite fanned out behind him. He stared into the hole for a spell, listening to the rain patter on the brim of his sombrero.

Brewer stepped up beside him. "Com'on, kid, let's get out of this rain."

"John Tunstall was the only man ever treated me like I was

free-born white. I swear on his grave, I'll get every last one of them sons a bitches that killt him if it's the last thing I do."

Ty led Lucy down the street to the widow O'Hara's. They walked in silence save the sucking sounds of mud under their shoes as they skirted puddles. She paused on the front porch out of the rain and lowered the parasol. She lifted red eyes to his.

"Come in?"

He nodded.

She opened the green door and stepped into a darkened foyer. Faint gray light seeped into the hall from the parlor and kitchen beyond.

"Is that you, dear?" Mrs. O'Hara appeared in the kitchen doorway, a backlit silhouette at the end of the hall. She nodded in greeting. "Marshal Ledger. Go on into the parlor. I've got a fresh pot of coffee. I'll bring you both a cup. You must be chilled to the bone."

Lucy hung her shawl on a peg in the foyer. She hung Ty's hat over it and led the way to the parlor. Gray light filtered through lace curtains gave the room a somber air that seemed to fit the occasion. The patter of rain on the roof accompanied the soft sounds of Lucy's skirts. Dishes clattered in the kitchen, the sounds of life going on. She settled on the settee, making room for him beside her. She folded her hands in her lap. Ty took his seat. Mrs. O'Hara bustled into the parlor carrying two steaming mugs of coffee. She handed one to each of them.

"Now, drink a little of that. It'll put some warmth back in you before you both catch your death." She watched them each take a sip. Satisfied she'd accomplished her purpose, she flounced back to the kitchen.

They sat for a time. Lucy lost in thought and Ty uncertain what to say. He shrugged into the silence.

"You know I'm sorry about all this, Lucy."

She tilted her chin. Her eyes met his. "All covers a lot."

He nodded. "I figure you loved him."

"I s'pose I did in a way. Not like . . ." She bit her lip, not sure what to say. "John was safe. Sometimes that means a lot to a girl. 'Specially when she's alone. I've been on my own ever since I lost my folks. It's been a long time. You get used to it. You think you don't need anybody, but that's not really how things are supposed to be. It's tempting to settle for something like safe."

He nodded again.

She drew a handkerchief from her sleeve and wiped her nose with a little sniff. "He wouldn't listen. I tried to warn him. Alex tried to tell him. Marshal Widenmann warned him too. He just wouldn't listen. He had it in his head how things were done a certain way. He gave no account to the notion that men like Dolan might not do things his way."

"Poor reason to kill a man."

"Most reasons are."

"What'll you do now?"

She shook her head. "I don't know. Alex was part owner in the bank and the store. I guess he owns it all now. It'll sort of depend on what he decides to do."

"So you plan to stay in Lincoln."

"For a time at least, I got no place else to go."

"Good."

She tilted her chin. "That mean something to you?"

"It does. I never felt right about the way we left things last fall. Maybe a little time will give me a chance to make that right by you."

She met his eyes level. "I'd like that, Ty Ledger."

★　★　★　★　★

McSween House

They gathered in the parlor fighting the effects of the rain for warmth. McSween and Widenmann sat in wing chairs. Brewer and his band of deputized Regulators stood, hats in hand.

"So what's to be done about it?" Brewer's question hung in the air.

"It's plain enough Brady won't do nothin'," the kid said.

"Rob, any word from Marshal Sherman on your jurisdiction?" McSween asked.

He shook his head.

The lawyer glanced around the room. "Well, Dick is still a duly sworn constable and we know who the killers are."

Brewer met his eyes. "So you're sayin' we finish the job Brady stopped us from doin'."

"That's an option. Any of the rest of you see another?"

The men responded with silence.

"Brady and Dolan must have had twenty men come after us that day. We don't have that kind of firepower," Brewer said.

"Ask Chisum for help," McSween said. "He's got as much at stake in this as we do."

"What do we do with the ones we catch?" Brewer asked. "Brady sure as hell won't lock 'em up."

"If Marshal Sherman gives me jurisdiction, we can lock them up at Fort Stanton," Widenmann said.

"What happens if he don't?" Brewer asked.

"I expect we could bluff our way there for a spell."

The kid spoke softly. "Lockin' 'em up won't be no trouble. Count on it."

CHAPTER NINETEEN

February 23rd

The rain cleared out overnight, taking the brief thaw with it. Clear morning skies turned sunny and cold. A wintery glow gave the parlor an illusion of warmth. A rap sounded at the door. Susan's heels clicked the polished wood floor to the foyer. The visitor's silhouette darkened the lace window curtain. She opened the door, unprepared for the visitor that awaited her.

Dolan smiled and tipped his hat. "Good afternoon, Mrs. McSween. Is Alex in?"

"Who is it, Susan?" He appeared at the study door across the parlor.

She stepped back. Dolan crossed the threshold.

"Jimmy Dolan, Alex, I wonder if I might have a word with you."

McSween knit his brow. "You picked a hell of a day for a social call, Dolan."

"Yes, well it's not purely social, and it's not unrelated to Tunstall's, shall we say, untimely demise."

"Untimely demise, murder you mean. But of course you wouldn't know anything about that, would you?"

Dolan reddened. He glanced at Susan and checked himself. "See here, McSween, I've come with a serious business proposition for you. Do you want to hear it or would you rather go on making wild accusations?"

"Very well then, right this way." He stepped into the study he used as an office, leaving Dolan to find his way across the parlor. A single lamp lit the desktop. He took his seat and waved Dolan to the visitor chair.

"All right, what's on your mind?"

Dolan took his seat. "Right to the point, I see."

"We've never had all that much to talk about, Dolan. Under the circumstance, I find the timing of your visit in poor taste at the least."

"I can't say I had any fondness for Tunstall, but you can't possibly blame me for what happened to him."

"Not so anyone could ever prove it. You do hold the lien on the Flying H herd. Who in their right mind would have put a hothead like Billy Mathews in charge of a posse made up of suspected rustlers to serve your court order? A sheriff who can't go to the privy without your permission, that's who. Proof is a matter of law. Circumstance and common sense indict you, Dolan."

Dolan sat back with a sour smirk. "Very imaginative, counselor, just the sort of wild raving Tunstall was so fond of." He let the comparison drip threat. "As you well know, the wheels of justice don't turn on circumstance and opinion. Now let's get down to business, shall we? I believe you have a minority interest in Tunstall's bank and store. Is that right?"

"I did."

"What do you mean you did?"

"We were partners. I had a minority position, but now, in the absence of a will, I own it all."

Dolan arched a brow, recalculating his position. "Then I'm talking to the right man. I'd like to buy both businesses. I'm prepared to make a fair offer following an examination of the books."

"You got a lot of nerve, Dolan."

"Call it what you wish, McSween. I call it good business.

This county isn't big enough for two mercantile stores. Tunstall didn't understand that. I'm sure an educated man, such as you, clearly sees the wisdom of such a conclusion."

"I see you had this county all to yourself until John Tunstall came along. He had the money to take you on. No one else did."

"Yes, well so much for history. I'm here to talk about the future, your future McSween. I'll come over to the store when it's convenient, have a look at the books and make you an offer. You'll pocket a tidy sum without any of the headaches of running a business."

"John had a very nice business established. If he hadn't, you wouldn't want it so badly. How do you propose to pay for it? We both know you're short on cash. Short enough to negotiate a loan of the county tax receipts."

"How I pay for it is none of your affair. I suggest you think about my proposal. It's the best offer you're likely to get."

"I'm not looking for an offer. I rather fancy finishing what John started."

"You do, do you? Tunstall didn't find his business all that rewarding."

"Is that a threat, Dolan?"

"Threat? Why would I do that? I've another way to deal with you, McSween. You know we've never satisfactorily settled that insurance claim you botched for us. I suspect a court might find you have some personal responsibility for the loss we incurred."

"You mean a court adjudicated by one of your Santa Fe pals."

"A court of competent jurisdiction."

"Ridiculous. Stick to bogus liens on horses, Dolan. They don't fight back."

"Now that sounds like a threat."

"No threat, merely a statement of fact."

"I took you for a more sensible man than Tunstall. It appears

I overestimated you." He stood. "I can find my way out. Good day."

Susan McSween waited for the front door to click closed. "I'm sorry for eavesdropping, dear. I can't believe the man's nerve coming here like this. What do you plan to do?"

"I hadn't really thought about the store or the bank until now."

"He's an evil man, Alex. John didn't have the sense to see that. Don't oppose him. Take the money. We can move on. With it we can start over in any number of places with more opportunity than Jimmy Dolan's Lincoln County."

"I'm surprised at you, Susan. John saw it as a business, but when he took on Dolan he made things better for the people here. Do you seriously want to sell out and give all that back to Dolan?"

"I don't want you to end up like John Tunstall. You know Dolan was behind John's killing. You said so yourself. Why, he as much as threatened you right here in your own home."

He made a steeple of his fingers, touching the tips to his lips in thought. "John had one thing right. New Mexico won't see statehood until we bring law and order to the territory."

"Let the professionals do that."

"Like Brady?"

"Like Rob Widenmann or Ty Ledger. You're a lawyer, Alex. You're not a lawman."

"Sometimes citizens have to stand up to rid the community of a man like Dolan. There are good people here with their lives invested in this county for better or worse. Dolan impersonates the law and then feels at liberty to break it anytime he pleases. It's got to stop before Lincoln can grow. We can't let him get away with it any longer. Dick Brewer and the Regulators are ready to take care of those responsible for John's death. With Chisum's help maybe we can put a stop to it."

"They weren't much help to John."

"John didn't know what he was up against. I do. John didn't protect himself. I'll not make the same mistake. If Chisum and Brewer stand with me, we can win. It's the right thing to do, Susan. It's the right thing to do."

She closed her eyes. It might be right, but right still got people killed.

Late afternoon sun tinted the cantina a rosy glow. The only time of day the place hid its dirt and scars. The kid stared at the whiskey in his glass. Waite kept an eye on him the way a man watches a coiled rattler just out of striking distance.

"It was Dolan that done it. Just as sure as if he put a bounty on his head like some folks say he done." He tossed off the drink and refilled the glass.

"You'll never prove that."

He scowled at Waite's logic. "Who needs proof? You know it. I know it. Every honest body in the county knows it."

"So, what do you figure you can do about it?"

"Nothin'. Unless maybe I go over there and shake the truth out of him."

"You must a really liked Brady's jail. I hear the food's shit."

"Piss on Brady. I'd welcome the chance to blow his sorry ass to hell."

"Kid, all this talk ain't doin' nothin' but gettin' you all riled up to no good."

He scraped back his chair.

"Where do you think you're goin'?"

"To have a talk with Dolan."

Waite stood and blocked his way. "I don't think that's a good idea."

"Shut up, Fred."

Billy pushed him out of the way.

Waite muttered under his breath and followed along, figuring he'd have to back the kid's play.

Dolan saw Bonney come out of the cantina with another of Tunstall's men trailing behind.

"Jasper, this looks like trouble. Go out the back way and find Sheriff Brady. Be quick about it, you hear?"

Jasper scrambled out from behind the counter, shuffling for the back door as fast as his wobbly old legs would carry him.

The Bonney kid looked like trouble. Ty hurried down the boardwalk with the thought he'd cut him off, find out what was on his mind and cool him off some. He managed to reach Dolan's store about the time Waite did. Billy had already gone inside.

"That looks like trouble."

Waite nodded. "Might be."

Ty led the way inside. Billy had his gun drawn, though not yet pointed at a surly Jimmy Dolan. He paid no attention to Ledger and Waite.

"What the hell do you want, Bonney?"

"You, Dolan. I want you for the murder of John Tunstall."

"I had nothing to do with it."

"You ordered it."

"You can't prove that."

"Who says I need proof?"

"You can't just bust in here making wild accusations at gunpoint."

Billy laughed. "Sure as hell looks like that's what I'm doin', except the accusation ain't wild. What are you gonna do about it, Dolan? Go ahead, make your play. I'd welcome the excuse to put a bullet in you the way your boys done Mr. Tunstall. You set him up to be killt, Dolan. You and your pet sheriff sent those men to kill him."

"You're crazy, kid. I got no idea what you're talkin' about. Now get the hell out of my store."

"I ain't goin' nowhere."

"Ledger, you're an officer of the law, arrest him."

"What for, Dolan? He ain't threatened you with that gun."

The front door burst open. "Hands in the air! All of you." Brady blocked the door, flanked by Hindman and Mathews. Brady and Mathews had their guns drawn. Hindman leveled a sawed-off shotgun. "One of you so much as moves, George here's gonna fill you full of shot. Get their guns."

Mathews relieved the kid and Waite of their guns. "What about him?" He pointed his chin at Ledger.

"Him too," Dolan ordered.

Ty glared at him. "Guess we know who's in charge now."

"Shut up, Ledger." Mathews lifted his guns.

"Lock 'em up." Dolan turned on his heel and went back to his office.

Brady stepped around the prisoners. "You heard the man. Keep your hands where we can see 'em. We're gonna take a little walk down to the jail."

Lucy glanced out the store window. The broom froze in her hand. She stared in disbelief. Sheriff Brady and his deputies marched Ty, the Bonney kid and one of Tunstall's Regulators down the street toward the jail at gunpoint.

"Alex, look at this!"

McSween came out from between the shelves and stood at her side.

"What do you make of that?"

"I have no idea."

"We've got to help them."

"It's Dolan's law. I don't know what we can do."

"We have to do something."

"Maybe I know someone who can." He peeled off his apron and left the store.

The cell door closed with a metallic bang. Ty grabbed the bars. "What's the charge, Sheriff?"

"I'll work on that some and let you know." He shuffled out, the door keys jangling.

Billy sat on his bunk. "What charge? The bastard's got Dolan's say-so. He don't need no more than that."

Waite shivered. "They don't waste no wood heatin' this place, do they?"

Billy stretched out on a bunk. "It gets colder at night, but you hardly notice for the food bein' so bad."

"There we was, havin' a nice quiet drink and you had to go off and poke your finger in the man's eye."

"The man's a murderer. I'd like to poke a lot more than his eye. I'll do just that, first chance I get out of here."

"Well, we ain't got John Tunstall to pull us out this time."

Ty dropped onto his bunk to the noisy complaint of the springs. "Rob Widenmann will get us out, I reckon."

Billy brightened. "In that case, I'm glad we brought you along, Marshal."

"I'd call it a pleasure, but I'd be lyin'."

February 24th

Brady worked a light coat of oil through the barrel of his gun with a short cleaning rod. The freshly cleaned cylinder lay on the desk empty when Widenmann barged into the office.

"Mornin,' Marshal. What can I do for you?"

"I hear you've got my deputy locked up. What's the charge?"

"Well, we haven't actually filed one yet. Most likely disturbin' the peace or something like that."

"Or something like that, what the hell kind of charge is that?"

"Mr. Dolan ain't decided what charge to press just yet. Ledger was with Bonney and Fred Waite when they busted into Dolan's store. Bonney was wavin' a gun around and makin' all kinds of wild accusations. Mr. Dolan took offense to it."

"What sort of accusations?"

"I don' know, somethin' about Tunstall's killin'."

"When did this happen?"

"Yesterday afternoon."

"Was the store open at the time?"

"I s'pose so."

"So they didn't break in."

"Not exactly."

"So basically you arrested them for sayin' somethin' Dolan took offense to."

"It's a county matter, Widenmann. You got no jurisdiction here. Now, if you've said your piece, get the hell out of my office."

"I want those men released now, Brady."

"You don't hear so good, do you? I said you ain't got no jurisdiction here. It's a county matter."

"I get jurisdiction when you interfere with a federal officer in the performance of his duty."

"What duty?"

"Investigatin' the death of a foreign national on our soil in case you've forgotten."

"What's that got to do with a civil disturbance?"

"About as much as a charge of 'or something like that.' Now you let those men go before I lock you up at Fort Stanton."

"I'd like to see you try."

Widenmann smiled, drew his gun and leveled it. "Even I can draw faster than you can put that gun back together. You're in a poor position to question my authority, Sheriff. Now release those men."

"Mr. Dolan ain't gonna like this."

"You think I give a shit? That's your problem. You're the one can't take a shit without Dolan's say-so and everybody knows it."

Lamplight spread a yellow halo across the desktop in the darkened office. Dolan hunched over the vellum in silhouette, his pen scratching a delicate cadence at the surface. He paused, collecting his thoughts over the circumstances of the insurance claim. He had to compose his allegation so as to implicate Mc-Sween in responsibility for his loss. He'd bring a civil suit to recover the sum of five thousand dollars. McSween, of course, would deny responsibility. They'd have to go to court, but with a little help from his friends, it would be the right court. He finished his thought, picked up the letter and blew the ink dry.

CHAPTER TWENTY

South Spring
February 27ᵗʰ

"So you figure you can put your bounty hunting aside and give her a proper home."

Roth met Chisum's eyes. The fire crackled. Mesquite smoke scented the air. Outside the wind howled. He nodded.

"What about that Crystobal fella down to Seven Rivers? He just gonna up and let bygones be bygones?"

"No. I'll take care of that first."

"I s'pect there's more where he come from."

Roth hated not having a truthful good answer. "None here just now."

"So there could be more?"

"I'd be lyin' if I said different."

Chisum let the words settle between them. He didn't like it, but at least the young man was honest. There was no denying the feelings between them. It was an age-old problem fathers faced, and he wasn't even her blood-kin father. He might be no more than the man who was there when the child needed a father, but that didn't change the feeling as far as he could tell.

"I'll take care of Crystobal. Then leastwise I can offer you a clean trail."

McSween indulged himself a sigh of relief as the ranch house came into view. The rumors had gotten to him. He'd been nervous as a cat on the ride down from Lincoln. Two warm sunny days and a promise of spring didn't help. He half expected shooting to start at any moment. Rumors said Tunstall was killed on Dolan's order. They said Dolan had offered a bounty on him when he refused to sell the mercantile and bank. The townsfolk were mostly sympathetic, but Dolan would have no trouble finding a gun to do his bidding if he wanted one. He needed help. He hoped he could count on Chisum.

He jogged through the gate and rode up the wagon track past the bunkhouse, barn and corral. He drew rein at the hacienda and eased down. A broad covered porch stretched across the front of the house and around the side to the southwest. He climbed the steps to the massive wooden door. The soft muffled sound of moccasins greeted his knock. Dawn Sky opened the door.

"Is Mr. Chisum in?"

"Who is it, Dawn?"

"Alex McSween," he called to the voice in the parlor.

Chisum appeared in the foyer. "Alex, come in, come in. What brings you all the way down here?"

"I'm afraid I've got some rather bad news. John Tunstall is dead."

"Dead?"

"Killed by Brady's men."

"I was afraid of something like that. Dolan ain't given to take matters lyin' down."

"No, he's not and these matters aren't over."

"Com'on. Take a load off your feet and tell me about it. You care for a drink?"

"I believe I would."

Roth stood up to excuse himself.

"Sit down, Johnny. You best hear this too. Dawn, bring us a drink and then have one of the boys take care of Mr. McSween's horse. He'll be joining us for dinner. The guest room's yours for the night, Alex."

"Thanks, John."

They settled into comfortable chairs set around a large adobe fireplace. The fragrant fire crackled against the onset of evening chill. Dawn Sky brought the whiskey bottle and glasses to the table beside Chisum's chair. She hurried off to the rest of her chores. Chisum poured. He handed one to McSween, another to Roth and sat back with his own.

"Now tell us what happened."

"Dolan got a court-ordered lien placed on the Flying H stock. Some claim of an unpaid debt by the previous owner. Brady sent some men to take the herd. They jumped John and his men moving the herd. John got separated from his men in the shoot-out. According to the story Brady's men tell, John refused to turn over the stock. They say he resisted when they tried to arrest him for obstruction. They claim they shot him after he shot at them."

Chisum took a swallow of his drink. "I never knew Tunstall to carry a gun."

"He bought one before he left for the ranch. Lucy thinks he was finally coming to believe Dolan might resort to violence. Brady claims it had been fired."

"Did Brewer or any of his men see what happened?"

"They were across the valley pinned down in the hills. Mathews and his men scattered after shooting Tunstall."

"Mathews? Brady put that hothead in charge?"

McSween nodded. "So they say."

"He might as well have tossed a stick of dynamite with a short lit fuse. Who'd he have with him?"

"Evans and his boys."

"Now there's a posse of upright citizens. Too bad we don't have eyewitness testimony. I'd bet there's more to that story."

"Sure there is. John was shot twice, once in the side and once in the head. He was murdered sure as we're sitting here, but that story will never be told." He finished his drink.

Chisum poured another round. "You said matters aren't settled."

"I had a minority partnership in the store and the bank. With John dead, I'm the owner. Dolan wants to buy me out. I told him no. Now, I hear he's put a bounty on me."

"He's declarin' war."

"That's why I'm here. We can't let Dolan get away with this. He's got to be stopped. I need your help."

"Are you suggesting we take the law into our own hands?"

"No. Justice Wilson issued warrants for those responsible. He appointed Dick Brewer constable. I'm saying we go after Brady's posse men with the law on our side."

Chisum rubbed his jaw, smoothing his mustache between his thumb and forefinger. "I'll have some of my boys join up with Brewer's men. Let's get after 'em."

"I need to ride down to the Flying H in the morning to speak with Brewer before I return to Lincoln."

"I'll send some of my boys with you. Johnny, you ride on up to Lincoln and let Widenmann and Ledger in on what we're planning here. Alex, you need to take one or two men back to Lincoln to look after you and Susan. Dolan starts to feel us closin' in on him, you'll be a target just like Tunstall."

"I don't mind saying I feel a bit like that already."

February 28th

Roth tossed the blanket up on the black's back in the gray light of predawn. His breath hung in the night chill. The black snorted and stomped anxious to be off. He hauled his saddle down from the rack and settled it over the blanket, feeling the fit to the withers. Satisfied, he lifted the stirrup fender over the seat and ducked under the horse's belly to snag the cinch. He came up with the strap and sensed her presence. He passed the strap through the cinch ring and up through the saddle ring. He turned to her.

She was little more than a silhouette in the dim light. A sparkle of light from somewhere caught her eye. She came to his arms. A light scent of cinnamon sweetened the comfortable smells of straw and horses. He held her soft and warm. She came to wish him a safe trip and to remind him to watch out for trouble. She needed no words to say these things. Her spirits must be quiet. If she sensed anything troubling, as she did at times, she'd say so.

"How long Johnny be gone?"

He shrugged against her. "Hard to say, couple days up to Lincoln, couple more down to the Flyin' H. After that, it depends on Brewer. I expect we'll ride out after Evans' men. We know where to find Brady's part of the bunch."

"You go after the bad man?"

She meant Crystobal. "I promised Señor John I'd clear him off my trail before we get married." She lifted her eyes to his. She didn't like the sound of that. "He's afraid for you, Dawn, like a good father should be."

"Dawn Sky afraid for Johnny."

"Don't be." He whispered into her hair. "I'll be the same sort of fearful for our daughter one day."

She favored him with one of those liquid looks that had no bottom. She touched her lips to his. He went lost in the sweetness.

"That'll sure 'nuff bring a feller home quick as he can." Put him in need of distraction too, he told himself. He turned to the cinch strap, double loop, finger snug, cross and tie. He lowered the stirrup fender.

She followed at his side as he led the black into the chill

morning air. A sliver of waning moonlight silvered black lights in her hair. He stepped into the saddle and settled. She touched his knee. He patted her hand. He eased the black clear and squeezed up a lope.

Chisum led McSween across the yard to the corral. Bright morning sun slanted over the eastern hills, with the promise of an early spring. Three men waited with their horses. Hired guns, McSween mulled the turn of his future. Two were tall and lean. One of them had the look of a schoolteacher in his long black frock coat. The third was average height. He wore baggy britches and a loose fitting serape.

"Mornin' boys." Chisum looked around. "Where's Johnny?"

The schoolteacher spoke up. "Rode out for Lincoln just before sunup."

Chisum nodded. "This here's Alex McSween. Alex, meet Doc Scurlock."

The man in the black frock coat pushed back behind the butts of the Colts slung on his hips touched his wide hat brim. He wore a sober expression with a prominent nose, lean cheekbones and neatly trimmed brown hair and mustaches.

"That there's Charlie Bowdre." Chisum gestured to the shorter man in a baggy double-breasted shirt. Plain featured, he had a weak chin that disappeared under a drooping mustache.

"The red-haired fella is Bill McClosky. He takes his paycheck from us these days, but he knows his way around Seven Rivers." The angular McClosky smiled at the mention of his history. The corners of his red handlebar turned up.

"You boys take Alex here over to the Flyin' H. Dick Brewer's gonna take some boys out after the men who killed John Tunstall. You go along with Dick and do like he says."

The men nodded. McSween turned to Chisum. "Thanks for your help, John."

"Least I can do. Hell, you're the one takin' all the risk. You take care of yourself and mind what I said about takin' a couple of the Regulators along to help out."

McSween shook his hand and collected his horse's rein, signaling the men to mount up. Scurlock picked up the lead and peeled away to the southwest.

Flying H
March 1st

Waite squinted against the glare of a low afternoon sun. He climbed up the bottom rail of the corral and looked northeast. "Riders comin'!"

Big Jim looked out from the loft above. Henry Brown left the hay he'd been spreading in the corral and crossed to Waite's side. Brewer, Bonney and Middleton tumbled out of the ranch house to the porch.

Brewer pursed his lips. "Any idea who it is?"

Waite shook his head.

"Spread out near some cover until we figure out who they are." The boys eased off, spreading out around the house, the barn, the hay wagon and a small stand of trees north of the corral.

Big Jim made them out. "Looks like McSween. I don't recognize the men with him."

Brewer adjusted the gun on his hip. "Hold your positions until we figure who they are."

The riders slowed to a trot as they approached the gate. McSween waved as if to signal all clear. Brewer recognized Scurlock and took the rest for Chisum men.

McSween and Scurlock drew rein. Scurlock grinned. "Bring 'em in, Dick. We ain't no trouble."

"Com'on in, boys." He let McSween step down. "This mean you got an answer from Chisum?"

"What does it look like?"

"Come in and tell me all about it." He turned to Middleton. "John, show Doc and the boys where they can bunk." He stepped aside and let McSween lead the way inside. The Bonney kid followed along. This was about avenging Tunstall. That made it his business.

McSween bent over the water bucket, took a dipper and drank. Water dribbled down his chin spreading dark red splotches on his cravat. He returned the dipper to the bucket and tossed his hat on the table. Dust mites boiled up in the sun splash where the hat hit the table. He pulled up a chair.

Brewer sat across from him. Billy stood in the shadows beside the door.

"Chisum's with us."

"It looked as much with all that firepower. The question is what do we do now?"

"Roth rode up to Lincoln to talk to Widenmann. In the meantime we'll use Wilson's warrants and your deputization. That way you and the boys can go after them with the law on your side."

"Good," Brewer said.

"That mean we can start huntin' tomorrow?"

McSween had almost forgotten Billy in the shadows. You could hear menace in the reference to hunting. "I'll go on back to Lincoln tomorrow. We should know if Widenmann has anything to add to what we've got in a few days."

Billy drew his gun. "I got everything I need right here, right now."

McSween held up a hand. "I understand your impatience, Billy. We don't want to do things the way Dolan and his crowd do. New Mexico needs real law and order and that means putting an end to the likes of Jimmy Dolan. You'll have your chance to see justice done by John Tunstall. Done the way he'd want it done, according to the law."

The kid holstered his gun, turned on his heel, cracked the door and went out into the sun glare.

"Can you control him, Dick?"

He knit his brow. "Maybe."

"I hope so. One more thing, Chisum thinks I should take one of the boys back to Lincoln with me. He thinks I'll be a target once Dolan gets the feeling we're closing in on him."

"John's smart."

"I thought so too."

"I'll send Big Jim back with you. He's like havin' a man and a half around."

CHAPTER TWENTY-ONE

Lincoln

March 2nd

Roth drew the black down to an easy jog at the east end of town. Lincoln stretched out like a sleeping cat, content under a noticeably warmer afternoon sun. The chill breeze, prodding tumbleweed down the street, lacked the sharp edge of bitter winter. Riding past Mrs. O'Hara's place, he wondered how Lucy was taking Tunstall's death. He'd never figure that one out. He thought sure she had her cap set for Ty once he got his wife's mourning out of his system. Maybe she got tired of waiting.

He glanced at Dolan's store. He had an odd sense of being watched. Dolan would be smart to keep an eye on things. If the man thought Tunstall's killin' settled things, he was in for a surprise. There were times when a man could push people. Sometimes you could push them pretty far, if you knew when to back off a little. Trouble was, men like Dolan didn't know how to back off. Sooner or later they pushed too far. That's when things had a way of snappin' back. Dolan was about to find that out.

He drew rein at the Wortley rail and swung down. Likely he'd find Ledger or Widenmann or both registered. He clumped up the step to the boardwalk and into the sepia-lit lobby. The clerk behind the counter dozed, perched on a stool that threatened to throw him. Roth's boot scrape snapped him awake.

"Uh, what can I do for you?" He blinked.

"I need a room."

"That'll be a dollar." He spun the register and reached for a key.

The marshals were both registered. "Either Widenmann or Ledger in?"

"No, sir. They'll likely be back for supper, Mr.—" He read the register. "Roth. Room three." He slid the key across the counter. "You want me to give 'em a message?"

"Yeah, tell 'em I'm in room three and to knock loud. I'm likely to be asleep."

"Sure thing. Down the hall, second room on the right. Stable's out back."

"Much obliged." He stepped back outside and collected the black. The stable around back of the alley had a watering trough beside the door. He let the black have his fill. Inside he found a vacant stall with fresh bedding. He pulled off his saddle and bridle and hung them on a worn rack. He found grain in a bin at the back of the stable with a scoop and a stack of buckets. He scooped grain into a bucket and carried it back to the stall. He climbed the loft ladder and pitched a forkful of hay into the stall. The black snorted appreciative. He climbed back down and placed the bucket of grain beside the hay. The black buried his nose in the bucket with another snort for his chores.

The room was small, spare and mostly clean. It had a bed that looked damn good after two nights of hard ground on the ride up from South Spring. He stretched out to wait for Widenmann or Ledger. His eyes drifted closed.

The knock at the door sounded like a gunshot. He jerked awake. "Yeah?"

"Johnny, it's Ty."

He rolled off the bed and shook the sleep from his head. Dull light seeping through the plain muslin curtains told him he'd dozed into sunset. He opened the door.

Ty chuckled. "Settled down life ain't that hard on a man. What brings you to town?"

"I come to see you and Widenmann."

"We just rode in. Rob'll meet us for drinks and supper."

Roth lifted his gun belt off the bedpost, strapped it on and picked his hat off the dresser. He followed Ledger out to the dining room. They grabbed a table and signaled the bartender for drinks. Widenmann arrived along with the whiskey.

"Bring me one too." He shook Roth's hand. "What brings you to town, Johnny?"

"Tunstall's murder."

"McSween and Chisum talked."

"They did. Chisum sent some of his men down to the Flying H to back up Brewer and his men. They're goin' after the boys Justice Wilson issued warrants for."

Widenmann stroked his mustache. "Dolan and Brady won't sit still for that. We've already seen how that works."

The bartender arrived with Widenmann's drink. He took a swallow. "I don't figure much good will come of Brewer's men going after the Brady posse."

"Rob, they murdered a man. Brady won't lift a finger. Hell, he was likely in on planning it with Dolan," Ty said.

"Likely so, but that don't prove it."

"That's how McSween and Chisum see it. Dolan's behind Tunstall's killin' sure as we're sittin' here. Provin' it starts with Brady's men. Chisum and McSween want to put the Regulators on the trail of Mathews and the Seven Rivers boys. Sooner or later somebody will talk. Brady will end up guilty or incompetent. Either way they figure to be rid of him. That should clip Dolan's wings. Who knows, maybe they get lucky and implicate him or he does somethin' foolish when they get that close to him."

Widenmann tossed off his drink and signaled for another round. "I don't know. It sounds good, but you push Brady and Dolan into a corner they'll fight for sure. Santa Fe won't like that. They'll play it like vigilante justice takin' over the county. If they call in the army, we could have a war on our hands."

"What's the alternative?"

"I don't know. I'd feel better if I had jurisdiction. McSween told me to try to get that on the grounds that Tunstall was a foreign national. I've sent a request to Marshal Sherman but I haven't heard anything yet."

"You threatened Brady with the fact that Tunstall was a foreigner to get us out of jail," Ty said.

"The bluff worked, but it was a stretch."

"Would you have locked him up?"

"Sure, but that don't mean I could make it stick."

The waiter arrived with the bottle. Roth poured a round. "So it's the same with these boys. The worst thing that can happen is a court throws out the charge. A lot of water goes under the bridge before that happens. Maybe enough water to get one of the sons a bitches talkin'. McSween will be along in a day or two. He'll help you put a legal shine on it."

"You goin' down to the Flying H, Johnny?"

"I am."

"Ty, you mind ridin' along so we have a witness account of what happens?"

Ty nodded.

"Good. Now let's get us some supper."

Flying H
March 4th

Roth and Ledger rode in under a cold drizzle and the watchful rifle sights of Henry Brown and Charlie Bowdre. The first gave an unpleasant promise of spring. The second a small sample of the considerable firepower assembled for the business at hand. They drew rein at the house and stepped down, shaking rainwater from slickers and hats. Brewer and Bonney waited on the porch. Roth led the way up the step out of the rain.

"Com'on in." Brewer extended his hand. "It may not be snow, but you boys look a might chilled."

Brewer led them inside. The ranch house looked like an armed camp. The Regulators scattered around the parlor. Doc Scurlock, Tom O'Folliard, Fred Waite and John Middleton huddled around a poker game in one corner. Frank McNab and Bill McCloskey dozed in their bedrolls. Bonney went back to cleaning his guns. Brewer gestured to a rough cut table near the stove.

"We got some hot coffee."

"That'd go mighty good." Roth spoke for both of them.

Brewer took the pot off the stove and poured two steaming cups. He set them on the table and pulled up a chair for himself.

Ty took a swallow. "Johnny tells me you're going to lead the posse."

"Mr. McSween and Chisum say I am."

"What do you plan to do?"

Brewer furrowed his brow. "We'll start with Evans and his boys. We can take care of them before Brady and Dolan find out we're on to 'em. There won't be much fight left in them once we've got 'em outnumbered."

Ty looked over the rim of his coffee cup. "Where do you plan to hold 'em?"

"Hold 'em?"

"Yeah, you don't expect Brady to hold your prisoners, do you?"

"I don't expect to hold no prisoners."

Ty set his coffee down. "You want the law on your side, don't you?"

He nodded.

"Then you'll take those men into custody and let a court decide their guilt."

"I said we wanted the law on our side. I didn't say we trust the territorial courts to do us justice."

"Serve them warrants fair and honest and even the territorial courts will back you. Turn this into a vigilante lynching and you won't have anybody back you. You'll be no better than Dolan and Brady."

"We'll give 'em a chance to surrender. I know those boys. They won't. They'll settle things the way they always do, with a gun."

"If you run the posse, Dick, it's your responsibility."

"And I'm tellin' you this posse better be ready for trouble."

Roth eased forward. "Com'on, Ty. I think we best see to them horses."

Ty caught his drift and scraped back his chair. "Thanks for the coffee, Dick."

"Hope it warms you up some."

Roth led the way outside. The rain had stopped. Dark woolen clouds rode off on a chill wind. They collected the horses and led them across the muddy yard to the barn. Ty led the steel-dust to an empty stall and ground tied him. Roth found another nearby. Saddle leather creaked as Ty threw up a stirrup fender.

"I got a bad feelin' about this, Johnny. Brewer might listen to reason but he's got some boys in there with quick triggers. How's he gonna keep a lid on the likes of Bonney?"

"They ain't regular lawmen. They see things different. You'll be along to show 'em the right way to do things. They're good men. It'll be all right. You'll see."

Ty hefted his saddle onto the rack and threw the blanket over it to dry. "I hope you're right, but like I said, I got a bad feelin' about this."

CHAPTER TWENTY-TWO

Seven Rivers
March 5th

A gentle breeze ruffled the horses' manes and tails. A dozen posse men fanned out along the crest of the ridge overlooking the ranch. They left no doubt for anyone below, they'd come in force. Brewer studied the house, the barn and the corral for any sign of movement.

"Looks like nobody's home again."

Ty leaned forward in his saddle intent on the barn. "Don't be too sure."

Brewer looked left and right. "All right, boys, we'll ease on in. Spread yourselves out. Any sign of trouble surround the place. Take your lead from me." He gave his horse its head and started down the slope.

Roth stayed near Brewer. Had Ty seen something in the barn? The doors were open, but sunlight revealed nothing more than dark shadow inside. Brewer drew a halt, hailing distance from the house.

"Hello the ranch. Officers of the law, we got a warrant for Jesse Evans."

Time passed. Brewer started forward.

"He's no here."

The muffled voice came from the barn. Roth smiled at the accent.

"That you Crys?"

"Sí, amigo. It is I, your worst fear. Have you brought enough friends to give you courage?"

"These boys came for Evans. I came for you, alone."

Brewer eyed Roth. "What the hell is this about?"

"Man's name is Crystobal. It's an old score. Long story, you ain't got time." He raised his voice. "So, Crys, you gonna come out of your hole, so we can have this out in the light of day?"

"You send your friends away, amigo, and Crystobal will grant your death wish."

Brewer scowled. Somehow he'd lost control of the situation. "You send Evans out first."

"Crystobal told you, he's no here."

"Who is then?"

"Only Crystobal and the mice."

He spat. "I don't believe the son of a bitch."

"Neither do I, I think he's tryin' to give cover to somebody. Send some men north and some south. They'll be in position in case anyone tries to make a break for it. That should flush this one out. We can deal with the rest of the place after I take care of him."

Ty tried to chase another uneasy feeling. "You sure about this, Johnny?"

He cocked an eye at his friend under his hat brim and nodded toward the barn. "I promised Chisum I'd take care of my unfinished business."

"Ledger, take half the boys south. I'll take the rest north. Good luck, Roth."

"I don't s'pect I'll need it."

The Regulators wheeled away. Time passed, waiting for the riders to clear the valley. The barn doorway remained dark. Wind swirled a thin sheet of dust across the yard. Roth stepped down and ground tied the black.

"The boys are gone, Crys. You comin' out or you plannin' to

shoot from ambush again?"

A silver concho flashed in the shadows beyond the doorway. "Oh, no, amigo, I'm coming out. I do not wish to miss the look in your eye when my bullets find you."

"I guess you must be much better now than you was the last time I shot you."

"The last time, luck was with you. Crystobal was not ready. This time is different. Crystobal is ready."

Ready, Roth reckoned.

The Mexican pistolero stepped out of the shadows into the sunlight, hands resting at his belt buckle. A crooked smile creased thin lips. He sidled away from the barn door and started toward Roth.

"I have waited for this moment, amigo. I waited those long days with my gut on fire from your bullet. I think I should return that favor. I think you should die slow. Slow enough to feel your gut burn."

Roth forced himself to concentrate on the Mexican.

Horses and riders burst through the barn door.

He filled his hands with fire and smoke. A gun exploded. His second blast burst the blue cloud. He spun to his knee and leveled his guns at the riders galloping away to the north. Something moved. He spun back to the left. Crystobal knelt in the dust holding the blood-soaked remains of his belly. Roth got up and walked slowly toward the fallen gunman.

He lifted eyes, rigid slits, his voice a barely audible croak. "You never looked. You should have looked." He coughed and spat a mouthful of blood. "This time Crystobal's gut does not burn. This time, Crystobal is . . . killed." He toppled forward, spilling a pool of bloody mud.

Horses pounded out of the south. Roth holstered his guns. Ty drew the steeldust to a sliding stop, the four riders behind him specters shrouded in dust.

"You all right?"

He nodded. "Two of 'em ran north. Brewer's on their trail."

"We best make sure they're makin' arrests and not nooses." He spurred the steeldust north and west followed by McNab, Scurlock, O'Folliard and McCloskey. Roth ran to the black, collected his reins, swung a leg up and spurred off on the heels of the dust cloud.

Frank Baker and Buck Morton wheeled northwest out of the barn, leaving Crystobal to his private revenge. Shots exploded behind them. Neither man looked back. Less than a half mile north of the ranch, riders broke on their back trail closing fast. Morton wasted two covering shots to no good effect.

"Save your bullets, Buck. You got no chance of even scarin' 'em at this range." Baker bent over his horse's neck, urging him on.

Morton managed to stay with him another half mile before his heavier mount began to slip behind Baker's wiry mustang. He chanced a glance over his shoulder.

"They're gainin' on us."

Baker took a look. "I'll pull up and take a couple of quality shots. You go on a quarter mile or so. Pull up and give your horse a blow. When I come by, you set up your shots, follow me and do it again. We'll spare our horses and slow 'em down some."

Morton nodded.

Baker pulled up behind a stand of scrub.

The first shot whined past Brewer's ear. He pulled up. *Son of a bitch, they forted up.* A second shot sent them scrambling. "Take cover, boys!"

By the time they found cover, the shooter broke up the trail and raced off to the north.

Brewer fumed at the trick. "After 'em!"

A quarter mile up the road they rounded a bend in the rocky terrain. A bullet sang off the rocks beside the trail, splashing stone chips on Billy's sombrero. He ducked instinctively as a second shot rang out. "Shit!" They wheeled their horses off the trail and into the rocks. The boys leaped down and spread out. The trail went still.

Brewer glanced at Bonney. "Did you see where the shot came from?"

"Nah."

"Anybody see it?"

No one answered. The silence broke to the retreating hooves of a galloping horse.

"Here we go again." Brewer leaped back into the saddle and spurred out after the shooter. A quarter mile up the trail he slowed into a blind turn, expecting more shots. None came. "Looks like they aim to keep us guessin'." He muttered more to himself than anyone within earshot.

"What?" Middleton drew his gun nervously.

"Nothin'. Keep goin'." They pounded down a flat stretch a quarter mile further to the base of a low rise. Two fast shots cracked out of a stand of scrub oak near the top. The posse scattered into flatlands that offered little cover. Another shot kicked dirt and scree in Brown's eyes. He returned fire, blazing three shots up the trail. The shooting fell silent.

Brewer lay flat on his belly behind a rock too small to conceal him. He peeked over the top. "Either we got him or he's fixin' to run again. Com'on boys get to your horses." The boys started to their feet. A volley of rifle fire spattered hot lead in their tracks. They dove back to whatever safety they could find.

"Looks like they finally mean it for a fight. Give 'em hell, boys." The Regulators opened fire on the tree clump. Powder smoke spread a blanket over both sides of the trail. Sudden realization hit Brewer, *no return fire.* "Hold your fire!" He put his ear to the ground. *Son of a bitch!* The gentle beat of a galloping horse told the tale. "He's runnin' again. Let's go."

Brewer led them out, mixing caution and speed. The sun sank deep into the afternoon. A mile further on, his gut told him they were losing ground. He guessed they were trying to string things out to sunset, hoping to get away in the dark. The next time he heard from his gut, he stared down the trail at a dry wash through a narrow cut. It had ambush written all over it. He drew rein.

"That don't look so good, does it?" Fred said.

Brewer glanced sidelong. Waite had a way with the obvious. "No, it don't and I don't plan on ridin' in there makin' out like an easy target, either. John, you take Fred and Henry around that thing to the west. Me and Billy will go around to the east. With luck, we'll come up behind the bushwacker."

Middleton nodded. He liked the idea.

They split up. Brewer and Billy circled east around the base of the ridge that made for the east wall of the wash. They picked their way slow and deliberate around to the backside of the ridge, expecting to come on trouble around every rock. Doubt gnawed at his gut. If they got this wrong, they'd lost a lot of ground and likely the game for today. They approached the back side of the wash with no sign of a shooter. He expected to hear shots from Middleton's men anytime.

Then he heard it. The rattle of a rock dislodged somewhere up ahead and the dull clacking sound as it rolled down rough hillside. He threw up a hand, met Billy's eye and stepped down. They drew their guns and eased forward. Sweat slicked his hatband though not from the heat. They reached the edge of the wash, nothing up above. Something scraped rock across the wash. *Shit!* It could be a shooter, or it could be Middleton and the boys. *Now what?* He had no good answer to the question.

"John, is that you?"

"Yeah."

Middleton popped up not twenty feet across the wash from where he and Billy stood. *Nobody here.*

That's when the shooting started up the trail. Lead gouged the rocks and whined along the back of the ridge along their exposed flanks. The Regulators had no choice but to dive into the wash for cover. The shots came from a rock stand further up the trail. They no more than got their heads down when the shooter turned his fire wide of the wash, scattering their horses. Brewer clenched his jaw. *These sons a bitches has really pissed me off.* All he got for his anger was dust sign and the sound of a galloping horse.

Well, he got a little something for his trouble. The pace of pursuit had slowed enough for Ledger, Roth and the rest of the boys to catch up.

Ty got the picture. Pretty good trick if they had a plan to make a good getaway.

"Dick, you keep up the chase. Make 'em think you're still playin' their game. Johnny, take Doc and Charlie. Swing east out of the line of fire. I'll take Tom and Bill west. We should be able to head 'em off a mile or so up the road. When you hear shootin' up ahead, Dick, give 'em hell."

Brewer nodded. "Givin' them bastards hell will be a pleasure if we get more for the effort than spent cartridges. Round up them horses, boys, and let's get after 'em." The Regulators fanned out in three directions.

An hour later, Ty spotted dust sign off to the east. He drew up and pointed. The sign stopped. Further to the south, gunshots popped in the distance. He winked at O'Folliard. "Looks like we got one." He wheeled the steeldust northeast, circled back to the south and drew rein.

Down the trail, one of the fugitives forted up in a rock stand.

Minutes later the second broke up the trail from the south. Ty let him draw even with the first.

"Now!" he spurred the steeldust. O'Folliard and McCluskey burst out of the rocks behind him. Gun drawn, he fired a warning shot. The rider slid to a stop. He swung his mount into the rocks with his partner.

Brewer and his men pounded up the trail from the south. Trapped, the mounted rider spurred his horse east. Roth and his men appeared out of nowhere, blocking his way. The Regulators closed in. Baker and Morton raised their hands and surrendered.

Brewer and his boys stepped down. "John, Henry, get their guns." He waited for the hardware to get collected. "Now, you two step down easy. Don't try anything funny. Nothin' would give us more pleasure than to fill your worthless hides with lead."

Baker and Morton stepped down. Morton looked sullen. Baker remained belligerent. "What the hell gives you call to come bustin' into our ranch and chase us half all over the county?"

"This here is a duly sworn posse and we got warrants for your arrest."

"On what charge?"

"The murder of John Tunstall."

"Shit." Baker spit. "We said all we got to say on that to Sheriff Brady. It's a clear case of resisting arrest and self-defense."

"Justice of the peace doesn't think so."

Ledger and Roth stepped down. Bonney stepped up beside Brewer, letting out his reata in a loop. "Enough jabberin' after these skunks. There's a stand of cottonwood up yonder just about their size."

"The hell, Brewer, you said you was a duly sworn posse. Last time I checked they don't go on and lynch men."

"Shut up, you murderin' son of a bitch, before I lose my good humor and gut shoot you for the slow death you deserve."

Brewer raised a hand. "Easy, Billy. We all know how you feel about John."

"You need to take these men to Lincoln and turn 'em over to the justice of the peace jurisdiction," Ty said.

Brewer braced. "What makes you think Brady'll sit still for that?"

"Those warrants say he's got no choice."

Baker chuckled.

"Shut up, Baker, before I let Bonney have you. I wish I was as all-fired sure as you, Ledger. This whole thing stinks from Santa Fe to Lincoln."

"McSween and Chisum are callin' the shots here and they want it done legal."

"The Marshal's right," McCloskey said. "These men is entitled to a fair trial."

Brown dropped his hand to his gun belt. "You need remindin' which side you're ridin' on this time, McCloskey?"

"I'm just sayin' these men and any of them others is entitled to a fair trial. I aim to see we get 'em back to Lincoln."

Brown started forward. Brewer checked him with a hand. "It's settled, boys. We take 'em to Lincoln."

CHAPTER TWENTY-THREE

*March 6*th

Warm weather stayed on, riding a southwest high desert breeze under a bright sun. The trail to Lincoln led northwest through the Flying H. Brewer led the posse with Middleton, Waite and Billy Bonney. The prisoners followed flanked by Bowdre and O'Folliard. Scurlock, McCloskey and Brown had the prisoners' backs. Ty and Johnny trailed behind with McNab.

Ty glanced at his friend. "You plannin' to ride all the way to Lincoln?"

"I got what I came for."

"Crystobal?"

He nodded. "With him off my trail, Chisum says he'll put aside his worries over me marryin' Dawn Sky."

"What worries? I mean, other than the fact it's you." He grinned at the jibe.

Roth chuckled. "He figures I made some bad enemies huntin' bounty. He doesn't want Dawn to wind up a widow. I can't say I blame him for that. I'm not partial to the idea, either."

"I wouldn't expect so. Seems like in the dead or alive business you'd only have to fret over the alives."

"Nothin' much I can do about any of 'em. Old Crys put the worry on Chisum's mind. With him out of the way, I s'pect Dawn will weary him of his worries."

"As only a woman can, my friend. Soon as she gets done wearyin' Chisum, it'll be your turn."

"You don't know Dawn."

"You don't know wed-locked women."

"I'll take my chances."

Ledger's smile crinkled the corners of his eyes. "Sooner or later, we all do."

"You plannin' to ride on to Lincoln?"

Ledger fixed on the prisoners and nodded.

"I was hopin' you'd ride down to South Spring and stand up for me at the weddin'."

"Hell, Chisum's got worry enough about you without that." They both laughed. "Truly it'd be an honor, Johnny, but I'm worried about seein' to it those men make it to a fair trial."

"They'll be all right. Brewer's made that clear. McCloskey will be along to keep an eye on things. How much more can you add to that?"

"I don't know. I just feel responsible."

"I understand, but you can't be the keeper of every name on those warrants. If those boys decide to ignore Brewer's order, what are you going to do about it?" He pointed with his chin. "I see a half dozen professional guns up there not countin' Mc-Closkey. In my business, I figure the chances. In case you can't guess, them chances stink."

"That's the difference between us. You figure chances. I uphold the law."

"Look, every last man jack of them swore the same oath as you. The carriage of justice will be right well guarded without you."

Ty scowled. "I s'pose you're right. You are about to get roped and tied, aren't you?" He parted with a smile. "That alone might be a sight worth seein'."

"Then you'll come?"

He nodded.

★ ★ ★ ★ ★

Flying H

The posse made the ranch just before sunset. They secured the prisoners in a storeroom and set about putting up the horses and preparing supper. The house glowed in golden lamplight when they sat down to fatback, beans and biscuits. Ledger and Roth joined Brewer and Waite at the table.

Brewer scraped a forkful of beans. "Fred, you and a few of the boys take the prisoners up to Lincoln in the morning. You'll likely have to stay on to hold them. You can take your orders from Justice Wilson."

"Marshal Widenmann will back you up if you need it," Ty said.

Waite turned to Brewer. "Who should I take with me?"

"Take the Kid, Doc and Henry."

"I'm on my way down to South Spring with Johnny, Dick," Ty said. "You best send McCloskey with them."

Brewer flicked his eyes to Ledger. He weighed the marshal's unspoken intent. "Take Bill along too then."

Waite met his eyes and nodded. He soaked up the last of his beans with a bite of biscuit and pushed his plate back. He pulled the makin's out of his shirt pocket and rolled a smoke. He scraped his chair back, took his plate to the washbasin and sauntered outside for a smoke.

Brewer finished his plate and followed Waite outside. Pale new moonlight painted the yard silver. Waite cast a dark shadow leaning against the corral rail, the orange glow of his smoke a pinpoint in the night.

Brewer ambled down to the corral. He propped a boot heel on the bottom rail and leaned against a post. He shook a dark line of fragrant tobacco into a paper, rolled and sealed it with a lick. He drew a lucifer from his vest pocket and scratched it on his rough canvas pant leg. The match flared smoky sulfur. He drew flame to his smoke and sucked a lung full of harsh satisfaction.

Waite's eyes creased at the corners, looking out over the corral. "Somethin' on your mind, Dick?"

"Santa Fe scum, they ain't never gonna see them two come to justice."

"Likely not."

"They're slippery bastards. You'll have to be real careful they don't make a break for it."

"Real careful would be easier without McCloskey."

"Still easier than havin' to deal with Ledger."

Waite lifted a sidelong glance. "McCloskey may forget which side he's on."

"That'd be a shame."

Waite flicked the butt of his smoke on a glowing arc into the corral and started back to the house. "It would indeed."

March 7th

Dawn turned the sky pink. Smoke poured out the stovepipe and drifted off on the breeze. The smells of cooked bacon and fresh coffee colored the morning air on the porch. Men spilled out into the yard and trooped down to the corral. They fed, watered and saddled horses. Ty found McCloskey saddling a sturdy buckskin.

"Mornin,' Bill."

"Mornin,' Ty."

"Roth wants me to ride down to South Spring with him. I can come along with you if you think you might need help."

"Brewer said his piece. I don't expect no trouble."

"Are you sure?"

He rested one hand on the butt of his gun and the other on the stock in his rifle boot. "Sure as I'm standin' here."

"I'm countin' on you to make sure those boys make it to Lincoln."

"We'll be fine. Nobody's going to lynch anybody while I'm around."

Ty met his eyes with a small nod and went off to saddle the steeldust.

South Spring

Late afternoon sky surrendered red-orange mountaintops and long purple shadows. Patches of yellow light dotted the dark outlines of the bunkhouse and hacienda below as Roth and Ledger rode out of the hills. They slow loped through the gate. Roth led the way to the house. Halfway across the yard a shaft of light appeared in the doorway. She stepped out into silhouette. Roth drew rein and leaped down. He bounded up the porch in one long stride and swallowed her up in his arms.

Ty stepped down, chuckling to himself. *Ground tied for sure, corral gate in sight.*

"Figured that for you, the way she run off from the supper table like that." Chisum filled the door frame. "I see you brought company. Dawn you best set another couple of places. Come in, come in." He clapped Roth on the back in something of an admission of defeat. He held out his hand. "Ty, good to see you."

The men filed into the dining room while Dawn Sky bustled off to the kitchen. Chisum took his seat at the head of the table.

"So, how'd you boys do?"

Ty scraped a chair back. "Baker and Morton are on their way up to Lincoln."

"You think Brady will actually hold 'em?"

"Brewer sent some of his boys along with them. They're to turn them over to Justice Wilson and hold them at his direction."

"That should work." He glanced at Roth, no need to ask the question. He felt Dawn enter the room behind him.

Roth met his eyes. "I got him. He won't cause any more trouble."

She rushed to stand beside him, hand on his shoulder.

Chisum knew when he was beat. "Oh, all right you two, it's plain you'll not give me a moment's peace until I give in. I expect that explains why Ty's here."

Roth smiled. "It does."

CHAPTER TWENTY-FOUR

March 8ᵗʰ

The stand of white oak along the creek bottom made a good place to camp some halfway up the trail to Lincoln. Waite pushed the best part of the last hour to get there before sunset. The shadows were long, the light gray and hazy by the time they drew rein and stepped down.

"Doc, you and Henry picket the horses downstream along the bottom. Bill, see if you can find us some firewood while me and Billy settle the prisoners."

McCloskey had a fragrant mesquite fire built and a pot of coffee on to boil by the time the evening star and a pale moon climbed up on the horizon. With prisoners and horses alike secured for the night, the men gathered around the fire. Bonney sat off by himself cleaning his gun.

Scurlock washed down the last of a hardtack biscuit with a mouthful of coffee. "I can't believe we're actually gonna waste our time turnin' them two over to Wilson and nurse maid 'em until they stand trial."

McCloskey didn't like the edge of suggestion in Scurlock's tone. "You heard Dick. McSween and Chisum want this done legal. We're servin' Justice Wilson's court."

"There you go again, McCloskey. You best remember which side you're on this trip." Brown didn't have much use for Mc-Closkey. It showed and he didn't give a damn if it did.

"I got no trouble rememberin' I'm on the side of the law, Brown."

The fire popped sending a shower of sparks into the night. Brown's eye caught the glint. "He says so like he's some expert on New Mexico politics, which is all this shit is. Dolan never lets the law get in the way when it don't suit his purpose. He'll have Brady take jurisdiction the minute we got them two in arm's reach."

"Best not be any politics." Billy spun the cylinder of his gun, checking the loads. "Either one of them sons of bitches tries to let them bastards go, I'll blow their sorry ass straight to hell. They can warm the place up for all the rest that had a hand in killin' Mr. Tunstall."

Scurlock smiled. "Billy may not say much, but when he does, he surly has a poetry way with his words."

McCloskey felt a little uneasy. Maybe he'd been a bit too confident about keeping a lid on the vigilante intentions of this group. He'd feel some better if Marshal Ledger were here about now. "No need for all them threats. You all heard Brewer. The law will handle this. Right, Fred?"

Waite squinted across the fire. "Dolan's law? Sure thing."

No help there. McCloskey felt alone. Well they'd got this far. One more day and they'd be in Lincoln. One more day and he'd have Widenmann and McSween to help keep a lid on things. For the moment he needed a cool head and a gun for a pillow.

Lincoln

The visitor bell seldom got Dolan's attention when he was in his office. This bell piqued his interest. He reached his office door to find Territorial Governor Samuel Axtell standing in the late afternoon sun splash at the front counter.

"Governor, welcome to Lincoln. I'm pleased to see you."

Tall and handsome Axtell had soft waves of brown hair, graying at the temples, and a dignified bearing. He wore a politician's affected smile and dark suit, calculated to impress thoughtful competence on those he met.

"Jimmy." He extended his hand. "Your telegram impressed me with the gravity of the situation here. I decided it merited my coming down here to have a look for myself."

Dolan took his hand. "The situation is serious. With your help, I believe we can manage the problem. Please step into my office." He showed Axtell in and closed the door. "Have a seat." He gestured to a side chair.

Axtell folded his frame into the offered chair as Dolan took his seat at the desk.

"Your telegram was somewhat brief. Tell me what's going on."

"You know we've had tension between the large and small ranchers in Lincoln County for years. Mostly the disputes were about public grazing land. Last year a man named Tunstall came to town. He bought a large ranch and cornered the market on the winter feed supply serving a number of small ranchers. Unfortunately he didn't always pay his bills. The Territorial Court granted me a lien on some of his livestock to satisfy a debt he owed me. When the sheriff attempted to serve the court's order, Tunstall resisted. He fired on the deputies. They returned fire. He was killed in the gunfight."

"Seems pretty cut and dried."

"There's more. Tunstall's business partner, a local lawyer named McSween, disputed the deputies' story. McSween convinced John Wilson, the local justice of the peace to issue warrants for the sheriff's posse men on murder charges. Wilson then appointed Dick Brewer constable to serve the warrants. Brewer managed Tunstall's ranch."

"Not exactly a disinterested third party."

"Wait, it gets better. Brewer raised a posse of Tunstall's hired guns to serve the warrants. Not only do these people defy Sheriff Brady's jurisdictional authority, they've turned the county into an armed camp. It's a powder keg ready to blow. I'm afraid we could lose control of the situation. If we do, we could be looking at all-out war."

Axtell rocked back in his chair, his brows knit. "Not the sort of thing we need when we're seeking statehood. What do you want me to do about it?"

"Justice Wilson created the jurisdictional conflict when he issued those warrants and appointed Brewer constable. It undermines Sheriff Brady's authority. Tunstall was already stirring up the Democrats to oppose Brady in the fall election."

"The Democrats, you say, we surely don't need to hear from that bunch." The governor drummed his fingers on the desk. "I can't order Wilson to withdraw the warrants on the sheriff's men. The Territorial Court will have to sort that out. That said, we can't have lawmen gunning each other down. Somebody's got to be in charge. I can order Wilson to withdraw his appointment of that constable if I call in the army to establish martial law."

"If you did, that should keep a lid on things until the Territorial Court convenes next month."

Axtell waved his hand. "I'll take the matter up with Justice Wilson. John is reasonable when he sees things clearly."

"I hope you're right."

"Leave it to me, Jimmy. I'll send word as soon as I've talked to him. If you need me, I'll be staying at the Wortley. Now, where can I find Justice Wilson?"

March 9ᵗʰ

McCloskey didn't sleep worth a damn. He had a bad feelin' that wouldn't shake. He got up when Doc stirred the fire to

187

light just before dawn. He took hardtack and water for the prisoners and went off to the trees where they were tied. He untied Morton.

Morton rubbed his wrists, working some feeling back to his fingers. "They're fixin to hang us, ain't they, Bill?"

"Shut up, Buck," Baker said.

"Ain't nobody gonna get hung unless a judge says so." McCloskey hoped he sounded convinced.

"I heard 'em talkin' last night. I swear they're fixin' to hang us."

"I said shut up, Buck!"

"I ain't shuttin' up, Frank. Bill here might be our onliest chance."

"Nobody's gonna hang anybody. You got my word on it." He untied Baker.

"Appears to me they got you outnumbered, Bill. You're in a poor position to be givin' assurance to such things."

"I got my eyes open and my guns handy, Frank. Now maybe you'd best take your own advice."

"Slip us a couple of guns, Bill. We'd even up the sides and get shut of these bastards."

"Hey!" Brown stood silhouetted in gray light. "You feedin' them two or jawin' over old times?"

McCloskey ignored him.

"Bring 'em on over here where we can keep an eye on things. Wouldn't want you to take a notion to let 'em go for old time's sake."

McCloskey stood. "You heard the man. Com'on, let's go."

"They's fixin' to hang us."

"Shut up, Buck."

The morning passed without incident. Waite and Bonney led the way, followed by the prisoners. McCloskey took the prisoner's backs flanked by Scurlock and Brown. They made Blackwater Canyon by midday. McCloskey began to relax. They'd make Lincoln by late afternoon and this little trip would be over.

Waite signaled a halt. He said something to Bonney and wheeled his horse around the prisoners. He drew up beside Scurlock.

"Well, McCloskey, this is it. What's the best way to kill these sons a bitches?"

Morton cut his eyes to Baker. Baker let his drift toward the canyon.

McCloskey felt the hair on the back of his neck rise. He eased off a breath. "Now, Fred, we been all through that. Brewer made it real clear. We're takin' these two into Lincoln. What happens from there is for a court to decide."

Waite shifted his chaw from one cheek to the other. He leaned over his saddle and spit a black-brown tobacco stream. "Dick made it real clear for Marshal Ledger. He had a different talk with me the night before we left. He don't think Dolan'll let them two come to justice."

"One man's opinion ain't reason to take the law into our hands."

"Enough of this shit." Scurlock wheeled his horse in front of McCloskey, boxing him in.

"Damn right." Brown drew and fired.

Baker and Morton bolted for the canyon.

The bullet hit McCloskey in the side, glanced off a rib and exited his throat just below the chin. He twisted in the saddle. "You back-shootin' son of a . . ." His eyes rolled white. The body slid out of the saddle.

"After 'em, boys!"

Billy put his heels to the roan, followed by gunfire. He filled his hand as the big roan pounded after the fleeing prisoners. He drew a bead on Baker. Tunstall's first killer danced on his sight. He settled into the rhythm of the horse's stride and squeezed. The Colt bucked. Baker jerked. Billy smiled that gap-toothed grin of his and fired two more shots. Baker pitched from the saddle. He slid to a stop beside the body.

One. He took some satisfaction. Up the trail Morton disappeared among the rocks at the mouth of the canyon. The Regulators swept past, hot on his heels. *This is where it begins, Mr. Tunstall.* He didn't feel like a kid anymore. He'd taken on a man's responsibility. They might call him "kid," but he'd show them. He meant business, deadly business.

He swept his eyes across the mouth of the canyon. He checked his gun, put his heels to the roan with a half smile and broke away to the east. He circled the canyon wall. Shots sounded below the canyon rim. He rode on. *Far enough,* he drew rein and dropped to the ground. He scrambled up the rise to the canyon rim, picked out a handsome boulder and looked down. Morton crouched in the rocks below, hidden from his pursuers. Billy cracked a crooked grin. He slipped his gun out of its holster, content to watch his prey for the moment.

"Give it up, Morton! You haven't got a chance."

Billy recognized Scurlock's voice. Morton twisted around, searching for a way out. On foot, the only good option pointed up. Sure enough, he started working his way through the rocks toward the rim. The climb would bring him up further north. Billy eased along the rim, cautious not to alert Morton to his presence. The unarmed man posed no threat, but he saw no point in spoiling the fun. He imagined the surprise and fear Morton would feel when he found himself looking down the muzzle of a gun held by John Tunstall's avenger. He settled into a crevice in the rock wall near the place Morton would come up thinking he might escape.

Minutes passed. A boot scraped a rock. The murderer eased

his way over the rim. He took off his hat and wiped sweat from his moon face on a sleeve. Billy cocked his gun. Morton froze. He turned slowly to the sound.

"Hello, Buck." Billy smiled, his vacant eyes mirthless. "You know I swore on John Tunstall's grave I'd kill every last one of you murderin' sons a bitches."

Morton's eyes went wide, white, staring. "Don't shoot, Billy. I didn't kill him, I swear. It was Evans and Mathews. Them's the ones you want."

"Your mama didn't never tell you to be careful of the friends you keep, did she? It might matter some who done the shootin,' but you was all in on it. Adios, Buck."

The muzzle flashed, the concussion charged a cloud of blue smoke. Red stain splattered Morton's belly. The gun exploded again, powder smoke masked another grin. Morton grabbed his mortal wounds in both hands as if to staunch the flow of life. His eyes turned wide in disbelief, pinched in realization. He staggered and pitched forward like an overstuffed sack.

Billy holstered his gun. Moments later Scurlock and Brown scrambled over the canyon rim. He looked up and met their eyes.

"What took you boys so long?"

Two.

Chapter Twenty-Five

Lincoln

Dolan clasped his hands behind his back and scowled at the sun-soaked muddy street beyond the store window. An ox-drawn freight wagon plodded past, the heavily loaded wagon plowing deep ruts in its wake. The bullwhacker flicked his profanity-laced whip across the backs of the mud-spattered yoke. The scene suited Dolan's troubles. Tunstall's death hadn't solved the problem. McSween had found a spine, likely with Chisum's help. The damn bank and store continued to bleed his profits. He had to put a stop to it, but how? McSween wouldn't be bought off. The civil suit he'd filed up in Las Vegas would distract McSween for having to defend it, but even he doubted it would stop him. The liquidity provided by the bank meant time was on his opponent's side. McSween had made it plain enough. He wouldn't be goaded into an excusable killing as easily as the fool Englishman, either. The longer it went on the worse things got. His cash receipts continued to decline. If that didn't change and soon, he'd find himself bankrupt. If he couldn't find a way to stop the lawyer legally, well then, he just might have to . . . *Wait, what the hell is this?*

Four heavily armed horsemen rode through town. Three of them led a second horse each with a blanket-shrouded body tied across the saddle. The only one he recognized was the gawky Bonney kid. Tunstall hired the boy, he seemed to recall. He guessed the rest for hired guns. Tunstall had hired more than a few. They drew rein at Brady's office and stepped down. The man who seemed to be in charge went inside.

Moments later he came out with Brady. The sheriff stopped at the first body and peeled back the blanket. He moved on to the second and the third. The leader handed Brady a folded document. Brady looked at it for a minute or two then shook his head. Dolan resisted the temptation to go over and find out what this was all about.

Brady shouted something over his shoulder toward the office. Deputy George Hindman scrambled out the door and down the steps. He collected the reins of the horses carrying the bodies and led them up the street toward the blacksmith's shop where they'd be measured for coffins. Brady exchanged a few more words with the leader, turned on his heel and stomped back into the office. Tunstall's hired guns led their horses down the street to the cantina. With the street clear, Dolan had all the suspense he could stand.

"I'll be back, Jasper." The visitor bell clanged as he swept out the door and down the street to Brady's office. He found the red-faced sheriff staring open-mouthed at his desk.

"What the hell was that all about?"

"You ain't gonna believe this."

"Try me. Who were the dead men?"

"Frank Baker, Buck Morton and Bill McCloskey."

"Who killed them?"

"That's the part you won't believe. Tunstall's hired guns claim they're a constable's posse. They said they had warrants for the arrest of those involved in killing Tunstall. That means they're still after more of my men. You said you would take care of that problem."

"I did. The governor is here. He convinced Justice Wilson to withdraw Brewer's appointment last night."

"Well the word never got to Brewer and it sure won't do

193

Baker and Morton no good. We can't have lawmen gunning each other down. Somebody's got to be in charge."

"The governor is calling out the army to declare martial law."

"They better get here quick. Brewer's got Tunstall and Chisum's hired guns organized into some excuse for a posse."

"What did McCloskey have to do with it?"

"He worked for Chisum of late. Tunstall's man, Waite, claims Baker shot him while he and Morton were tryin' to escape." Brady pulled his desk chair back and sat heavily, rubbing the bridge of his nose between thumb and forefinger. "I don't like this one bit. They bring any of those men to trial somebody's liable to talk."

"Nobody's going to trial, Brady. Now shut up and listen. Brewer and his so-called posse killed those men without legal sanction. You go along to Justice Wilson and you get warrants on Dick Brewer and every last one of McSween's and Chisum's gunmen, including the Bonney kid. The charge is murder."

South Spring

They kept the nuptials simple. The black-robed Padre Bernardino officiated. Short and plump with a shiny bald pate fringed in brown hair, he performed his solemn duties with a jolly disposition. Chisum gave the bride away. Ty stood up for Johnny. Dawn Sky chose the big black cowboy Deacon Swain for her witness. The ex-slave took the responsibility in sober humor, mindful of his unfamiliar presence in the big house. Caneris was the only other guest. They moved the parlor furniture away from the fireplace to allow them all to gather around.

The padre began with a cherub-like smile. "Dearly beloved, we are gathered here today to join this man and this woman in the sacrament of holy matrimony."

The words took Ty back to a small white church on a hill east of Cheyenne. The day he made Victoria his wife was the happiest day of his life. Now she was gone, her life cut short by a vicious killer. Had it been a year already? It had. He still felt the hollow place she left in his life. Avenging her killing staunched his rage. That only made room for the hurt. Would he ever know that joy again? Lucy smiled in his mind's eye. Maybe, maybe one day he could.

They had something between them. They'd both felt it the time they first met in Dodge. A casual conversation, nothing more, he'd walked away then. He hadn't seen her again until last year. So much had happened. So much had changed and yet, the feeling was still there. It touched a nerve raw with grief in Denver last spring and then again later in Santa Fe. It got the best of them on a hillside in Lincoln last summer. He'd walked away again. She turned to Tunstall. The Englishman's death left no reason they couldn't try again, if she was willing. It seemed like she might be. The padre called him back to the moment.

"Do you, Nathaniel John Roth, take this woman, to have and to hold . . ."

Nathaniel? Ty arched an amused brow at Roth.

He scowled in reply.

"For rich or for poor, in sickness and in health until death do you part?"

"I do."

"Do you Maria Dawn Sky take this man . . ."

Ty smiled at Roth's surprise. Two could play this game.

She turned to Roth, misty eyed. "I do."

"I now pronounce you husband and wife. You may kiss the bride."

He didn't have to ask twice.

Ty took Johnny's hand with a chuckle. "Congratulations, Nathaniel."

"Don't start with me."

"I noticed you got a surprise of your own."

He turned to Dawn. "I didn't know your name was Maria."

"Padre said I must have a Christian name when he baptized me. He gave Dawn Sky that name."

"I'll stick with Dawn."

She smiled. "I like Johnny too."

"Well, that's settled." Chisum handed glasses of whiskey to Johnny and Ty. He turned to Johnny and Dawn. "Let me offer my best wishes for all the happiness life can bring to your marriage."

Ty lifted his glass. "I'll drink to that."

They did.

"When are you heading back to Lincoln, Ty?" Chisum said.

"I plan to start back in the morning."

"Good, mind if I ride with you?"

"Hell, no, I'd be glad of the company."

"I need to spend a few days up there. It'll let the newlyweds have the run of the house."

Roth lifted his glass. "That's a mighty fine wedding present, John. Thanks."

"Hell, that ain't your wedding present. Com'on step outside with me for a minute." He led the way out to the porch, followed by Johnny and Dawn. An unseasonably warm taste of spring blew up from the south, stirring waves on a golden sea of winter grass. It ruffled the hair at Dawn's shoulders. Chisum swept an arm northeast. "See that section?"

Johnny nodded.

"That's your wedding present, clear to the river. You can put your house right there."

"I, I don't know how we can thank you, John."

"Don't. It means I won't have to break in a new housekeeper. At least until this one gets busy with little ones of her own.

Now let's go back inside and give this wedding a proper celebration."

Chisum and Ledger didn't wait breakfast for the newlyweds the next morning. They saddled up and rode northwest under a sky patched in cottonball clouds. Chisum sat a long-striding, big-boned buckskin, setting a brisk pace. Morning chill gave way to a softer spring warmth. The hillsides hinted green traces of new growth. Here and there a touch of color promised the arrival of spring flowers.

"If you don't mind my asking, what brings you up to Lincoln?"

Gray eyes lit the shadow beneath his hat brim. "Time I talk to McSween and get a feel for how Dolan's reactin' to our people goin' after Tunstall's killers."

"You need a trip to Lincoln to figure that out?"

He pursed his lips. "Not how he's takin' it, if that's what you mean. The question is what's he gonna do about it?"

"He's likely to figure it for a county matter and no business of constables appointed by a justice of the peace."

"Yup. He can disagree all he wants. Talk is cheap. Doin' somethin' about it is another matter."

"He's got some guns."

"He does. We've got more and that's before we finish servin' those warrants. He'll read them tea leaves and reckon he's got to do somethin' before we get too much advantage on him. The question is what?"

"He'll tip his hand sooner or later. Marshal Widenmann and I will keep an eye on things." The conversation fell silent for a mile or so.

"There's a creek up yonder." Chisum waved a gloved hand toward a stand of cottonwood off to the west. "We can water and rest the horses a spell."

The horses caught the scent of water and picked up the pace without encouragement. They splashed into the gurgling stream, swollen with spring runoff and dropped their heads to drink. Chisum and Ledger stepped down.

Ledger cupped a handful of clear cold water to his mouth. It tasted sweet. Even the dribble running down his chin felt good. Chisum stood by, his sun-bronzed square jaw set above the collar of his canvas coat. His steel-gray hair turned white at the sideburns.

"That was a mighty generous wedding gift you made Johnny and Dawn Sky."

"Best way I could think of to keep her close by. I love that girl like a daughter. I always knew she'd up and marry one day, but an old man like me didn't have to like the idea."

"I've known Johnny a long time. He'll be good to her."

"Hell, I know that. If I didn't think so I'd have run him off at gunpoint. It's nothin' personal. An old man gets set in his ways. He don't have to be cheerful over the loss of the daughter he never had."

"You haven't exactly lost her and you ain't that old, either."

His eyes creased at the corners. "I know."

CHAPTER TWENTY-SIX

Lincoln

A sudden rap at the door intruded on McSween's concentration. He flicked his watchcase open and checked the time with a frown. He wasn't expecting anyone. The knock sounded again, insistent.

"Coming." He hauled himself up from behind his desk and crossed the parlor to the lace-curtained front door. *Brady, what the hell did he want?* He opened the door.

"Sheriff, afternoon. What can I do for you?"

"McSween." He held out a thick packet. "This summons come down from District Court in Las Vegas. Consider it served."

McSween opened the packet and glanced at the heading. The documents were addressed to him as respondent in a civil suit filed on behalf of James J. Dolan as plaintiff in the matter of recovering five thousand dollars in proceeds forfeited in settlement of a certain insurance claim filed . . .

Brady produced a receipt and pen with a mocking smile. "Sign here."

Chisum and Ledger drew up at the Wortley hitch rack, cold and tired after a long day in a chill rain-soaked saddle. The lobby door opened to a grim-faced Rob Widenmann. He stopped in his tracks.

"Afternoon, Marshal."

He nodded. "Chisum, I'm glad you're here. You too, Ty. I was just on my way over to see McSween. If you have the time, you might want to come along. It'll save me havin' to chew these oats twice." He stepped down to the street and collected his horse.

"Somethin' the matter?"

"Depends on who you ask." He stepped into the saddle and swung away up the street.

Chisum pulled a puzzled look. Ty shrugged and squeezed up a trot after the marshal. Ty saw him first. He caught Chisum's eye and lifted his chin toward the visitor leaving the McSween house.

"Brady," Chisum said. "Wonder what that's all about."

They dropped rein at the McSween house and trooped up the walk after Widenmann. McSween answered the door at the first knock. He clutched a stack of official-looking papers in his hand.

"To what do I owe the honor of such a distinguished delegation?"

Widenmann cut past the pleasantries. "We need to talk. May we come in?"

The lawyer stepped back from the door with a shrug. "Have a seat in the parlor. My office won't hold a meeting this size."

They scattered to seats around a comfortably appointed room muted in gray light seeping through lace curtains. The soft patter of rain on the roof filled the silence.

"I'd offer you refreshments, but I'm all thumbs in the kitchen until Susan returns from the bank."

Chisum raised a hand. "None needed, thanks anyway. All right, Marshal, out with the mystery."

"Brewer's men caught up with Frank Baker and Buck Morton."

"We know. Ty here was with them."

Widenmann arched a brow at Ledger. "Were you with them when Baker and Morton took a fatal case of lead poisoning?"

"No. Damn it. I was afraid of somethin' like that. McCloskey and I both were. Bill said he could handle it."

The marshal smoothed his mustache. "Well he couldn't. He's dead too."

"What happened?"

"According to them left to tell about it, Baker and Morton killed McCloskey while tryin' to escape."

Ty scowled. "They were unarmed and in custody when I left them. Somebody must've made a bad mistake."

"Kind of unusual given all those experienced men, don't you think?"

McSween sat back riveted on Widenmann. "Are you suggesting our men murdered Baker and Morton."

"I am and likely McCloskey too if he was of a mind to stop the killin'."

"That's a pretty strong charge," Chisum said.

"There's more. According to Justice Wilson, the governor hit town night before last."

Chisum arched a brow. "The governor? What the hell is he doing here?"

"Called to investigate the events attending to Tunstall's death."

"Called by who?" Chisum said, exchanging a glance with McSween.

"Wilson didn't say. The governor told him he's calling out the army and declaring martial law. He ordered Wilson to withdraw Brewer's appointment as a constable. Wilson did. Yesterday, Brady showed up demanding warrants for Brewer and his men for the murders of Frank Baker and Buck Morton."

Chisum clenched his jaw. "Well, I guess we know how Dolan plans to protect his side of this thing."

"Brady can't prove his allegation and them who can, won't talk. We all heard what the Kid said at Tunstall's funeral. Ty and McCloskey both had concerns over the mood of Brewer and his men. You two pay those men. Throw the army in here to back Dolan's sheriff and we've got an ugly situation on our hands."

"You don't know it was vigilante justice, Rob," Chisum said. "Baker and Morton was rustlers and gunmen long before they murdered Tunstall."

"They were accused of murdering Tunstall. Guilt is for a court to decide, not a posse."

"Gentlemen, please." McSween raised a hand for calm. "Marshal, I'm sure if you talk to Dick Brewer he can vouch for his men. John and I certainly support the need to keep our men on the side of the law. Brewer's orders were clear."

"Brewer made that clear to all his men," Ty said.

Widenmann chenched his jaw. "Brewer wasn't with the men who brought in Baker and Morton."

McSween knit his brow. "If Wilson withdrew Brewer's appointment, the serving of those warrants comes into question."

"According to Brady it becomes a question of murder," Widenmann said.

Chisum scowled. "Brady's been a busy boy. That was him leavin' when we rode up, wasn't it, Alex?"

McSween nodded. "He came to serve a summons in a civil suit Dolan filed against me over an insurance claim that I settled for the Fritz family estate. I suspect it's his way of pressuring me to sell him the bank and the store. I'm sure he'll offer to drop the suit if I sell."

"Hell, this whole thing smells from here to Santa Fe. We may have to appeal to a higher authority before this is all over."

"What authority do you have in mind that's higher than Santa Fe?"

"Territorial governors are appointed by the president."

"You know President Hayes?"

"No, but I know somebody who does."

"Who's that?"

"My lawyer."

The visitor bell clanged near closing. Lucy looked up from a bolt of fabric and smiled. *Ty, god, he looks good.*

He returned her smile. Sunset slashed the rumpled banks of gray cloud in the west. Golden light slanting through the store window fired her hair. Her eyes turned liquid in the muted glow between the shelves. She put aside what she'd been doing and crossed the store.

"Hi, cowboy, it's been a while."

A long-ago whisper echoed. "Too long." He took his hat in hand.

"When did you hit town?"

"This afternoon. I thought I'd come by and see if maybe you'd like to have supper."

She smiled again. Her eyes glittered as she held his. "I'd like that."

Susan McSween watched from behind the teller counter, losing her place in balancing the drawer. She knew they were friends. The marshal had walked Lucy home a time or two. She'd always assumed where John was concerned it was no more than that. Lucy surely leaned on him during the funeral, but this was plainly something more.

"I was just about to close up. It won't take but a minute." She went to the counter and began totaling up the day's receipts.

Ty noticed Susan and waved. She smiled. "You'll be all right if I steal Lucy?"

"Oh, I'll be just fine. Big Jim here keeps an eye on the place. He'll see me home."

French dozed on a chair propped up against the back wall of

the store with a sawed-off shotgun cradled in his lap. *Good,* Ty thought, comforted by the protection and yet disturbed again at the need of it.

Lucy went to the window and turned the sign to *closed.* "Well that's that. See you in the morning, Susan." She threw her shawl around her shoulders.

"Good night, Lucy."

She took his arm and let him lead her out the door to the clang of the bell. They strolled along the boardwalk toward Mrs. O'Hara's in silence.

She rested easy on his arm, the feeling more comfortable than he remembered. "It's still there."

She picked up his meaning with no more preamble than that. "Always has been."

"But I thought . . ."

"You think too much."

"How was I supposed to know?"

"Listen to your heart for once."

"Oh, that."

"Yes, that."

The next sound that passed between them was the familiar squeal of Mrs. O'Hara's gate. Lucy opened the door and let them in. The house smelled of fresh baked bread. It set Ty's mouth to water.

"Now this is the way a home ought to smell."

"It is, isn't it? One of these days you'll have to get to work on that, cowboy."

"Lucy, dear, is that you?"

"Yes, Mrs. O'Hara. Look who followed me home."

She stuck her head out of the kitchen, no more than a silhouette at the end of the dimly lit hall. "Is that Marshal Ledger? Well bless my soul. It's been too long. Come on in and let me have a look at you. I've missed you even if our friend there hasn't had the good sense to."

He shuffled down the hall feeling a bit sheepish. "Don't blame Lucy. I'm the one stayed gone."

"Well, either way, it's nice to have you back."

"Give me a minute to freshen up, Ty. You're in better hands than you know."

Susan McSween let herself in the front door. She heard male voices coming from the parlor. She found Alex there with Rob Widenmann and John Chisum.

"John, what a pleasant surprise." She favored him with one of her most fetching smiles.

"Mrs. McSween, how very nice to see you."

"Please, John, you must call me Susan. Alex, why didn't you tell me John was in town?"

"I didn't know."

"No matter." She smiled again. "You simply must stay for supper. You too, Marshal. Now, Alex, serve our guests a drink while I stir up some supper."

She set off for the kitchen with a flounce in her skirts and a warm flush in her cheeks. *John Chisum.*

They had the Wortley dining room pretty much to themselves. The McSweens invited Chisum and Widenmann to supper, so apart from a lonely drummer, the Wortley had just about run out of guests to serve. Just about, but not quite. They had a quiet drink and ordered the special, stewed chicken and dumplings. Ty caught the flicker in Lucy's eye as she glanced behind him.

"What is it?"

"Interesting."

"What's interesting?"

She lifted her chin toward the door. "Dolan just came in with none other than Governor Axtell."

"Chisum had the right of it."

"Had what right?"

"The governor got Justice Wilson to withdraw Brewer's constable appointment. Brady got arrest warrants issued on Dick and the boys charging them with the murders of Baker and Morton. Chisum said it smelled from here to Santa Fe. That pair back there give off the odor he was smellin'."

"Well, they got their heads together thick as thieves."

"One's a thief. The other's a politician. Come to think of it, thief about sums it up."

After dinner, Ty paid the bill and started for the door with Lucy on his arm. Dolan and Axtell were indeed deep in conversation. So deep they didn't notice the couple approach their table.

"So, when do you think the army will get here?" Dolan said.

Axtell bit off his response. Dolan glanced over his shoulder and scowled.

"Evenin', Governor." Ty touched his hat. "Dolan. Enjoy your dinner."

Outside Lucy took his arm. "They didn't look any too pleased to see us."

"Pretty close to being caught red-handed. Did you hear what Dolan asked the governor?"

"Something about the army."

"He wanted to know when the army would be here. Dolan doesn't have enough guns to take on Brewer and the boys. If they bring in the army, the Regulators best make themselves scarce."

"Let's not spoil a lovely evening with any more talk of such ugliness."

They took a leisurely stroll back to Mrs. O'Hara's. Bright moonlight silvered the street. Chill night air frosted their breath.

When they reached the front porch, Lucy took his hands in hers.

"Care to come in?"

"I'd like that."

She led him inside. The scent of fresh bread lingered in the air. He followed her into the parlor. She lit an oil lamp, trimmed the wick low and settled on the settee. She arranged her skirt to make room for him beside her. He took his intended place. She wriggled under his arm and put her head to rest on his chest.

"There, that's better."

"It is." He paused. "I'm sorry."

"Sorry for what?"

"For takin' so long to figure things out."

"You had to get over your grief. I'm the one who should be sorry. I'm the one who didn't wait."

"Who could blame you for that?"

"Me."

"You?"

"Yes, me. John came along after you left. He was safe and convenient. I needed respectable work. If it had ever come to more than it did, it would have been unfair to him. I took advantage of him. I didn't love him."

"Well, I'm still sorry for takin' so long to figure things out. I never should have put you through that."

She lifted liquid eyes to his. "And just what exactly did all this figuring come to?"

The kiss came easy, sweet and soft and slow. Her fingers twined his hair. Time froze, warm and moist turned liquid, urgent. Her head went light, the air consumed of nourishment.

"Oh, yes." She breathed. "That never went away."

"Yup, I finally figured that out."

"Good." She hugged him fiercely. "Don't ever let go again."

"I don't reckon I could."

She kissed him hard. "Good."

He smiled warm. "Well, little lady it's gettin' late. We have your reputation to consider."

"It's a little late for that, cowboy."

"Not in Lincoln."

Chapter Twenty-Seven

Flying H

Widenmann and Ty rode into the ranch with late afternoon sun warming their backs. The marshal stepped down, looped a rein over the worn rail and clumped up the step. Brewer waited on the porch.

"Marshal, Ty, what brings you two all the way down here."

Widenmann took his hand. "We need to talk, Dick."

"Sounds serious. Com'on in." He led the way to the kitchen table. "Care for a cup of coffee?" They nodded as they pulled up chairs. Brewer poured three steaming cups and took his seat. "Now, what's on your mind, Rob?"

"The Baker and Morton killin's."

Brewer shrugged. "I 'spect the boys told you. They jumped McCloskey and made a run for it. Seems pretty cut and dried to me."

"Maybe too cut and too dried," Ty said. "McCloskey and I both heard the hangin' talk when those men were arrested. I had concerns they might not make it to Lincoln. So did McCloskey. He told me he'd handle it. Maybe he tried and got himself killed for it."

Brewer scowled. "You sayin' my boys lied?"

"I'm sayin' it's as likely as a competent man like McCloskey makin' a mistake fool enough to put a gun in the hand of Baker or Morton."

"That's pure speculation, Ledger."

"Not much different than Mathews and his boys sayin' Tunstall fired on them."

"That's different."

"Is it?"

Widenmann raised a hand. "Ease back, you two. What's done is done. I'm more concerned with what happens from here on."

"You want the rest of them warrants served?"

"I do, but we've got a problem."

"What's that?"

"Dolan put Governor Axtell up to pressurin' Justice Wilson. Wilson suspended your constable appointment. You ain't authorized to serve them warrants."

Brewer shrugged. "That seems easy enough. You deputize me and the boys and we're back on the case."

"I don't have jurisdiction, at least not an obvious one."

"What do you mean by obvious?"

"I've been thinkin' on the ride down here. There might be a way. I'd be stickin' my neck out from here to Santa Fe, but there might be a way."

"How's that?" Ty said.

"Tunstall did business with the army. That makes him a federal contractor, sort of. I could claim jurisdiction based on that. At least until some higher-up told me I couldn't. If things was to go right, it might not matter by then."

"There you go." Brewer beamed. "Problem solved."

"Not so fast, Dick, I'm the one with my neck stuck out here. I want those men brought before a court of law for a proper trial. Understand?"

"Enforcin' the law can be a messy business, Rob. You know that."

"I do. I also know angry men sometimes take the law into their own hands. I'll not be responsible for sworn deputies takin' to vigilante law. Is that clear?"

"Crystal."

"Good. Now let's quit all this fussin' and have a drink like we was all on the same side."

Brewer smiled. "Sounds good. You all right with that, Ledger?"

Ty nodded.

Across the parlor in the bunk room the Kid spun the cylinder of his gun, checking the loads.

Peppin Ranch

George Peppin didn't get many visitors. A half dozen armed men riding into his place had him reaching for his Winchester. As they drew closer, he recognized Dick Brewer. His wariness faded into curiosity. *What was Tunstall's foreman up to with a bunch of hired guns?* He didn't have to wait long for his answer. They drew rein at hailing distance.

"Yo the house."

Peppin put up his rifle and stepped out to the porch unarmed. He waved them in.

"Mornin', Dick."

"Mornin', George."

"You boys are a long way off Flying H range to be lookin' for strays."

"We're not lookin' for strays."

"Somethin' must be right important, then, to bring you boys out in force like this."

"We've got warrants for the arrest of Jesse Evans and Buckshot Roberts."

"My, my. What's the charge?"

"The murder of John Tunstall."

"You don't say. Where's Sheriff Brady?"

"Brady's not involved. We're deputy US marshals. You have any idea where Evans and Roberts might be?"

"I ain't seen 'em if that's what you mean. Jesse's place is down to Seven Rivers, but you know that."

"We've been there. Evans wasn't around."

"Buckshot's got a place over toward Blazer's Mill. That's the best I can do to help you boys."

Brewer touched his hat brim. "Much obliged, George."

The posse wheeled away southwest. Peppin watched them go. *Deputy US marshals. I wonder if Jimmy Dolan knows.*

Lincoln

"I tell you, Jimmy, Brewer and them Regulators of his are still after us. I was damn lucky to spot them a comin', or they'd have got me sure."

"Simmer down, Jesse. Let me think a minute. Wilson rescinded Brewer's constable appointment. That means McSween and Chisum have decided to take the law into their own hands. Governor Axtell has asked the army to intervene. Now's the time to call them out. I'll ride over to Fort Stanton myself to make the request. For the time being you can lie low here."

A soft knock sounded at the office door.

"Not now, Jasper, I'm busy."

"George Peppin is here to see you, Mr. Dolan. He says it's important."

"Now what?" The desk chair groaned, announcing his decision.

"You stay out of sight, Jesse. I'll see what George wants."

Dolan stepped out to the store and closed the office door.

"George, what can I do for you?"

"Jimmy. More like what I can do for you. Can we go into your office?"

Dolan glanced around. The store was empty. "No one here but Jasper. Say your piece."

"It sounds like Rob Widenmann deputized Dick Brewer and a

bunch of Tunstall Regulators to serve murder warrants on Jesse Evans and Buckshot Roberts."

"So that explains it."

"Explains what?"

"I heard Brewer was lookin' for Evans. Thanks, George. You've been a big help." He reached over the counter and grabbed a handful of cigars. "Have a cigar."

Peppin stuffed them in his vest pocket. Dolan returned to his office.

"You hear that?"

Evans nodded. "Now what?"

"We mostly stick with our plan. You hide out. I've got a telegram to send to clear up this US marshal business. Then we call out the army."

Santo Fo

T. B. Catron read the telegram with a shake of his head. Dolan had more problems down in Lincoln than a prime herd with a case of hoof-and-mouth disease. The governor thought he had the situation under control when he returned from his trip down there. Things didn't stay fixed for long. He'd have to tell the governor, but first he'd take care of Dolan's problem.

"Wiley!"

The bird-like secretary appeared at the office door. "Sir?"

"I need to see Marshal Sherman this afternoon."

"Very good, sir."

Lincoln

Brady shoved another log in the potbellied stove and closed the door with a scrape of metallic complaint. Outside the wind howled. Spring snow swirled down the street, holding the town hostage to winter's stubborn grip. Boots clumped the boardwalk. The sheriff glanced toward the door. Dolan's frame filled the doorway with a chill gust.

"Afternoon, Mr. Dolan. What can I do for you?"

He closed the door. "More like what can I do for you, William."

Brady looked puzzled. Dolan crossed the office and tossed a plain envelope across the desk. Brady slit it open with a pocketknife. "It says here I'm appointed special deputy US marshal. I don't understand."

"It means you're Widenmann's new boss. It means you have the authority to call off his dogs."

"What if he don't go for that?"

"Lock him up."

"On what charge?"

"Who gives a shit?"

"I gotta charge him with somethin'."

"Call it insubordination."

"What?"

"Insubordination, disobeyin' an order."

"I reckon I can use that. I doubt I can spell in-so-board-in-a-nation."

Widenmann and Ty pulled their mounts down to a trot at the east end of town. After a long day in the saddle fighting wind-driven snow, both were ready to light down. Ty cut his eyes to the marshal.

"You goin' to the hotel?"

He nodded. "You?"

"I'll swing in at the store to say hello to Lucy."

A knowing look flickered across Widenmann's eye. "No sense lettin' them supper plans get away without you."

He wheeled to the rail, hiding embarrassment under wind raw-reddened cheeks. The marshal jogged on up the street to the Wortley, drew rein and stepped down. He tethered his horse and climbed the step to the boardwalk. He just about had the registration signed when the lobby door opened.

"Widenmann, I thought that was you."

He glanced over his shoulder. "Sheriff," he greeted Brady.

"Not just sheriff anymore. Special deputy US marshal to you."

"What?"

"Yup, the appointment come down from Santa Fe day before yesterday."

Widenmann eased around to face Brady. "Funny, Marshal Sherman never sent word he was thinkin' about doing that."

"Guess he left them orders up to me."

"He did, did he, and what orders would those be?"

"You're to turn the Tunstall investigation over to me."

"To you? Hell that'd be like askin' a fox to guard the henhouse."

"Watch your mouth, Widenmann. You're relieved as of now."

"If you don't mind, I'd like to wire Marshal Sherman to confirm that."

"No need. I got the badge and the appointment letter goes with it right here."

"All the same, I'd like to hear it from him. Now, if you'll excuse me."

"Hand over your badge."

"Not until I hear from Marshal Sherman."

"Hand it over now."

"I said no."

"Suit yourself. George!"

Deputy George Hindman stepped through the back door to the lobby with a sawed-off shotgun leveled at Widenmann.

Brady smiled smug. "Now, if you don't mind, I'll take your badge and your gun."

"On what charge?"

"In-sah, in-so-bor, ah hell, disobeyin' an order. If we hurry, we can get you over to the stockade at Fort Stanton before sundown."

Chapter Twenty-Eight

They had a pleasant supper and enough sparkin' to leave them both breathless. By the time Ty started back to the hotel they were both thinking about warm weather and an evening ride into the hills. The idea had Ty thinking they'd find something more there than they did the last time.

The lamp in the hotel lobby burned low. The clerk dozed on a stool behind the counter. He woke to Ty's boot scrape, blinked behind smudged spectacles and fixed on him.

"Marshal Ledger, I didn't know if you'd be coming in. I thought maybe he'd got you too."

Ty wrinkled his brow. "Who'd got me too?"

"Sheriff Brady, or Marshal Brady, I guess now."

"What are you talking about?"

"I'm not sure I understand it all. Sheriff Brady come in this afternoon while Marshal Widenmann was checkin' in. Brady told the marshal he'd been appointed special deputy US marshal. It sounded like that made him Marshal Widenmann's boss. Brady told him he was takin' over investigatin' the Tunstall killin'."

"He's what?"

"Marshal Widenmann didn't much like it, either. He said he wanted to hear that firsthand from Marshal Sherman. That's when the trouble started."

"Trouble?"

"Yeah. That's when Sheriff Brady or Marshal or whatever he

is now, asked Marshal Widenmann to hand over his badge. He refused. Deputy Hindman showed up with a shotgun and they arrested him."

"Arrested him! On what charge?"

"Brady said something about disobeyin' an order. They took him to the stockade at Fort Stanton."

"And you think they might be after me?"

He shrugged. "I don't know. You ride with Marshal Widenmann, I just thought maybe."

What the hell is goin' on? His mind raced. "Do you have a room for me?"

The clerk nodded. He picked a key off the board behind the counter and turned the register around for Ty to sign in.

Ty laid a dollar on the counter. "Mind if I don't sign? I'd just as soon no one knows I'm here until I figure out what the hell is going on."

The clerk took the dollar. "I ain't seen you in more than a week."

Fort Stanton

Civilian visitor privileges weren't standard issue in a military stockade. Fortunately, Ty's friend, Colonel Dudley, arranged a pass with no questions asked. He followed the sergeant down a dark corridor between two rows of bare cells. The chill air smelled an odd mixture of disinfectant and urine.

"You got a visitor, Widenmann." He opened the cell door. "Call when you're finished."

Widenmann sat on a bunk made up with a coarse wool blanket. "Ty, good to see you, I was afraid I might rot in here before anyone figured out where I was."

"What the hell are you doing in here, Rob?"

"Good question. Somebody got to Marshal Sherman. Whoever it was persuaded or ordered him to appoint Brady a special deputy marshal. I'm guessin' Dolan wanted me off the Tunstall investigation and that was the fastest way to do it."

"You think it was Dolan?"

"He's got influence in Santa Fe. Brady's not smart enough to figure this out let alone get me locked up in here."

"Why lock you up here? What's wrong with the jail in Lincoln?"

"Smart really. I'm a civilian prisoner in military custody. The army is just holding me. Brady is the arresting federal officer. I've got no appeal, unless I can get to Sherman or a federal judge. Neither one is handy. I'd have more options in civilian custody."

"I can't get you out of here the way you got us out of the lockup in Lincoln."

"Nope. That's the point. What you can do is have McSween get to work on it. Maybe he can figure something out."

"I'll go see him right away."

"Be careful. If you'd been with me they'd likely have locked you up too. Stay clear of Brady until we get this sorted out."

"I plan on it. Guard!"

The sergeant major announced Ty.

"Colonel Dudley will see you now."

Ty stepped into the office. He cocked his head toward the door. "May I?"

Dudley nodded. The door clicked closed.

"Have a seat, Ty. How did it go with Widenmann?"

"What's to say? They've got us in a box. We don't have many options."

"I'm afraid you're right. In fact that box is about to get deeper."

Ty wrinkled his brow. "What do you mean?"

"Governor Axtell has requested army support for the civil

authority in Lincoln."

"What does that mean?"

"I'm sending a troop into Lincoln to support Sheriff Brady."

"You can't be serious."

"I'm afraid I am."

"Can't you question that based on the situation?"

"I could try, but my orders come down the War Department chain of command. They get it from the president, who authorized intervention at the governor's request. So in the end, Governor Axtell is the controlling legal authority. All I can do is follow orders."

Lincoln

McSween rubbed his chin between thumb and forefinger considering the facts as Ty described them. The desk lamp cast a long shadow against a bookcase lined with neat rows of leather-bound law books. An island of light floated across the desktop, painting both men in sober masks of light and shadow.

"Rob probably has the right of it. This is some of Dolan's work. He's the only one around these parts with the kind of influence it'd take to force Sherman to reverse himself. Brady won't drop the charges. The post commander's hands are tied. Sherman could order him released, but whoever put him up to appointing Brady in the first place won't sit still for that. Maybe we could persuade Sherman to order him transferred to Santa Fe. If we get him out of Lincoln, the political pressure should cool off and Sherman can find a way to release him."

"But what about Tunstall's murder?"

"Well, we still have you and all of Brewer's duly sworn deputy marshals. You ought to be able to finish serving the rest of the warrants."

"Well, all those duly sworn deputies will only stay that way as long as Brady doesn't catch up with them. He's about to get some help in catching up with them from the army."

McSween rubbed the bridge of his nose. "All right, we need to get word to Dick. He and the boys need to lie low for a spell until we deal with the Santa Fe problem."

"How are you going to do that?"

"I'm not sure. Chisum says his lawyer knows President Hayes. I need to talk with John. We need to get Evans or one of his boys to implicate Brady or Dolan or both."

"I don't know, Alex. All of that strikes me as a long shot."

"Likely is. We both know Brady and Dolan had a hand in John's murder, whether they were there or not. They may be long shots, but they're the only ones I can come up with. You go along down to the Flying H and tell Dick what's happened. I'm going to South Spring. We need help. It's time for Chisum to get involved if he cares to win this thing. Come along, I'll show you out."

McSween led the way through the darkened parlor by the dim light, spilling from the office door. He clasped Ty's hand at the front door. "Make sure you know where to find Dick and the boys once we've sorted this out. I'll see you at South Spring in a few days."

The door latched shut behind Ty.

"You're going to South Spring?" Susan stepped out of the shadows, ghostlike in a flowing nightdress.

He nodded.

"I'm going with you."

"What about the store and the bank?"

"Lucy can take care of things here. Dolan has his problem with you. I'm your wife. Truthfully, I don't feel safe here."

"Yes, my dear, I see your point."

By the time he left McSween, the hour had passed time for respectable calling. He paid it no mind. He had to see her before he left town. No telling how long he'd be gone this time. He couldn't just disappear, not again, not now.

He'd never been to the upper floor of the widow's house. He had a vague sense of direction from hearing Lucy come down. The rest was guesswork helped some by a bright full moon, painting the scene a ghostly white. Lace curtains on the front bedroom window, plain cotton on the back. The back of the house overlooked open plain. She likely had the back bedroom. He tossed a pebble up to the window he hoped was Lucy's. It clattered against the glass and bounced off the sill. Nothing. He tried again. Two pebbles this time. They made twice the clatter. Nothing. *Hell, he might wake the dead before he woke whoever was in that room.* Then again maybe he had it wrong and no one was in there. He bent to find stones for one more try. The back door creaked.

"Ty, is that you?" Her voice was hushed.

"Yeah." He went to the back porch. The moon gave her an otherworldly glow an Indian might have taken for a night spirit. She motioned him into the darkened kitchen. No man with red blood would mistake her for a night spirit when she melted in his arms. He found her lips, soft and liquid. He traced the smooth curve of her spine to the small of her back, her skin warm to his touch beneath a light night shift.

"What a nice surprise."

Her breath tasted sweet in his mouth. She wriggled close and held him tight, the press of her hips saying more than words.

"What brings you by?"

"You."

She purred when she smiled. "I like the sound of that."

"I had to see you before I left town."

"Where are you going?"

"I'm on my way down to the Flying H to see Brewer. Brady's arrested Rob. He's got him locked up over to Fort Stanton."

"Brady? Stanton? What's that all about?"

"Dolan's playin' politics to get Rob off the Tunstall case. Mc-Sween figures he's after me too. I need to get out of town and lie low for a spell."

"Oh."

He heard her disappointment. It gave him a warm feeling he held tight.

"How long will you be gone?"

"Hard to say. I'll send word when I can."

"Damn, just when I was gettin' used to havin' you around again, cowboy."

"I don't like it, either."

"Good."

She kissed him, soft and innocent, still plain with want.

"Lucy, I'd like you to quit workin' at the store."

"Why? Alex and Susan need me."

"Dolan is uppin' the stakes in this game. I'm afraid shootin' might start any time now. I don't want you mixed up in the middle of that."

"I've been takin' care of myself a long time now. I can handle it. Besides, like I told you before, a girl's gotta eat."

"This is different."

"No, it ain't. But you can make it different."

"I plan to."

A smile wrinkled her moon-frosted nose. "What's that supposed to mean?"

"Ah, well, you know. We've known each other a while now and we keep . . ."

"We?"

"I keep, well maybe we should. Lucy, would you?"

"Ty Ledger, are you askin' me to marry you?"

"I, ah, I guess I am."

"I thought you'd never get around to it, cowboy."

"Well?"

"Well what?" Moonlight caught a misty liquid in her eye.

"Will you?"

She kissed him with a fire fair near to burst his britches buttons.

CHAPTER TWENTY-NINE

Flying H

Ty pushed hard, making the ranch in a day and a half. He loped into the yard under a bright blue midday sky, drew rein at the corral and swung down. Fred Waite eased out of the barn holding a rifle he put up when he saw who it was.

"Where's Brewer?"

He tossed his head. "In the house."

"Will you take care of my horse, Fred? He's had a hard trip."

"Sure thing." He set the Winchester beside the barn door and took the lathered horse's lead.

Ty set off for the house on a long stride. Early spring sun promised a warm afternoon. He took the porch steps in a clump as Brewer opened the front door. The Bonney kid hovered at his shoulder.

"Ty, what brings you down here?"

"A bit of trouble we need to discuss."

"Come in." He stepped back. The Kid melted into a far corner of the room. Brewer crossed the cabin to a long wooden table. "Coffee?"

Ty nodded. He pulled back a chair. Brewer poured two cups from a pot on the stove and took a place across from him. He passed a steaming cup of "been standing there"–strong coffee across the table.

"Brady's arrested Widenmann."

"On what charge?"

"Obstruction. Brady ordered him off the Tunstall case. Rob refused."

"Brady can't order a US marshal to do anything."

"He can now. Sherman appointed him special deputy. He's got Rob locked up over at Fort Stanton. McSween doesn't see an easy way to get him released. Somebody pressured Sherman to get Brady appointed. Sherman's got no good reason to listen to McSween."

"Dolan."

"That's how I figure it. There's more. Governor Axtell has asked the army to assist civil authorities in maintaining law and order in Lincoln County."

"What's that supposed to mean?"

"It means Brady will be coming after you boys with an army escort. This thing is comin' to a head. McSween is on his way to South Spring to get Chisum's help, for all the good that does. The truth is, we can't stand up to the army. You and the boys need to clear out of here. Our only choice is to take to the hills until we figure out what to do next."

Brewer braced himself with a sip of coffee. "So, what about Tunstall's killers?"

"McSween says we're all still duly sworn deputies. We can finish serving the warrants as long as we don't get caught."

"What the hell is that going to accomplish?"

"Maybe one of them will talk. Maybe somebody will implicate Brady or Dolan or both. It's not much, but it's the best we've got for now."

The Kid rested a hand on the butt of his gun. *Like hell it is.*

Brewer pushed his chair back, having reached a decision. "We'll clear out of here as soon as we pack our gear."

"I'll ride down to South Spring to stay in touch with Mc-Sween and Chisum. Where can I find you boys if we need to?"

"There's an abandoned rock house in the hills across the Pecos from Roswell at Bottomless Lakes."

"I know it."

"We'll scatter when we leave here so as not to leave much by way of a trail. We'll drift up there by our separate ways. We should be there in a few days' time."

South Spring

McSween wheeled the buggy through the gate at a jog and nosed the bay mare up the road to the house. Susan rode silent beside him, suffering the effects of the journey. He bore a grim set to his jaw. He'd brooded over the situation on the long ride down from Lincoln. By every estimation he could conceive, the battle for Lincoln was about to be joined. Much would depend on his ability to persuade Chisum to see things his way. With Chisum's help, Dolan must surely see himself overmatched. He drew lines at the house, set the brake and stepped down. He came around to offer Susan his hand down. She accepted it stiffly and followed him up the porch step. The Navajo girl answered his knock.

"Is Mr. Chisum in?"

She nodded and opened the door.

"Who is it, Dawn?" Chisum called from the parlor.

"Alex and Susan McSween," she answered.

Chisum's shadowed frame filled the sun-washed arched parlor entry. "Alex, what brings you down here? And Susan, what a pleasant surprise."

She locked her eyes in his with a small smile that said more than simple greeting.

"The situation in Lincoln has taken a turn for the worse. I hope you'll excuse the intrusion. We need to talk."

Chisum broke away to the lawyer. "Of course. You sound ominous."

"I'm afraid I am."

"Come in." He led the way to the parlor.

A tall, impeccably tailored English gentleman rose to greet them. Despite his years he gave the appearance of having been forged out of steel from the crisp cut of his iron-gray hair and beard to the icy glint in his slate eyes. Even his suit appeared struck by a smith.

"Alex, Susan, may I present Montegue Leverson. Montegue, this is Alex and his lovely wife, Susan McSween."

Leverson bowed stiffly.

"I believe I mentioned Montegue to you, Alex. His law practice is in Colorado, but he finds time to represent me when matters warrant. Alex is a lawyer himself, Montegue. He's the man I mentioned in regard to the troubles in Lincoln. Have a seat."

McSween took a seat on the sofa facing the fireplace. Susan favored Chisum with a warm glance and took a seat beside her husband. Leverson and Chisum took seats flanking the hearth glow.

"I'm afraid matters in Lincoln are coming to a head. It appears Santa Fe is taking a hand on Dolan's behalf. Marshal Sherman appointed Brady a special deputy marshal."

"Brady. Why would he do that?"

"It smells like Dolan's friends in the Santa Fe Ring. Brady ordered Widenmann off the Tunstall case. When Rob questioned the order, Brady arrested him. They've got him locked up in the stockade at Fort Stanton."

"Smart. No local jurisdiction to appeal to," Leverson said.

"There's more. Governor Axtell has asked the army to support civil authorities in Lincoln."

"Brady," Chisum said.

"The governor visited Lincoln at Dolan's request."

"So where does that leave us?"

"We still have Deputy Ledger and Brewer's men to serve the

rest of the warrants as long as Brady and his army escort don't catch up with them. Ty rode down to the Flying H to warn Dick. He'll take the boys into hiding. Ty will be along to let us know where to find them."

Chisum rubbed his chin. "It looks like things is coming to a head."

"That's why I'm here, John, We need help if we hope to win."

Chisum sat back, folding his hands in his lap. "I reckon we all knew it'd come to this sooner or later. You can count on me, Alex."

Flying H

Captain Purington called a halt in the hills northeast of the ranch. Brady drew rein at his stirrup. A troop of black cavalry strung out behind them. Purington extended the glass from its pouch at the cantle of his McClellan saddle. He fitted the eyepiece and swept the ranch yard below.

"Looks pretty quiet down there. How do you want to proceed, Sheriff?"

"We need to search the place. We may be met with armed resistance. What do you suggest, Captain?"

"With your permission, Sergeant Cahill and a detachment will accompany you to the ranch for your inspection. I will hold the balance of my command in reserve in the event of hostilities."

"Very good."

"Sergeant Cahill!"

"Sir?"

"Detail six men to accompany the sheriff."

They found the ranch deserted.

The steeldust loped northeast through rolling hills above the Pecos valley. Crisp late March wind bit around the edges of his canvas coat. Thoughts of Lucy warmed him inside. He'd surprised himself with the proposal. Not that he'd made it, but that he'd made it just then. He'd left her to uncertainty once before. He wasn't about to do that again. He needed to get her out of the store. If Brewer and his Regulators caught up with Mathews, or Chisum and his boys got Evans, Dolan would go to war sure as hell had fire and brimstone. Big Jim was one good man. Good or not, one wouldn't be enough.

He crested a rise southwest of the ranch. It looked like Roth had started clearing land for a house northeast of the hacienda. He smiled, remembering the satisfaction of building a house for Victoria. He wondered how she'd feel about Lucy. He guessed she'd understand. He'd need to give some thought to a more settled down life for Lucy, one where he could build her a house with a happier ending.

He slow loped through the gate up to the corral and drew rein. Deacon Swain stepped out of the barn.

"Mr. Ty, I didn't hear you was comin'."

"Oh, you know, Deac, that old bad penny turns up every once in a while."

He chuckled. "Yes, sir, it sure do."

"Chisum around?"

"Up to the house with Mr. McSween. Let me look after your horse. You go along and see him for yourself."

"Much obliged." He handed over the reins and crunched across the yard to the house. Dawn Sky answered his rap at the door. "Evenin', Mrs. Roth." She smiled, darkened by a blush. "I wonder if I might have a few words with John."

"That you, Ty?" Chisum called.

"It is."

"Show him in, Dawn."

He found Chisum, Leverson, McSween and Johnny in the parlor. The men rose to shake hands.

"Grab a seat. Dawn's fixin' supper. We got room for one more, Dawn?"

She nodded.

"How did it go with Brewer?"

"He and his boys are on their way across the river to Bottomless Lakes. With any luck, they'll get lost before Brady and his cavalry troop catch up with them." He glanced at McSween. "Truth is, you and I might be smart to join them."

"You think they might come looking for us here?"

"Right after they find the Flying H deserted."

"Ty's likely right," Chisum said.

"I suppose that would be best." He turned to Susan. "That's rough country and company, my dear. Are you up to it?"

"If I must."

"She's more than welcome to stay here."

"That's most generous of you, John," McSween said. "You'll be safe and comfortable here, my dear."

"I'm sure of it." She met Chisum's eyes. "Thank you."

"Good, that's settled. We'll leave in the morning," Ty said.

Dawn appeared in the parlor archway. "Supper is ready."

They settled around the dining-room table to roast lamb, chiles stuffed with a mild cheese, tortillas and coffee. Ty took one look at the spread and couldn't resist.

"You eat like this regular, Johnny?"

Roth bobbed his head around a mouth full of lamb.

"That explains that little extra paunch you've packed on."

Roth looked at his belt buckle. "Not yet, pard, but you can keep eatin' them beans as long as you like."

After supper, Roth walked down to the bunkhouse with Ty. He paused under a clear star-studded sky. Lingering chill in the air reminisced of winter.

"I need the return of a favor."

Roth eyed his friend. "You ain't fixin' to get yourself captured by C'manch, are you?"

Ty chuckled, "Nothing as dire as that. I need a witness."

"Who you plan on shootin'?"

"Nobody. I need a witness to a wedding."

Roth smiled. "Well, it's about time. I thought you'd blown it for sure when she took up with Tunstall. Maybe you owe Dolan something after all."

"I wouldn't have a man shot over such a thing."

"Bad gallows humor, sorry. Well, I'd be happy to return the favor. When's the big day?"

"We haven't picked one yet. I just sort of asked her before I left Lincoln."

"You plannin' to stay around here?"

"I don't know. I'll need to find steadier work than part-time deputy marshalin'."

"Lincoln could use a good sheriff."

"I'm likely on the wrong side of those politics."

"You might not be if Brady and Dolan end up in the middle of Tunstall's killin'."

"That's a lot of ifs."

"What about cattle ranchin'? You done it before. Hell, you know more about cattle than I do."

"That takes money. Money I haven't got."

"McSween's got a bank. Banks make loans."

"I hadn't thought of that."

"Maybe you should."

"Maybe I should."

CHAPTER THIRTY

Deacon Swain saw them come. It took him back to the war. Black bluecoats, he'd been one fighting for an honorable cause. This cause didn't strike him as the same. He propped his pitchfork against the barn and hurried up to the house. He rapped on the door. Dawn Sky greeted him with a question in her eye.

"Company's coming. Mister John might like to know."

Chisum appeared in dim light behind her.

"Who is it, Deac?"

"Army, Mr. John."

"Must be Brady. Thanks, Deacon." He turned to Susan. "If you'd like to disappear, I'll handle this."

She straightened her shoulders. "That's very kind of you, John, but I'll not hide from injustice like some common criminal. Alex isn't here. He's the one they're after." She led the way out to the porch.

Chisum stood at her side. The captain drew the column to a halt. Brady stepped down.

"Chisum. Mrs. McSween. Is your husband here?"

She shook her head.

"Where is he?"

"Away on business."

"Where?"

"He didn't say."

"You expect me to believe that?"

"I don't care what you believe."

"We've got warrants for the arrest of a number of men known to be in his employ."

"I don't know anything about that."

"If he's hiding them, he's an accessory to murder."

"I'm looking at an accessory to murder."

Brady turned scarlet. "I've also got a court order for your husband to appear before Judge Bristol in a civil matter. If he doesn't come along voluntarily, he'll be found in contempt of court and I will be forced to arrest him."

"Turn himself in to you? Why would he sign his own death warrant?"

"It's the law."

"That'll be enough, Brady. Mrs. McSween is a guest in my home. The men you're after aren't here. Now, I suggest you get off my land."

"Just like that."

"Just like that."

"Mrs. McSween, George Purington, at your service. If your husband is willing, I am authorized to take him into protective custody. I assure you no harm will come to him at Fort Stanton."

"I've already told you, my husband isn't here."

"Perhaps when he returns, at least consider it. Sheriff?"

Brady stepped into his saddle. "This ain't over, Chisum."

"No, it's not."

Brady and his cavalry wheeled away to the gate at a lope.

"Deac?"

"Mr. John."

"Ride on over to Bottomless Lakes. Tell Mr. McSween Sheriff Brady's been here. He's wanted at court."

The fire burned low, coloring the parlor in a mesquite-scented warm glow. They sat quietly on opposite ends of the settee, absorbing the events of the day.

"You stood up to him. I admire the pluck."

She turned to his profile, silhouette in shadow sparked by firelight reflected in one eye. "I can't abide the man's gall. I appreciate you standing by me in the end."

"It's been quite a day."

"I'm afraid it's only the beginning."

"Yes. I don't know about you, but I believe I could use a drink. Would you care for a glass of sherry?"

"That sounds so proper. If you don't mind, I'd rather have a whiskey."

He arched a brow. "Woman after my own heart." He rose to fetch the drinks.

She watched. You don't know the half of it.

He returned moments later. Amber liquid shrouded in cut crystal danced in the firelight. He offered her a glass.

She accepted it, her hand lingering on his. She patted the sofa beside her.

He eyed the invitation as though seeing it for the first time. It was unexpected. It wasn't surprising. He sank slowly beside her, uncertain he may have mistaken her. She lifted her glass to his and took a swallow. The whiskey warmed. The air hung still, heavy with promise.

"You're a special woman, Susan. Alex is lucky to have you."

"Alex is playing a fool's game. We both know he'll go to his grave with Tunstall."

"Then why fight it? Take Dolan's offer and start over somewhere."

She shot him a look, liquid fire in her eye. "John Chisum, I'm surprised at you. You'd never do such a thing."

"What I would do doesn't matter. We're talking about Alex."

"We are and he's about to get himself killed."

"You could convince him to stop."

She laughed. "No more than I might convince you." She tossed off her drink.

"Care for another?"

She set her glass on the table, ignoring the question. "I couldn't convince either of you to give it up. I could give you something to think about that Alex simply doesn't understand."

"What's that?"

She turned to him. She took his glass and set it beside hers. The air turned warm and moist. She leaned toward him, her lips parted. Time dissolved.

Bottomless Lakes

Wanted at court, what does that mean? It means the time has come to settle this thing.

"What do we do now?" Ty said.

McSween returned from his thoughts. "I'm going to South Spring to talk to Chisum. Then I'm going to Lincoln."

"I'm going with you." *I've got to get Lucy out of that store before this goes bad.*

The Kid glanced at Brewer. *His eyes said some of us best go too.*

CHAPTER THIRTY-ONE

South Spring

They gathered around the dining table with the supper dishes cleared away. Chisum sat at the head of the table flanked by McSween and Leverson. Ty and Johnny kept to their places. Susan retired to the kitchen to help Dawn Sky with the dishes. Over supper Leverson summarized the barrage of letters he'd sent on behalf of the Chisum-McSween faction. He forcefully portrayed Santa Fe Ring corruption extending from Governor Axtell to US Attorney Catron to District Attorney William Rynerson and Judge Bristol's court. He petitioned President Hayes to call off the army and remove both the governor and the US attorney. His letter writing campaign included influential political figures in positions to lend their voices to the chorus of appeals reaching the president.

"Most impressive, Montegue," McSween said. "Do you think your campaign will be successful?"

The lawyer shrugged. "One never knows in such matters. Suffice it to say we've done all we can. Now it is up to the wheels of power to grind."

Chisum turned to Alex. "So how do we play this whilst those wheels grind?"

"Brewer and his men have resumed the search for Mathews and Roberts. If your boys go after Evans and his bunch, Dolan just might get the message. If we make a big show of force it might convince him he can't win."

"He's got too much at stake. You're thinkin' like a lawyer, Alex. Same as Tunstall. This'll all settle in gunplay before it's done."

"Remember, we're serving arrest warrants. We want those men taken alive."

"Of course we do, but you know as well as I, we don't always get what we want. Johnny, tell the boys to get ready. You're ridin' down to Seven Rivers in the morning. If Evans ain't there, you'll be on the trail as long as it takes to find him."

Roth nodded. "You plannin' to ride with us, Ty?"

"No. I'll ride to Lincoln with Mr. McSween. I got some unfinished business up there."

Roth grinned. "She wouldn't be workin' for Mr. McSween would she?"

McSween arched a brow.

Ledger ignored the question.

"Well, you two best not go back to Lincoln alone," Chisum said. "I'll take Frank, Charlie and Tom and ride with you. That way Brady won't be so quick to throw you in the Fort Stanton stockade with Widenmann."

McSween nodded. "Thanks, John. Much obliged."

"I shan't be left behind in this," Leverson said. "I shall accompany you as well."

Ty squinted into the last rays of a flaming sunset beneath a billowing mountain of purple cloud. Blue shadow spilled down the distant hills crawling east toward the onset of night. He made out a trace of smoke sign.

"Frank, take a look."

McNab followed the jut of his chin.

"Why would you camp here when you're so close to Lincoln?"

"Because you're stayin' out of Lincoln for a reason. Let's

have a look." McNab led off toward the sign followed by Ledger, Bowdre and O'Folliard. Thirty minutes later they came up behind a rise close enough to smell a mesquite fire. McNab drew a halt and stepped down.

"Wait here, boys, while I go in and have a look." He climbed the rise and disappeared in a black shadowed grove of juniper. Minutes later he came back down the tree line. Chisum had caught up by then along with the buggy carrying the McSweens and Leverson. "It's the Bonney kid and a couple of Brewer's boys. I thought it might be." He collected his reins and stepped into the saddle, signaling the others to remount.

He led them out around the hill and drew rein in sight of the fire. "Yo the fire!" As expected the men scrambled for their guns. "Easy, Billy. It's Frank McNab and a few South Spring boys. We've got Mr. Chisum and the McSweens with us."

"Ride on in easy so we can see you."

Ty smiled. The Kid's reedy adolescent voice managed a little authority. They rode in and stepped down. The men stood to greet them. Waite shook McNab's hand.

"Coffee's made. Fire's there for cookin'. We wasn't expectin' company so we didn't fix up any extra."

"We can take care of ourselves. What are you doin' out here?"

The Kid spoke up. "Waitin' to get the lay of the land before we ride in and tip our hand."

"Makes sense," McSween said. "Mind if we join you."

"That's fine for you and the boys, Alex," Ty said. "I got personal business in Lincoln. I'm gonna ride on in."

"Best stay out of sight."

"Count on it."

Lincoln

Dolan picked up his cards. He squinted in the dim lamplight. He'd set up the game in the back room at the store where the boys could stay out of sight. The room smelled of burlap covered packages and crated stores mingled with coal oil and cigar smoke. He shifted his cheroot from one cheek to the other, allowing his eyes to slide from Evans to Roberts to Coe. None of them showed anything. He fanned his hand, two pair, jacks and sixes. The bet checked to him.

"Five to see 'em."

Evans lifted an eyebrow and tossed in his call. Roberts followed. Coe folded. Dolan laid down his hand. Evans tossed in a pair of Queens. Roberts had aces. Dolan scooped up the pot.

"Pleasure doin' business with you boys."

"I need a drink," Evans said.

"The bottle's behind the counter. Glasses are on the shelf above."

Evans fetched the whiskey and glasses. He passed the glasses followed by the bottle. "So you don't figure lockin' up Widenmann settled the Tunstall flap."

Dolan took a swallow. "If McSween was of a mind to give it up, he'd sell out and move on. I reckon he's got Chisum backin' him up and likely figures that for enough."

"How long you want me and the boys to hang around town waitin'? I ain't complainin' about the hospitality, but all this card playin' is costin' me money."

"Hell, Jesse, wait long enough your luck is bound to change."

"How long?"

"Long enough for McSween to show his hand. I expect we'll hear from him soon enough."

Ty rode into the east end of town, dark and still in the early evening. A cold steady rain had boiled up out of those deep purple clouds. The street turned to a muddy sludge. The lace curtains at Mrs. O'Hara's gave a warm glow. He stepped down at the gate and looped a rein over the fence. The gate squealed its familiar welcome. He stepped into the porch shadow out of the rain and rapped on the door. High button shoes tapped the polished floor with a faint rustle of petticoat. The door swung open. Lucy's eyes lit. She rushed into his arms, holding him tight with no thought to the cold and wet of his slicker.

"I've missed you."

The whisper felt warm against his chest. "I've missed you too."

She pulled back. "Have you had any supper?"

He shook his head.

"Bring your horse around back where he won't be so noticeable and come in the kitchen. I'll fix you something."

He kissed her.

"Hold that thought, cowboy. Hurry back." She watched him walk back to the gate, turned and hurried back inside.

Ty led the steeldust around the house. The rain lifted. The clouds broke, revealing the evening star in the eastern sky followed by a milk-white moon. He dropped his reins to a ground tie and loosened the cinch. He pumped a bucket of water and left the horse to graze. Lucy let him in the back door. Mrs. O'Hara stood at the sink, finishing up the last of the supper dishes.

"Marshal Ledger, it's nice to have you back even if it means skulking about in the night."

He removed his hat and slicker with a smile and hung them on a peg beside the door. "You'd best call me Ty, ma'am. We're pretty near gonna be family."

"So I hear. Congratulations to both of you. Now, Lucy, that pot of stew should still be warm. This man looks as though he could use a bite to eat. I'll be upstairs with that dress I'm hemming if you need anything." She took herself off down the hall to the stairway.

Lucy tested the stew kettle. "This could use a little warming." She stirred the stove to light and set the kettle on to heat. "Care for some coffee while we wait?"

He nodded.

She poured two cups and set them on the kitchen table. "So what brings you back to Lincoln?" She took a seat.

"You, of course." He sat down.

She smiled. "I like that. Then again, with men there's likely some other reason to go along with that one."

"The Regulators are camped outside of town. They're fixin' to serve the rest of the warrants for Tunstall's murder."

"You won't get mixed up in that, will you?"

"Not as long as they stick by their oaths and uphold the law."

"Do you think they will?"

"I hope so."

She checked the kettle. "Stew's ready." She served him a bowl with a slice of fresh bread and sat down to watch him eat. "You still staying clear of Sheriff Brady?"

He nodded around a mouth full of stew.

"Well, you can't stay at the Wortley then."

"The clerk hid me out the night Brady arrested Rob."

"It's too risky. You'll stay here. You can bed down in the parlor."

"What will Mrs. O'Hara think?"

"She likes you near as much as I do. As long as we don't compromise propriety, she'll be fine."

Ty unsaddled the steeldust and picketed him for the night while Lucy cleaned up his supper dishes. She led him down the hall to the parlor. The soft glow of a single oil lamp trimmed low lit the room. She made him comfortable on the settee and sat beside him. He wrapped his arm around her and drew her to his chest.

"That feels good." She purred. "Like all's right with the world."

"It does."

The tick of the parlor clock and the rhythms of breathing marked the passage of time. At length she lifted her eyes to his and patted his chest. "Well, cowboy, it's comin' time for a respectable girl to turn in. You can bunk here. It ain't much, but it's better than the hard ground outside."

"You sure Mrs. O'Hara won't mind?"

"Not as long as we keep it respectable. She never quite forgave me for when I was seein' John."

"I knew there was a reason I liked her."

"Truth is she knew me better than I knew me then."

He bent to her lips. Soft sweetness melted. He folded her in his arms. A flood of hunger blotted light and time.

"Oh, Ty." She put a hand to his mouth with a shudder. "There ain't nothin' respectable happening inside this body. It's time I went upstairs."

"There's only one way out of this."

"I know. When?"

"Soon as I figure a way to support you."

"I don't eat much."

He chuckled. "A young 'un might."

She kissed him. "See you in the morning, cowboy."

CHAPTER THIRTY-TWO

April 1ˢᵗ

Thick gray clouds poured out of the mountains, cloaking predawn light in the promise of more rain. The Regulators drifted into town in pairs to avoid attracting attention. The Kid and Fred Waite jogged their horses up the street from the east end of town. Billy eased his horse over to the old Torreon tower, built in the early days of the settlement to defend the town against Indian attacks. He stepped down beside a stand of white oak. Waite followed.

"What are we doin' here?"

The Kid squinted across the mud-clotted street. "Brady and his deputies gotta pass this way to get to the McSween store. A day don't pass that Brady don't check that for his boss. That adobe wall over yonder will give us our best shot at 'em."

"Shot? I thought we was supposed to arrest Mathews."

"Oh, yeah, right. I almost forgot."

As the gray light brightened McNab and Middleton rode in. They dropped rein behind the Tunstall store and wandered into the white oaks with Fred and the Kid.

Bowdre and O'Folliard rode in thirty minutes later. The Kid waved them into a vacant lot behind the Torreon wall.

"Any sign of 'em?" Tom asked.

"Not yet. They'll be along sooner or later. Did McSween come in with you?"

"He figured to hang back until we had the street clear," Charlie said.

"He don't trust Dolan much, does he?"

"Would you?"

Billy smiled his crooked smile. "No further than the barrel of my gun."

Bowdre stared out the window. "You figure they'll put up a fight?"

"Only if we give 'em the chance."

Lucy hurried off to the store. Mrs. O'Hara spoiled Ty with a breakfast fit for a king. As he lingered over coffee he mulled the situation. Lincoln was too small to hide in. Still there were a couple of things he needed to do. McSween returning to town might throw a match on dry tinder if Dolan was of a mind to bring the dispute to a head. He'd lie low in the store where he could keep an eye on Lucy in case things went bad. That would put him between Dolan and McSween's return to town.

He spotted Bowdre and O'Folliard from the widow's parlor window. He thanked Mrs. O'Hara for her hospitality and slipped out the back door. He saddled the steeldust and rode east to the edge of town. He circled north to the crest of the ridge leading down to the river. He turned west and worked his way through the trees behind the buildings lining the north side of the street until he reached the back of the Tunstall store. He found the Regulators' horses picketed there with more in the lot further west behind the Torreon Tower. He dropped from the saddle and ground tied his horse. He climbed the step to the back door and knocked. The floorboards within creaked under the big man's bulk.

"Who is it?"

"Ty Ledger."

The door opened. Big Jim stepped back. "Glad you're here.

The boys is gatherin' up the street. What's up?"

"They plan to serve the warrant on Mathews."

"I need to get out there."

"How many men you figure you need to arrest one man?"

French returned a vacant stare.

"Go on if you feel the need. I'll keep an eye on things here."

French started for the front of the store.

"Remember, Jim, you need to arrest Mathews. You tell those boys for me. A judge will decide his guilt or innocence."

French gave a half nod and disappeared.

Lucy followed his back as she came to meet him behind the store. "I'm glad you're here." She came into his arms and let him hold her. "They're gathering up the street at the Torreon. Do you think there'll be trouble?"

"I hope not, but there's a lot of itchy trigger fingers about to face each other."

Her eyes turned liquid. "Promise me you'll be careful if things go bad."

"I'm always careful. That's why I want you out of here."

"I know. I'm just not used to bein' looked after that way."

"Best get used to it."

"I, I plan to." She tipped up on her toes and kissed him.

By nine o'clock the Regulators had assembled at the Torreon. They fanned out behind the adobe wall. The Kid took the east end where he had a view down the street to the west end of town. The clock crawled through the early morning. Commercial traffic slowed to a trickle, as though the town sensed trouble and held its collective breath. A chill northwest breeze blew ripples on the puddles collected in the street. The men hunkered down behind the wall cutting the wind. The Kid kept a sharp eye.

★ ★ ★ ★ ★

Chisum led the way into the east end of town. Alex McSween drove the buggy carrying Susan and Leverson. Chisum drew rein. A cold northwest wind rippled the puddles on the drab deserted street. Susan shivered beside McSween. Blustery wet weather sometimes kept street traffic down. Sometimes. This had a different feel. The House loomed over the far end of town where the road wound away to the west. Chisum's buckskin stomped, slapping a muddy splash. Trouble lurked somewhere between that hoofprint and Dolan's commercial fortress. He could feel it. He squeezed the buckskin up the street.

The Kid squinted at the rider and buggy coming down the street from the east end of town. Chisum and McSween, it had to be. He cut his eyes west. Three men spilled out of Dolan's store and started down the street as if a welcoming committee sent to greet the visitor.

"Here they come." He filled his hand. The others scrambled into position. Brady ambled toward them flanked by Hindman and Mathews. The Kid eyed Mathews, walking on Brady's outside shoulder. He might have to go through the sheriff to get to Tunstall's killer. *Tough, Brady had it comin' too.*

Time slowed. The three men seemed in no hurry. All three wore guns, nothing heavy. It didn't appear they expected trouble. Hindman gave a casual glance at the horses standing hipshot in the oak trees beside the Torreon as they drew close. He made no remark, not realizing they meant trouble until it was too late.

The Kid let them pass along the wall and the guns hidden there. When they reached his position, he stood up with a grin.

"Morning, Sheriff."

Brady paused as though accepting a citizen's greeting and turned. The gap-tooth smile registered identity. He reached.

247

The Kid's muzzle flashed twice before his hand slapped leather. The top of the wall exploded in blooms of powder smoke. Hindman dropped in a puddle with a mighty splash like a sack half filled with potatoes. Mathews bolted across the street for cover. The Kid followed his jerky gait with shots, kicking clods of mud into the wind. The deputy ducked out of sight.

Ty bolted out of his chair at the first sound of gunfire. He dashed into the front of the store both guns drawn. Lucy froze, round-eyed.

"You get down and stay down."

"What is it, Ty?"

"Trouble." The visitor bell sounded alarm as he ran out the door. He turned up the street. Two bodies sprawled in the mud just past the Torreon. The Bonney kid appeared gun in hand followed by Big Jim French.

Further up the street a second burst of gunfire split the air. The Kid jerked and turned his gun on four men running from the direction of Dolan's store. Other Regulators returned fire from positions behind the Torreon wall. Big Jim ran down the street toward Ty. The Kid limped back behind the wall.

Jesse Evans led the House gunmen. Ty made out Buckshot Roberts and George Coe's cousin Frank. He fired twice, giving Big Jim cover as he ran to the store. The Dolan men were forced to take cover, trading volleys with the Regulators forted up behind the wall. The standoff fell silent as suddenly as it started.

McSween pulled the buggy to a stop beside Chisum. A cloud of gunsmoke drifted over the Torreon wall. Two bodies lay in the street. Other men further up the street fired on the wall. From their position, he guessed them for Dolan men. That made the men behind the wall Regulators. Bodies in the street could only mean the worst.

"Let's find some cover," Chisum said.

McSween wheeled the buggy into an alley. He helped Susan down. They'd find their way back to the store when the shooting ended.

Behind the wall McNab took charge. There'd be hell to pay now.

"You hit bad, Billy?"

"Nah, took a little piece out of my ass is all."

"Then let's get to the horses and get shut of this place."

They collected the horses before the Dolan men recognized they were moving. They swung to saddle leather. McNab led them north into the trees lining the ridge and down the wooded hillside to the river.

"Horses movin'!" Evans dashed across the street. He jumped the wall followed by Roberts and Coe.

The Regulators sleighed and slid through the white oak, pursued by a buzzing swarm of futile fire chewed up in the trees overhead. They broke onto the river's edge and galloped east out of town, trailing a froth of silver white foam.

The visitor bell startled Lucy. She let out the breath she'd been holding at the sight of Ty with his guns drawn. She'd hidden Big Jim in the cellar. She struggled to cover the trap door with a pickle barrel.

"Here, let me give you a hand with that. You look guilty as sin."

"What happened, Ty?"

"The Regulators tried to take Mathews. Brady and Hindman ended up shot. Evans and his boys joined in. I don't know who started it, but I figure it's a war now. The Regulators made a run for it. Dolan's men will come lookin' for me and Jim."

"You can hide in the cellar too."

"No, save that for him." He went to the window and looked up the street. "Here they come. I'll draw 'em off out the back when they get here. Jim, keep an eye on her until we decide what to do next."

A muffled mumble sounded up through the floor.

"I'll be back as soon as I can sneak into town."

"Be careful, Ty."

He met her eyes. "I will." He started for the back door as boots sounded on the boardwalk. He left the back door trail open and dashed for the steeldust. The visitor bell sounded behind him. He leaped into the saddle and put heels to flanks in a sprint to the tree-lined ridge. Guns charged at the back door. Bullets rattled and whined harmlessly through the trees as he disappeared down the slope.

He followed the river east and turned south well out of town. He eased up on his horse. *Now what?* However it started, it had started. Blood spilled on both sides. Blood and greed provided more than enough cause for war. The law in Lincoln lay dead in the street, not that Brady's brand of law ever amounted to much. McSween might see reason, but between the bank and the store, he now had a big stake in this fight. Dolan had his stake all on the line. He'd give no quarter. Widenmann would help if he weren't stuck in the stockade at Fort Stanton. *Fort Stanton, that's it.* He circled back west.

Fort Stanton

Ty made the fort by late afternoon. He rode straight to Colonel Dudley's office and stepped down. The sergeant major greeted him in the small regimental office.

"Afternoon, Marshal Ledger. Is the colonel expecting you?"

"He's not, Sergeant. This isn't a social call. It's official business."

"I see. I'll tell him you're here."

"No need, Sergeant." Dudley filled the doorway to his office. "Something serious, Ty?"

"I'm afraid so, Nate."

"Come in then."

Ty followed Dudley into his office.

"Have a seat. Now, what's the trouble?"

He spun out the events of the morning over in Lincoln. Dudley listened intently stroking his chin as he finished.

"So you say Brady is dead."

"Best I could tell."

"That doesn't leave much by way of civilian law over there."

"Deputy Sheriff Mathews seems to have gotten away, though the Regulators hold a federal warrant for his arrest on murder charges."

"And the Regulators are deputies of Marshal Widenmann who is no longer in charge of that case."

"What we've got over there, Nate, are two armed camps fixin' to go to war. Isn't there something you can do?"

"I can't just ride over there and declare martial law. The governor requested that we support the civil authorities."

A knock sounded at the door. "Begging your pardon, sir, a rider is here from Linclon requesting support following the shooting of the sheriff this morning."

"Very well. Ty, I'm afraid I'll have to attend to this."

"But you'll be sending troops in to support the Dolan faction."

"I'm sending troops to support civil authority. Those are my orders."

"But that's who you are going to assist."

"I'm sorry, Ty. I can try reporting the situation to my chain of command, but I wouldn't hold out much hope without a change in the governor's order."

McSween led the way to their home through the back of the alley. Susan followed with Leverson and Chisum. He let them in by the back door. Out front the street swarmed with Dolan men searching for any Regulators who might still be in town. As late afternoon sun sank to the mountaintops, a new commotion sounded in the street. McSween pulled back a lace curtain.

"Look at this."

Chisum joined him at the window. A troop of cavalry loped up the street, pennants snapping in the breeze. The column halted up the street at the House. Dolan clumped down the steps to meet them. Captain Purington dismounted to greet him. Moments later George Peppin joined Dolan and the captain. Dolan gestured toward the McSween house. Peppin, the captain and a detail set off down the street. Dolan returned to his store. Peppin and the cavalrymen presented themselves at the McSween front door with a stout knock. McSween and Chisum exchanged a glance as the lawyer went to answer the door. Leverson followed at his shoulder.

"George, what can I do for you?"

"That's Deputy Sheriff Peppin, McSween. We come to search your house."

"When did you become deputy sheriff?"

"Shortly before Sheriff Brady's demise."

"Any such appointment expired with the sheriff."

"I'm all the sheriff we have in Lincoln for now. We're going to search your house."

"Search my home, what for?"

"For the men responsible for the shootings this morning."

"There's no one hiding here."

"We'll see about that."

"Do you have a search warrant?"

Peppin fingered the badge on his chest. "This is all the warrant I need."

"Oh, but it's not!" Leverson said.

"Who the hell are you?"

"Montegue Leverson, attorney at law. The law requires that you have a warrant to search a citizen's home. In this case it is doubtful you have the authority to obtain one regardless of what you may have pinned to your shirt."

Peppin gaped at the Englishman.

"Mr. McSween, Captain George Purington at your service. Recently I spoke with your wife at the Chisum ranch. I am authorized to offer you protective custody at Fort Stanton. I suggest you accept that offer and come along quietly. The situation in Lincoln has deteriorated since the shootings this morning. I am under orders to support civil authorities. That means searching your home. Now, I suggest you accept my offer. I can assure your safety at Fort Stanton."

"Captain, I'm appalled at your suggestion of an illegal search!"

"I was addressing Mr. McSween, Mr. Levinson, or whatever your name is."

"It's Leverson and you, may I remind you, are an officer of the United States Army. You are sworn to uphold and defend the Constitution. The Constitution protects this man's home in the absence of a search warrant."

"To hell with the Constitution, I'm here to keep the peace. Now, Mr. McSween, will you accept my offer or not?"

McSween turned to Chisum. "What do you think?"

He paused. "We are in a poor position to protect you here. It might be best."

McSween met Susan's worried expression.

"And my wife?"

"If you wish," Purington said.

"Very well."

Office of the Governor
Santa Fe

Axtell held Dolan's telegram up to catch the last light before sunset. He scowled. The situation in Lincoln had gotten worse. Sheriff Brady gunned down in the street along with one of his deputies. Dolan claims the McSween-Chisum faction is responsible. The small ranchers have plainly had enough. Both sides were arming themselves. According to Dolan, the situation was a powder keg about to break out in open war. He had to do something to restore order, but what? Call out the army again? Publicly admit that civil order had broken down with the prospect of statehood on the horizon. That would never do. Hell, he'd have to answer to Elkins for that. He wanted another term. That didn't include getting crosswise with the real power behind the Republican machine.

He needed something, something that appealed to both sides. He needed to buy time. If he could reestablish law and order the whole mess might blow over. He drummed his fingers on the desk, letting evening shadows gather around him. He fished in his vest pocket for a lucifer and scratched it on the sole of his shoe. A bright flare pierced the gloom hissing acrid sulfur scent. He lifted the chimney to his desk lamp. The wick caught. He shook the match out and trimmed the wick. The chimney spread a soft glow across his cluttered desktop.

That's it. He nodded to himself. He'd appoint a grand jury and not just any grand jury. He'd make it an honest grand jury, one likely to find fault on both sides. Dolan wouldn't like it, but how much damage could it really do him? It ought to stop the shooting for a spell. More important, it would send the right message to Washington about New Mexican law and order. *Yes,* he nodded. *That's it.*

CHAPTER THIRTY-THREE

Flying H

The Regulators rode into the yard. Brewer took one look at the spent horses and knew there'd been trouble. McNab left his horse to the boys at the corral and made his way to the house. Brewer waited on the porch. He read the man's expression.

"Trouble, Frank?"

He nodded.

"Come in." Brewer led the way inside. "What happened?"

"Brady went for a gun. The Kid shot him. Somebody shot Hindman too. Next thing you know, Dolan men come runnin'. We shot it out on the street."

"What about Mathews?"

"He got away."

"Who was with Dolan?"

"Evans, a couple of his boys."

Brewer sat at the table deep in thought. "This ain't over, Frank."

"No, it ain't. It won't be until we get the rest of 'em."

"You figure Evans and his boys will stay in Lincoln?"

"I wouldn't. Would you?"

"No, I reckon they'll lay low down at Seven Rivers."

"They'll steer clear of the Pecos valley. Likely ride south through the Tularosa."

"That's where we'll cut their trail."

★ ★ ★ ★ ★

Blazer's Mill
April 4ᵗʰ

Blazer's Mill made a convenient rest stop for travelers on the road between Lincoln and Mesilla. The settlement served as home to the Mescalaro Agency. The large agency building and Dr. Blazer's two-story home sat atop a low hill. The agency building also housed Dr. Blazer's onetime dentist office and a restaurant catering to travelers operated by the agent's wife. Further down the hill, a sawmill powered by Tularosa creek stood beside a small general store and post office. Two small adobe homes stood opposite the mill across the dirt ruts that passed for a street. A blacksmith shop, barn and corral meandered up the hill from the houses to the agency.

Brewer and the Regulators rode in under a blazing midday sun. The posse included George Coe, John Middleton, Henry Brown, Charlie Bowdre, Fred Waite, Frank McNab, Tom O'Folliard, Doc Scurlock, Jose Chavez and Billy Bonney. They drew rein and stepped down at the corral. They watered their horses and put them up for a rest. Brewer led the way up the hill to the restaurant. He paused to catch Middleton's eye on the porch.

"John, pull up here and keep an eye peeled. We'll have a plate sent out to you."

Middleton nodded and settled onto a bench overlooking the settlement as Brewer and the boys trooped inside. Within minutes Middleton's head dropped to his chest. He snapped awake and swatted belatedly at the buzz of a fat black fly. Fighting the fly fought sleep. A lone rider appeared out of the distant sun haze, a dark figure, riding a mule. He watched the rider come. His stomach growled. *Where the hell is that plate?* The rider made a good excuse. He entered the restaurant and found Brewer.

257

"We've got company."

Brewer, Coe and Brown followed Middleton back out to the porch. The rider drew rein at the post office and stepped down. Brewer squinted into the sun. "Any idea who that is?"

"Buckshot Roberts," Coe said.

"We got a warrant for him. I want this one alive."

"He ain't likely to go easy given the way things has gone so far. Let me have a talk with him. Maybe I can persuade him into surrendering."

"What makes you think he'll listen to you?"

"We're neighbors. He'll talk to me without goin' for his gun. He gets wind of any of the rest of you, there'll be gunplay."

"Good luck."

Coe started down the hill. Brewer and Brown turned to go back inside.

"Dick, don't forget that plate," Middleton said.

Finished with his business at the post office, Roberts drew the Winchester from his saddle boot and started up the hill to the restaurant and a hot meal. The sight of George Coe coming toward him registered an alarm. Coe might be a neighbor, but he'd sided with the McSween-Chisum faction. He may even have been among those who gunned down Brady and Hindman. Coe smiled and waved. Roberts hefted the Winchester and waited.

"Afternoon, Buckshot."

"Coe."

"We need to talk."

"Can't figure what for. I'm after some lunch. It's a free country. You can walk along and say your piece if you want." Roberts continued up the hill following a tumbleweed pushed along in the wind.

Coe fell in beside him. "There's a posse in the restaurant, Buckshot. They got a warrant for your arrest."

He stopped. "On what charge?"

"Tunstall's murder." Roberts glanced back down the hill at his mule. "Forget it. You'll never get away."

"You gonna stop me?"

"Not me. Dick Brewer's got ten armed men in that restaurant. The only smart thing to do is give up. Brewer will see to it you get a fair trial."

"Right, same as Baker and Morton."

"They brought that on themselves, same as you if you try to run. Now, why not hand over that rifle. We'll get some lunch and get you locked up safe and proper."

"Bullshit. I might believe you, George, but some of them in there has blood on their hands."

"Now, don't go jumpin' to conclusions. Com'on and sit a spell. I bet we can work out a deal." He led the way down the porch away from the restaurant door.

Roberts mulled his situation. It didn't look good. Ten guns to one got a man dead. "What kind of deal you talkin' about?"

"You didn't kill Tunstall, but you know who did. You could trade your testimony for safe passage. Most judges would treat a man kindly for that."

Wrinkled brows gathered, bunched in thought. Coe had a point. *Was Mathews and Evans worth dyin' for?* He thought a bit more.

"Buckshot Roberts ain't no sellout."

Inside the restaurant the Regulators finished their meal. What passed for patience had worn thin. Bowdre stood across the table from Brewer.

"Coe ain't gonna talk Roberts into surrenderin'. Would you after what happened to Baker and Morton?"

"Not likely."

"Com'on, Dick, let's get this over with."

"All right, men, this is it. We give him his chance. Let's take him alive if he'll let us."

Bowdre led the way outside with his gun drawn at his side. The sight of the Regulators filing out of the restaurant startled Roberts. He stood with the Winchester leveled at his right hip. Bowdre cocked his gun.

"Hand that rifle over to George and put up your hands, Roberts. You're under arrest.

Roberts stepped back from Bowdre's advance separating himself from Coe. "Not a chance."

Two shots exploded. Roberts' shot knocked Bowdre down. The bullet glanced off his belt buckle, hitting Coe in his gun hand. Bowdre's bullet hit Roberts in the groin. The old man staggered with a grunt, straightened himself and levered his Winchester, firing from the hip. His first shot hit Middleton in the chest. A second blast erupted without pause, striking Doc Scurlock's still holstered gun. The Regulators scattered for cover, firing wildly. Roberts swept the yard with the rifle muzzle. The Bonney kid had aim. The Winchester kicked. A nick in the arm bought time.

Roberts backed down the hill toward his mule, stitching the agency yard with covering fire. He reached one of the adobe houses across from the mill as his rifle clicked empty. A bad situation had gone worse. He looked down the hill to his mule. He had a box of cartridges in the saddlebag. He just might make it. Then what? He doubted he could ride with his wound, let alone long enough to get away. He ducked into the house for cover. Slowly his eyes adjusted to the dim light, searching for ammunition. He'd sure as shit backed himself into a corner now. Coe might have pulled off his deal, but with three or four of them sons a bitches down, there'd be no deal makin' other than decidin' who got the kill shot.

Then he saw it. He hobbled across the room, using the useless Winchester for a cane. An old .50-caliber Sharps buffalo gun stood in the corner with a box of bullets on the table beside it. *Well I'll be. It's a fightin' chance.*

He grabbed the rifle and the cartridges and limped back to the door. Using the door frame for support, he slumped to the floor. He opened the box of shells, cracked the breach and slipped a heavy-caliber bullet into the chamber. Pain radiated from his wound. His pant leg felt cold and sticky wet. Fatigue pressed against his eyelids. His breathing came ragged.

The hillside was quiet. The Regulators waited, guns trained on the house where Roberts holed up. Brewer and McNab stood beside the agency building. McNab scratched his chin. "Looks like we got us a standoff, Dick. What do you figure to do?"

Bullshit! Brewer fumed. The gut-shot old bastard knocked down five good men. "Burn the son of a bitch out."

"That should work. How do you want to play it?"

"Slip on down to the blacksmith shop, Frank. I'm goin' down the creek bank to the sawmill. Give me time to get in position, then see if you can get him talkin'. Tell him we're gonna burn him out unless he gives up. If he doesn't give up, he may show himself trying to get a shot off. If he does, I may be able to get a shot at him."

McNab nodded and moved off down the hill.

Brewer crunched down to the creek bank, out of sight of Roberts' position. He made his way down the creek bed to the mill. He crawled up the bank to a pile of logs stacked beside the mill.

"Roberts!" McNab called. "It's no good. You're surrounded. Give yourself up or we'll burn you out."

A shadow moved beside the dark doorway.

"Go to hell!"

Brewer fired.

The bullet whined through the open doorway and bit a chunk out of the adobe back wall. Roberts risked a glance out the door. Powder smoke drifted off from the woodpile beside the mill. He eased himself down to his belly and backed away from the door covered in shadow. He set up his shot at the woodpile and waited for the shooter to show himself. Time passed. Sun glinted on a gun barrel. The heavy muzzle wavered before his aim. A hat crown moved atop the log pile. The shooter's head came up to take aim. The Sharps exploded in a deafening roar that reverberated in the small room. A cloud of powder smoke filled the darkened doorway. The shooter's head burst in red mist and bone splinters.

"Got him!" The victory crow choked to a cough.

The Regulators watched in disbelief. Dick Brewer dead was more than they could stomach. Fred Waite scuttled down the hill to McNab.

"He ain't worth it, Frank. He can bleed to death for all I care. Let's get out of here."

"Hitch a team to that wagon at the corral for Dick's body, Middleton, Coe and Bowdre. The rest should be able to ride."

Waite set off for the corral.

"You've cost us more than you're worth, Roberts. Your ticket to hell is already punched. Die slow."

Roberts laughed, punctuated by fits of coughing.

CHAPTER THIRTY-FOUR

Flying H

The ranch house looked like a field hospital left over from the war for all the wounded and injured lying around. Middleton was flat on his back nursing a chest wound. Bowdre suffered little more than a belly ache, thanks to his belt buckle. Coe wasn't so lucky. The surgeon at Fort Stanton amputated his damaged trigger finger. Scurlock had a bad bruise and the need of a new gun. The Bonney kid paced the house like a caged cat, paying scant heed to his sore ass and bandaged arm.

"First Mr. Tunstall, now Dick. Who's going to run this outfit next?"

Waite looked up from cleaning his gun. "I say Frank. Anybody say any different?" Nobody did. "Frank, you're captain of the Regulators. What's our next move?"

"We still got killers to bring down, but first we better get some of you boys up and about."

"We wouldn't have got near so shot up if we'd just killt the son of a bitch," the Kid said. "Playin' lawman is dangerous."

He got some murmurs of agreement Ty didn't like. "You boys got them badges to enforce the law. You take up murderin' the accused, the law will treat you no better than them."

The Kid laughed. "We killt 'em all so far. The only thing we're arguin' over is how many of us get shot in the bargain."

"The Kid's got a point," McNab said.

Waite nodded.

263

Ty didn't like the sound of it. Brewer couldn't control these men. McNab, it appeared, lacked Brewer's resolve. He needed to talk to McSween. *He needed to get Lucy out of that store.*

Lincoln

He rode down the riverbank north of town. Sunlight filtered through the trees dappled the hillside. The river rushed downstream swollen with spring runoff. The gurgles and splashing swallowed the occasional scrape of the steeldust's hoof on a stone. The riverbank told him when he'd reached the center of town. The muddy scars of the Regulators' escape were plainly visible coming down the hillside. A little further upstream, his trail led to the back of the store.

The steeldust charged the hill, fighting for footing on long powerful strides. The big gelding crested the ridge at the back of the store and shook off the exertion. Ty stepped down and dropped him a ground tie. He climbed the steps to the back door and paused. He knocked, remembering Big Jim should be watching over the place.

"Who is it?"

"Ty." The door squeaked open. "How are things?"

"Quiet as a church, for now."

"Good." He stepped past the big Regulator into the store. He nodded to Susan as he passed the teller cage. The store was empty. He found Lucy dusting a shelf. She ran into his arms and hung on hard.

"I've been so worried. We heard about that awful business at Blazer's Mill."

"I wasn't there."

She sagged against him, her worry spent. "Com'on." She took him by the hand and led him to the back door. "Susan, can you watch the store for a few minutes?"

She smiled.

Ty paused at the teller cage. "Is Alex in?"

"He's in the office at home."

"Good. I need to speak with him."

Lucy led the way out into the sunshine on the back loading platform. The door clicked closed, leaving them alone with the rustle of the trees and the soft sounds of rushing water. She turned into his kiss. Sun and chill breeze, the faint twitter of birdsong, lost in a warmth that touched her essence.

"There, that's better." She hugged him. "I was so frightened for you."

He lifted her chin. "No. I'm the one frightened for you. You've got to get out of the store. That shoot-out last week got way too close to the woman I love."

"Ty Ledger, you said it."

"Said what?"

"You said you love me."

"Aw, you knew that."

"Maybe deep down, I hoped, but it's nice to hear you say it out loud."

"Now, don't you go and get me all distracted. I mean it."

"Of course you do. I love you too."

"Not that. I mean it about the store."

"Then you don't love me." She put on a pout.

"You got me all twisted up. You know I love you."

She smiled. "I like that. Com'on, sit a spell." She sat on the top step. Ty sat beside her. "I can't just walk out on Alex and Susan. We've got Big Jim to look after us. I'm more worried about you runnin' to every gunfight in the county with them Regulators."

"I'm not runnin' with the Regulators. They were deputized marshals but they're behavin' like vigilantes. I need to see Alex about that and don't change the subject."

"It's a woman's place to change the subject. I'll think about

it while I'm waitin' for a certain tall Texan to make an honest
woman out of me. Tell you what, since you're skulking around
town the way you are, I'll make up a picnic and meet you up on
the hill north of town around sundown. You remember the
place?"

"There you go changin' the subject again."

Her kiss ran deep with promise.

He caught his breath. "I guess it's all right."

"What?"

"Your changin' the subject."

She bit his lip. "'Course it is."

McSween heard the knock. *Who the hell comes knocking on the
back door?* He left his desk and went to the kitchen door. Ty
Ledger, that makes sense.

"Come in, Ty. I'm glad you're here."

"We need to talk."

"We do." He led the way to the office. "Have a chair." Mc-
Sween settled behind the desk. "So what's on your mind?"

"I've just come in from the Flying H. The Regulators replaced
Brewer with Frank McNab as captain."

"Frank's a good man."

"He's a gunman. Those men don't sound like a posse
anymore. They sound like vigilantes. Every attempt they've
made to serve those warrants has ended in killin' without a
single arrest."

"I know it looks bad. We need real law in Lincoln. That's
what I want to talk to you about. Governor Axtell has convened
a grand jury to investigate everything that has been happening
here. They should be here next week."

"Won't the Santa Fe boys just whitewash things Dolan's
way?"

"Maybe some but there is undeniable dirt on both sides of

the street. New Mexico's chances for statehood depend on law and order. Congress will be looking over their shoulder on this one. They've got to play it straight or some of us will make sure the right people know about it. Axtell knows that. He's chosen jurors with sympathies on both sides."

"So what does that have to do with me?"

"One of the things the jury will do is recommend appointment of a sheriff to fill out the balance of Brady's term. I think you're just the man for the job. You've got the background. You're new here so you don't appear to have strong ties to either side."

"You won't fool Dolan with that."

"I'm talking about appearances for those looking over the jury's shoulder. God knows it won't be easy for them to find anyone in this county who fits the bill any better than you. If you're willing, I think I can arrange it."

It did solve the problem of havin' a job to support a wife. That is, if she'd still have him as sheriff of this hornet's nest. "See what you can do."

Sunset painted the hills purple against an orange and crimson sky. Black traces of cloud drifted along like smoke sign. He waited with his blanket spread on the hillside overlooking the town below. A lone rider loped through town, splashed across the river and mounted a climb into the hill. He smiled.

Billy Mathews scratched his chin, watching her ride out of town. Odd time of day for a ride, he thought. She'd been seein' Ledger since Tunstall's death. He disappeared after the Brady ambush. Too much for coincidence, it gave him a hunch. He left the cantina and collected his horse in the gathering gloom.

★ ★ ★ ★ ★

Lucy drew rein. "You lost, cowboy?"

"Not now." He took her by the waist and lifted her down. She smiled up at him in the last fading glow. His kiss drew her up on the tips of her toes. She hung on tight.

"Hungry?"

"I could stand a second helping of that."

"Save room for dessert." Her lashes dipped.

He untied the basket from her saddle and carried it to the blanket. Lucy set about laying out the contents while he led her buckskin mare to a grove of trees where the steeldust cropped spring grass. She served ham and biscuits, apple pie and cider.

"What did you and Alex talk about?"

"He wants me to take the sheriff's job."

"You're not going to do it, are you?"

"I need a job to support a wife."

"Maybe so, but not that job. This county's at war. You'd be a target for both sides."

"I might be able to stop the war."

"What makes you think that?"

"McSween and Chisum control one side. I can reason with them. Dolan dances to the Santa Fe tune. Those boys want statehood and that means law and order. They'll lean on him."

"You're dreaming. Ty, you're not serious, are you?"

"Who knows if it will happen, but I'd think on it."

"And you want me out of the store."

"That's different."

The rifle report chased the bullet whine to a clot of dirt that burst behind him.

"Get down!" He pushed Lucy to the ground and covered her with his body. He drew his gun and searched the darkness off to the west. "When I tell you to go, run for the trees. Understand?" She nodded.

He crawled off the blanket into the ground shadow. He made a guess at the shooter's position. "Go!" He fired and scrambled away from the muzzle flash. Return flashes exploded fifty yards further to the west. Ty fired behind them and moved again. Lucy made the trees safely. The shooter fired again. This time Ty did not return fire. He had the shooter's position. He moved forward, hugging the ground shadow. Minutes passed. He advanced slowly, steadily.

The sound of someone running disturbed the dark stillness. Ty fired. A horse and rider burst from the rocks above, silhouetted against the night skyline. In an instant the shadow melted into the darkness, trailing a cloud of starlit dust.

Ty stood and holstered his gun. He started for the trees. "He's gone. You all right?"

She emerged from the trees. "I'm fine. Are you?"

He took her in his arms.

"Who was it?"

"No idea, but I reckon I won't be gettin' his vote."

"You are serious."

"This territory won't be fit for decent folk until this thing is settled. Somebody's got to do it."

"Just don't make a widow out of me before I'm a bride."

"I'll do my best."

"Mrs. O'Hara says you can bunk in the parlor tonight. I think she likes having you around."

"You ready to go back to town?"

She held his eyes. "After dessert."

CHAPTER THIRTY-FIVE

Lincoln County Courthouse
April 18ᵗʰ

"All rise. The grand jury for Lincoln County, New Mexico Territory, is now in session, the Honorable Warren H. Bristol presiding. Be seated."

Rain pelted the roof and windows in a muted patter. Thunder rumbled in the distance. The small courtroom was crowded to standing room only. Nearly everyone in the county had a stake in these findings. The white-haired judge in his black robe took his seat and addressed the jury box. "Has the jury concluded its findings?"

The foreman rose. "We have, Your Honor." He handed a stack of papers to the bailiff.

"The bailiff will read the findings into the court record."

"With respect to the murders of Sheriff William Brady and Deputy George Hindman, the jury finds probable cause to charge the following individuals: Henry Brown, Fred Waite, William Bonney and John Middleton."

"So ordered." The judge rapped his gavel.

"With respect to the murder of Andrew Roberts, the jury finds probable cause to charge the following individuals: Henry Brown, Fred Waite, William Bonney, John Middleton, George Coe and Josiah Scurlock."

"So ordered."

"With respect to the murder of John Tunstall, the jury finds probable cause to charge the following individuals: Jesse Evans and William Mathews. With respect to the murder of John Tunstall, the jury finds probable cause to charge James Dolan as an accessory to capital murder."

The crowd broke into a stunned buzz.

Bristol banged his gavel. "This court will come to order!" The crowd fell silent. "So ordered."

"With respect to the allegation of cattle rustling, the jury finds probable cause to charge Jesse Evans and James Dolan."

"So ordered."

"With respect to the allegation of embezzlement against Alexander McSween, the jury finds no cause to indict."

"Case dismissed."

"With respect to the appointment of acting sheriff for Lincoln County to serve until the next election, the jury recommends the appointment of George Peppin."

"So ordered."

The bailiff folded the papers.

"This court stands adjourned."

"Son of a bitch!" Dolan paced his office in a black rage. Evans sat beside the desk, keeping out of the storm path. "Appointing an honest jury to keep up appearances is one thing, having them take McSween's side is another. At least we got Peppin appointed sheriff. He can serve warrants on those indictments handed down on McSween's people. This war ain't over by a long shot. We're not going to take this lyin' down. You get the boys ready, Jesse. We're goin' Regulator huntin'." He continued pacing in thought.

"What happened?"

"Come in." McSween stepped back allowing Ty into the foyer. He closed the door. "I don't know what happened. I thought I had it all arranged. Maybe Bristol got wind of it or maybe Dolan. Whatever happened, Dolan's got himself a sheriff. I expect he'll use that to start rounding up our men."

"Short of having them hide out, there's not much we can do about it."

"There is one thing."

"What's that?"

"Marshall Sherman is short one special deputy."

Rio Hondo
April 29th

Deputy Sheriffs Jesse Evans, Billy Mathews and Manuel Sagovia camped in the hills west of the main ford connecting the Pecos River valley ranches and Lincoln. Evans reckoned it a good place to hunt. Men need supplies. Supplies meant travel to Lincoln. Sagovia kept watch in a rockfall near the crest of a hill, overlooking the ford. Evans and Mathews dozed in the shade of a juniper stand beside a wash running with snowmelt.

Sagovia came alert. Three riders appeared in the hills south of the river, making an unhurried pace northwest. "Riders come."

Evans scrambled up the side of the wash, leaving Mathews groggily rubbing his eyes. He settled in beside the Mexican. "I'd know that big roan anywhere. It's the Bonney kid."

"His amigo is Frank McNab. I don't know the other one."

Evans squinted off to the north. "They'll cross at the ford and climb that draw yonder." He pointed a mile up the trail. "Com'on, let's fix a little surprise welcome for 'em."

Thirty minutes later, McNab, Bonney and Bowdre reached the river and stopped to water their horses.

"How do you plan to play this, Frank?"

The Kid was always one step ahead. Not a bad thing if a man

planned on stayin' alive. "Well, we ain't gonna ride down the main street in broad daylight. I figure we can sneak into Mc-Sween's store the back way along the river. We can pick up our supplies and maybe spend the night there."

"Back of the store's better than hard ground, but not much fun," Bowdre said.

"Show our faces in the cantina and we're likely to get our asses shot off. I expect McSween can find us a bottle. We'll make our own fun."

The Kid spat. "Fun hell, Frank, there ain't a girl between us."

"That Sample girl works in the store," Bowdre offered.

"You two simmer down. You're talkin' about Ty's girl."

The Kid grinned. "I almost forgot."

"Best not." McNab squeezed his horse into the river and splashed across. A mile further north the trail climbed into a narrow draw. Bowdre and the Kid settled into file behind McNab as they wound their way up a steep stony slope. A large rockfall spilled down the last fifty yards to the summit, forcing the riders to pick their way forward.

Rifle shots cracked from the rocks above on both sides of the draw. McNab jerked in the saddle at the first volley and toppled from his mount. Bowdre and Bonney wheeled their horses and returned fire as they fought their way back down the trail to cover. Rifle fire chewed at the rocks, bullets sang showers of rock chips.

"Sons a bitches got Frank."

Bowdre vented his fury in futile fire. "Now what do we do?"

"Cover me. I'm goin' up top and clear them bastards off our trail."

"Hell, Billy, there must be at least three of 'em. What kind of odds is that?"

"My kind." He grabbed the Winchester from Bowdre's saddle

boot and tossed it to him. "Cover me." He pulled his rifle, ducked around a high side in the rockfall and started to climb.

Bowdre fired harassing shots up the draw to no effect, other than drawing meaningless return fire. Meaningless that is until the shooting painted targets for the Kid. Minutes later the Kid's rifle spoke up. The shooting up top got hot for a time and then fell silent.

"Damn!" the Kid shouted. "They're runnin' for it."

Flying H

The Regulators gathered in the ranch house parlor. Bowdre recounted the events of the ambush. They'd taken McNab's body to Lincoln. They'd slipped into town the back way, picked up their supplies and reported McNab's death to McSween. He took care of reporting the murder and turning over the body to the sheriff.

"Who done the killin'?" Scurlock demanded.

"Didn't get a good look at 'em," the Kid said.

"They got to be Dolan men," Bowdre said.

Scurlock cut his eyes from one man to the next. "Then I say we pay Jimmy Dolan a visit." Murmurs of agreement went round the room.

"I say Doc's our new captain," the Kid said.

"I don't know about that. That job doesn't do a body any good."

"Someone's got to do it, Doc. I say it's you."

US Marshal's Office
Santa Fe

Sherman sat at his cluttered desk reading McSween's request. He'd seen this coming before he even filed his report on Brady's death. Special deputy appointments were serious business. So were their deaths in the line of duty. He knew Axtell had ordered a grand jury convened in Lincoln. The governor took great pains to maintain appearances beyond reproach. He'd read the findings in the newspaper. The proceedings must not have gone according to everyone's satisfaction. Likely it had something to do with the appointment of an interim sheriff. Chisum's lawyer had stirred up an official inquiry into the situation in Lincoln. McSween and his friends had some influence higher up the federal ladder than the Santa Fe Ring. He could almost hear the telegraph chatter from Lincoln to Washington. It might be good if he were seen to be above the partisan squabble.

McSween wanted him to appoint a new special deputy. Ty Ledger was a good man. The reports coming out of Lincoln County were disturbing. It amounted to open warfare. He could appoint a special deputy, but how much would that accomplish? Under the circumstances it might amount to signing Ledger's death warrant. What the governor needed to do is use the army to declare martial law. He'd give McSween his special deputy. No point in fighting him on it, but he'd also make his point about martial law with the governor.

Chapter Thirty-Six

Lincoln
May 2ⁿᵈ

That many horses on Lincoln's quiet street made enough noise to get noticed even at a walk. Ty glanced out the sheriff's office window at the commotion. Doc Scurlock led a half dozen heavily armed Regulators up the street. The situation had trouble written all over it. He'd stopped by the office to notify Peppin of his appointment as special deputy US marshal. The sheriff had a stack of warrants for men on both sides and nary enough jail cells to hold half of them. In this case he was out with a posse lookin' for the men about to shoot up his town.

Ty pulled a sawed-off shotgun down from the rack beside the door. He opened the cupboard below and picked out a box of shells. He broke the action, loaded both barrels and snapped the weapon closed. He stuffed his shirt pocket with shells. He stepped onto the sun-soaked boardwalk just as the shooting started up the street.

He ran toward the sound, his boots pounding a hollow beat on the planks. Rounding a gentle curve in the road, he saw Scurlock and his men shooting in the general direction of Dolan's store at the west end of town. This made for an interesting confrontation. He'd ridden with these men. Now he wore a badge duty bound to protect the other side.

He slowed as he drew near. The Regulators were scattered along the street and around to the west of the store. They fired from the backs of skittish mounts prancing and circling in the dusty street. He recognized the Bonney kid, Bowdre, O'Folliard, Waite and Brown.

Scurlock shouted. "Throw down your guns and come out, Dolan. You're under arrest."

"Go to hell, Scurlock!" Gunfire punctuated the reply.

Ty ran toward the store, judging the Regulators might still consider him a friend. He skidded to a stop short of the store close to Scurlock. He pointed the scattergun to the sky and let go with a blast from one barrel. The report got their attention.

"Hold your fire, all of you!"

"Stay out of this, Ledger. This is US marshal's business."

"It ain't anymore, Doc. I'm the new special deputy for Lincoln County. You and your boys are not my deputies."

"You tellin' me you side with the son of a bitch what killed John Tunstall?"

"I'm sidin' with the law."

"Then why aint't you locked that murderer up? The grand jury indicted him for an accessory."

"The grand jury indicted most of you boys too. We ain't got enough jail cells for all of you. You'll get your days in court soon enough. Now put up those guns and get the hell out of town."

"Don't make me laugh, Ledger, we got you six to one. Now get the hell out of our way while we still remember you was a friend once. Com'on boys let's burn the son of a bitch out."

"Doc, I got one shell left in this gun." He jacked the hammer and leveled the muzzle at Scurlock's head. "One of your men makes a move and I'll blow you to kingdom come. Now put up those guns and get the hell out of town."

Scurlock stared down the shotgun. Certain death stared back in the dark bore. He read Ledger's eyes. He'd do it sure as hell. *Hell,* he wasn't ready for that party just yet.

"Put up your guns, boys." He cut his eyes to the store. "This ain't over, Dolan. It ain't ever gonna be over until we get what we come for." He wheeled his horse and spurred up a gallop. The Regulators followed down the street out of town.

Dolan stepped out of the store gun in hand. "Much obliged, Ledger. I hadn't counted on you for that kind of help."

"Don't make too much of it, Dolan. I got a job to do. That don't mean I like all of it. The blood on your hands started all this. Don't think for a minute I forget that." He turned on his heel and walked back to the office.

Dolan watched him. He'd been lucky. Ledger was honest. Another man might have sold him out to his friends. That was a problem. What the hell was he gonna do with an honest lawman? First an honest jury, now an honest US marshal. Santa Fe owed him plenty.

Seven Rivers
May 15th

They rode out of the hills. Dark shadows, horses and riders painted black in twilight, floating on a misty carpet of dust. Seven heavily armed men. They surrounded the ranch yard on three sides and drew rein. Rifles appeared from saddle boots.

"Evans, you're surrounded. You and your men come out with your hands where we can see them." Scurlock waited. "You hear me, Evans? Surrender or we'll burn this shack you call a ranch down around your ears."

"He ain't here."

"Who is here?"

"Nobody, just me, Manuel."

"Where is Evans?"

"Looking for you."

Scurlock laughed. "He ain't tryin' very hard. I'm easy to find. All right, amigo, since you're all alone, you best come out with your hands up." No answer. "You got two minutes to show yourself or we burn the place down with you in it." Nothing.

A lone horse and rider burst from the back of the house, galloping northwest. The Kid put his spurs to the big roan. He slapped his rifle into the saddle boot and drew his gun, quickly closing the gap on the fleeing Manuel Sagovia.

The Dolan man turned in his saddle feeling the press of his pursuer. His eyes went wide white.

The Kid leveled his gun and fired. Muzzle flash bloomed white light and powder smoke. He fired again, close enough to hear Sagovia grunt. He slumped in the saddle. The Kid fired a third time, knocking the man from his horse. The body bounced on the hardscrabble high desert and rolled into the base of a sage bush. The Kid pulled up the roan and holstered his gun. *Five, Mr. Tunstall. More comin'.*

South Spring
June 21ˢᵗ

Chisum, McSween, Scurlock and Roth sat around the dining-room table. The doors and windows were thrown open, allowing a pleasant summer breeze to cool the house. McSween called the meeting to break the news.

"Sheriff Peppin and his posses are combing the Pecos River valley, lookin' for our men."

Chisum rubbed his chin. "You knew Dolan wouldn't sit still after Ledger was appointed special deputy. It looks like his Santa Fe friends plan on playin' both sides of the street."

"I don't think so. They'll put up the appearance of law and order, but underneath it, they'll back Dolan."

"So we got Ledger. They got Peppin. It looks like a standoff to me."

"Don't be too quick to count on Ledger," Scurlock said. "He run me and the boys off when we tried to arrest Dolan."

McSween nodded agreement. "Doc's right. Ledger will

uphold the law. He may see most things our way, but he won't take sides."

Chisum looked from McSween to Scurlock. "So where does that leave us?"

"It's open war," Scurlock said. "Evans and his boys are out lookin' for us. You can bet Peppin will have a Dolan posse lookin' for us too."

McSween frowned, massaging the bridge of his nose. "So what do we do, Doc?"

"Let 'em find us someplace where we can have it out on our terms."

"Legally we can defend our property," McSween said.

"I don't want to try defending the Flying H cheese box."

Chisum nodded.

"Riders comin'!" The warning brought the meeting to an abrupt halt.

"Now what the hell?" Chisum let the question trail over his shoulder as he led the way to the front door. Caneris stood in the yard pointing to a group of riders coming hard.

"It's Billy and the boys," Scurlock said.

"What lit a fire under their tail?" Roth said.

"That." Doc pointed to a cloud of dust rising on the Regulators' back trail.

The Kid slid his roan to a stop and jumped down. He stuck a thumb over his shoulder. "Peppin's comin' with a big posse. Must have Evans' boys with him."

"All right, boys, inside," Chisum said. "The adobe on this house is better than Fort Stanton."

The Regulators scrambled inside and fanned out to cover windows and doors. The posse men burst into the yard and drew rein.

"Yo the house! This is Sheriff Peppin, Chisum. You're harboring wanted criminals. Give 'em up or we'll come get 'em."

"Turn your murderin' cattle thieves around, Peppin, and get the hell off my land."

"Fan out, boys!"

The posse surrounded the house and opened fire. Bullets bit the adobe walls and whined away in a stony shower.

Scurlock made his way around the house, making sure they had any blind spots covered. "Hold your fire, boys, unless you've got a good shot. This ain't goin' nowhere unless they rush us."

The shooting died out in frustration in less than an hour. The hacienda absorbed everything the posse men had to offer. The afternoon lengthened in shadow. Nightfall would change the situation.

McSween and Chisum huddled in the parlor with Roth and Scurlock. "What do we do come nightfall?"

"If they think they've cover, they might try to rush us," Chisum said.

"They might." Scurlock nodded.

"So what do we do about it?" McSween asked.

"We make sure we see them first," Roth said.

Doc cocked an eye. "What are you thinkin', Johnny?"

"We put a couple men on the roof. Station a few more under cover in the yard. If they try to move in, we give 'em a surprise."

Doc nodded. "I'll take care of it."

Evans found Peppin just past sunset.

"How long you figure they can stay forted up in there?"

"Hard to say. I figure we can try to rush them once it gets good and dark."

"I don't know about that. Look at that evening star. Looks like a clear night. Pretty close to full moon too."

"There's a creek that runs back of the hacienda. It should give us cover to get close."

★　★　★　★　★

Evans led five others down the creek bed toward the back of the hacienda. They kept to the shadows as best they could against the glow of starlight. The moon with its bright white light had yet to reach full height in the night sky. He signaled a halt at the closest point to the back door, a black shadow across a small vegetable garden. He cocked his Winchester and looked to his men. Their eyes met his alert and ready. He turned up the bank.

A rifle cracked. The bullet struck the creek bank at Evans' boot, showering him in rock chips. He jumped back searching for a target. A second shot exploded, sending a geyser of water up from the creek bed. The muzzle flash came from the roof. Evans returned fire. With the element of surprise lost and facing a shooter with the advantage of height, Evans signaled his men to pull back down the creek bed. The night fell silent.

At daybreak, Charlie Bowdre watched the posse men preparing to depart. He climbed down from the roof and went inside through the back door.

"They're fixin' to leave."

"For now," Scurlock said.

McSween sat in the parlor with Chisum.

"I've had about enough of this cat-and-mouse game. I'm ready to go home. It's time for a showdown. We can occupy the store."

"And your house," Scurlock added.

McSween and Chisum exchanged glances. Stern resolve united them. They nodded.

"It's settled then," McSween said. "Give me a couple of weeks to stock the store with ammunition."

Roth didn't like the sound of it. Ty would get caught in the middle of the coming fight, trying to keep the peace. He'd get himself killed sure as hell.

McSween started for home the next morning. Roth brooded in silence, clearly preoccupied. Chisum sensed his unease.

"You've been real quiet, Johnny. What's eatin' you, boy."

"That powder keg is gonna blow in Ty's face."

"Likely so."

"He'll get his law-abiding ass shot to hell in the middle of a war."

"Tough time to be a lawman."

"I got to go to Lincoln and warn him. Get him out of there if I can."

"Hell, all you'll do is get yourself caught in the middle of it just like him. You've got a wife now, responsibilities. Leave it to the professionals."

"I am a professional. I owe my life to Ty Ledger. I'd be C'manche buzzard bait if it hadn't been for him. I just can't leave him hung out on his own."

"What about Dawn?"

"She'll have to understand."

"This is the kind of trouble I was afraid of. Why'd Ledger take that job in the first place? He had to know it'd come to this."

"He needed a job. He's fixin' to marry Lucy Sample."

"I thought you two would go into the cattle business together. Hell, I'll stake you to a herd to get you started if it'll get the badge off his chest."

"It might, but knowing Ty, not before this is over."

Chisum set his jaw. "Do what you have to. Just don't make a widow out of that girl."

★ ★ ★ ★ ★

Lincoln
June 23rd

Roth rode into town braced by hot summer wind. Dust swirled down the street, pushing tumbleweeds out of the west. He drew rein at the Wortley hitch rack and stepped down. He found Ty tending the steeldust in the stable. He smiled and extended a hand.

"Good to see you, Johnny. What brings you to Lincoln?"

"We need to talk."

"That sounds serious."

"It is."

"I was just about to have some lunch. We can talk over that."

"Food sounds good about now." They started for the back of the hotel. "How are things in town?"

"Pretty quiet since Scurlock and the boys tried to take on Dolan last month."

"Quiet for now."

Ty smelled trouble.

"Lucy still workin' for McSween?"

"Yeah. Don't matter how hard I try, I can't seem to talk her out of it."

Roth fell silent as they passed through the lobby on the way to the dining room. Ty led the way to a corner table. The waiter came over.

"What'll it be, Marshal?"

"What's the special?"

"Ham and mashed."

"That'll be fine."

"Make it two," Roth said.

The waiter went to the kitchen. Ty fixed on his friend. "What's on your mind, Johnny?"

"The Regulators are coming back to town in force."

"Shit! I was afraid of that. When?"

"Couple of weeks, I expect. McSween needs that much time to stock the store with ammunition."

The waiter arrived with two steaming plates. Ty glanced away as though he'd lost his appetite.

"What are they plannin'?"

"Evans and his boys have been lookin' for them. Peppin's got posses joined in the hunt. They caught up to the Regulators down at South Spring. They pulled back after a two-day gunfight, but that ain't nowhere near the end of it. McSween and Scurlock figure to occupy the store and McSween's house and wait for Dolan to make his play. That way they have the cover of protecting their property."

"Son of a bitch! That explains why Dolan's men have been so scarce the last few weeks. It ain't bad enough they're ridin' the county shootin' at each other. Now they're fixin' to turn Lincoln into a battlefield. Between one side and the other, there ain't enough men left to keep the peace."

"That's the way I see it."

"What the hell am I gonna do?"

"Quit and get out of town."

"You know I can't do that, Johnny."

"You will if you got a lick of sense."

"There's got to be a way." He cut a forkful of ham and chewed lost in thought. "Dudley, that's it!"

"The army?"

"I'll get him to send troops and declare martial law."

"You think he'll do it?"

"He's got to, or we'll have us a civil war here. I can ride over to the fort in the morning and have a talk with him."

"Mind if I ride along?"

"I'd be glad of the company. First, though, I gotta get Lucy out of that store, now."

Lucy turned from the shelf she was dusting at the sound of the visitor bell.

"Hey, cowboy." She shook her head. "I'm still not used to callin' you Marshal. Was that Johnny rode by a bit ago?"

"It was." He gave her a peck on the cheek.

"What brings him to town?"

"Can we go out back and have a talk."

"Sure. Why so serious?"

"I'll tell you out back."

She led the way. "Susan, can you watch the store for a few minutes?"

Susan smiled with a wave.

Outside they sat on the wagon-loading platform. "What's wrong, Ty?"

"The Regulators are comin' to town. They mean it for a showdown with Dolan and his men. They plan on forting up here in the store and the McSween house. I don't want you anywhere near any of that."

"Oh, my! Does Susan know?"

"It's McSween's plan so I'd expect she does. I know we've had this conversation before, Lucy, but this is different. They're gonna turn this town into a battlefield unless I can stop them."

"You stop them! How can you possibly do that?"

"Ask Colonel Dudley to declare martial law."

"You think he will?"

"I sure hope so. In the meantime you need to get out of here."

"I can't just walk out and leave things."

"Lucy, this is war!"

"I'll tell Susan. The minute the Regulators get here, I'm leaving."

"Promise?"

"I promise."

He kissed her proper.

CHAPTER THIRTY-SEVEN

Fort Stanton
June 24th

"Colonel Dudley will see you now." The sergeant major stepped aside allowing Ledger and Roth to enter the office.

Dudley stood at his desk to greet them. He extended a hand. "Ty, what brings you by? This doesn't have the look of a social call. Anything I can do for you?"

Ty took his hand. "I'm afraid it's not a social call, Nate. You remember my friend, Johnny Roth"

"I do. Have a seat." Dudley returned to his desk. "What's on your mind?"

Ty took his seat. "We need help with a situation in Lincoln. The McSween and Dolan factions are gunning for a showdown. I haven't enough men to stop it. I need you to send troops to town and declare martial law."

Dudley made a steeple of his fingertips. "I've heard reports that sound serious."

"Damn serious."

"I can't just do that on my own authority. The governor would have to ask for that kind of help."

"I don't know if we've got that kind of time."

"I'm sorry, Ty, that's all I can do. You'll have to make the request to Governor Axtell's office. I'll arrange for you to use the post telegraph."

"Who knows if the governor will consider the request coming

from me? Most folks think I'm aligned with the McSween faction. I doubt Dolan's Santa Fe friends will do much for me."

Dudley shrugged. "All you can do is try."

Roth didn't pretend to have Dawn Sky's gift of vision, but he had a pretty good idea of how this would turn out. Riding back to Lincoln he posed the question.

"What do you figure to do if Axtell doesn't send troops?"

"Damned if I know."

"Ty, you can't stop this by yourself."

"I can try."

"You might as well put a gun to your head and pull the trigger. You'd have a better chance of missing than stopping what's coming."

Ty cut his eyes to his friend. He was probably right.

"Look, Ty, you don't need this job. I don't know much about the cattle business, but Chisum says he'll stake us to a herd to get started. You can support a family that way. I plan to."

"That's a generous offer, Johnny. It's tempting."

"Forget tempting. Hand McSween his badge and take the offer."

"I got one last card to play."

"What card?"

"Maybe I can talk sense to McSween."

Roth pulled a frown. "Talk then. Just don't take a bullet for a one-street town hell-bent on destroyin' itself."

Lincoln
June 26th

Ty waved at Lucy as he passed the store. Summer sun bleached the sky a pale blue. Hot breeze swirled dust devils down the street. He seemed not to notice, preoccupied at what he might say to McSween. He turned up the walk to the porch. His boots scraped the porch planks. His knock sounded hollow within. Moments later the lawyer's heels answered, clipping the polished wood beyond the door.

"Ty." He extended a hand. "Come in, come in." He showed him into the parlor. Golden light flooded the room through lace curtains. "Plenty hot out there today."

"It is."

"Step into the office here and have a seat. I expect you didn't drop by to discuss the weather."

He took the offered chair. "No, I didn't."

McSween took his seat. "What's on your mind?"

"Call it off, Alex."

He braced. "Call what off?"

"The showdown with Dolan."

"How do you know about that?"

"Roth is my friend."

"I see. All right, Ty, look, it has to happen sooner or later. We simply mean to dictate the terms. All you have to do is stay out of the way."

"I can't."

"It's none of your affair."

"You made it my business when you got me this badge. My job is to keep the peace. You're plannin' to turn this town into a battlefield. I can't allow that."

"You can't stop it."

"I can try."

"Look, Ty, I consider you a friend. I wouldn't want to see you get hurt, but if you get in the middle of this, I can't be responsible for what might happen. I'd rather see you resign until this is over."

"I took an oath. I have a duty to uphold the law. I can't walk away because you've decided to have it out with Dolan. Think about what you are doing? A lot of people on both sides stand to get hurt. Think about Susan. Do you want that?"

McSween paused. "No, I don't want that, but we can't let the people of this county continue to live under Dolan's thumb. He's got to be stopped."

"This isn't the way to do it."

"What do you suggest?"

"Look, the grand jury handed down the indictments. I'll serve the warrants. Let the courts decide the matter. You're a lawyer, you should understand that. You've got the store and the bank. You've already broken Dolan's stranglehold. Be patient."

"Tell that to Dolan. You don't have enough men or jail cells to serve those warrants. If you did, you'd have done it by now. The store and the bank are exactly the point. Dolan won't let them survive. He tried to buy them. I refused to sell. Now he's out to destroy me by force. Look at what happened to McNab. We can't wait patiently while Dolan picks us off one ambush at a time. You can't stop him. We have to."

"What if I can stop him?"

"I don't see how."

"I've asked the governor to call out the army and declare martial law."

"Hmm, that might work. What makes you think Axtell will do it?"

"That little inquiry Leverson started. It got me this badge. Sherman knows what's going on. I suspect Axtell does too."

"I hope you're right about that."

"He sent us an honest grand jury, didn't he?"

"If Axtell sends in the army to deal with Dolan, my men will stand down."

"Good." Ty rose and took McSween's hand. "I can show myself out."

Outside, he took a deep breath. *Maybe. The governor had to come through.*

Office of the Governor
Santa Fe

Martial law. Axtell stared at the telegram from the special deputy marshal in Lincoln. He had reason to believe the situation down there would come to an armed showdown in the county seat. He represented that the McSween faction would stand down if the army were brought in to keep the peace. The army, martial law, it looked bad and that's all there was to it. He drummed his fingers on the desk. McSween agreed. What about Dolan?

Jimmy was damn unhappy when Sherman appointed—he glanced at the telegram—Ty Ledger a special deputy. What about Dolan's man Peppin? Clearly this was a civil matter. The sheriff ought to have jurisdiction. If they needed army help he should ask for it. Dolan had warned him that Tunstall was threatening to stir up Democrat opposition to Brady. Maybe McSween inherited that notion along with the bank and the store. It smelled like Ledger might be McSween's man. Martial law, he really wanted no part of that except as a last resort. Best see what Jimmy thinks.

Lincoln

Oppressive heat made the office feel like an oven. Dolan sat in his shirtsleeves, his coat thrown over the back of his chair. His visitor sat in a barrel-backed chair across from the desk, his coat draped over his knee.

"How is the posse comin', George?"

Peppin scowled. "Slow, Jimmy. Chisum and McSween hired a lot of men between 'em. Evans has lost more than a few. We got the word out, but the way I make it, we're still outnumbered. Any word from Jesse on how he's makin' out huntin' down

Regulators?"

"No word since the dustup down at South Spring. I expect that says it."

"So the sides ain't evened none."

"Likely not. How long before you can raise some more men?"

Peppin shrugged.

A floorboard creaked beyond the office door, announcing the old clerk's approach. Dolan glanced at the door. "What is it, Jasper?"

"Telegram from Santa Fe, Mr. Dolan." The old scarecrow shuffled across the office and handed over an envelope.

Dolan took it and tore it open. The signature line caught his eye, *Axtell*. He read the message. Damn. He knit his brows and read it again.

"Somethin' the matter?"

"Ledger asked the governor to call out the army and declare martial law in Lincoln. He says the marshal expects trouble. He says McSween will stand down if the army's called in."

Peppin furrowed his brow. "McSween will stand down, stand down from what? What do you suppose he's got up his sleeve that's got Ledger worked up enough to call for the army?"

"You suppose Chisum and McSween have figured out they've got us outnumbered?"

"Maybe, but what could they do with that?"

"Draw us into some kind of showdown. If they planned on trying something like that, where do you suppose it would be?" Dolan said.

"No tellin' for sure. If it was me I'd look for someplace that gave me an advantage."

"That could be a lot of places. Ledger did ask the governor to call out the army to declare martial law here in Lincoln. Maybe he knows something."

"That could explain it. So what do you tell the governor?"

Dolan smiled. "We don't need the army, yet. The sheriff will let him know when we do."

CHAPTER THIRTY-EIGHT

July 14ᵗʰ

They rode in under a blazing summer sun. Dark forms emerging from heat waves shimmering on the road into town. Ledger and Roth watched the street from the boardwalk. Scurlock tipped his hat as they passed. The Kid favored Ty with his gaptooth grin. Roth counted ten of them including McSween. Big Jim, standing guard in the store made eleven, ten professional guns. They put up the horses in the corral behind the store in a field next to the Torreon Tower.

Moments after they did, true to her word, Lucy left the store. She crossed the street to where Ty and Johnny stood. She held Ty's eyes, hers filled with concern.

"You go on down to Mrs. O'Hara's. We'll keep an eye on things here."

She hesitated. "Who'll keep an eye on you?"

"The army, I hope."

It didn't reassure her.

"Me, for sure," Roth said.

"Go along now. Dolan's men are ridin' around lookin' for this bunch. Nothin's gonna happen till they find 'em. I'll be by a little later."

"Come for supper." She hurried along.

Scurlock took control of the store with Bowdre, Middleton, Brown and Coe. Alex and Susan McSween opened their house

295

to the Kid, Tom O'Folliard, Jose Chavez, Eugenio Salazar and Big Jim French. They settled in to wait.

Time passed. Word spread. Peppin and Dolan met in the office at the House.

"Cigar, George?"

"Don't mind if I do." He selected one from the box and bit the tip. He scratched a lucifer and held it. Dolan puffed his smoke to light. Peppin lit his.

"So, how do you want to play this, Jimmy?"

"I've sent word for Evans to bring in his boys. We'll set up shop at the Wortley. You take a couple of your men and take control of the Torreon. Then we wait."

"Wait for what?"

"For the cavalry to arrive."

"Cavalry?"

Dolan nodded. "You remember I told Axtell we didn't need the army, yet?"

He nodded.

"You sent him a telegram this afternoon that said we do."

"I did?"

"You did."

"What did I say?"

"You told him we didn't need martial law. You said you needed troops to put down a civil disturbance in Lincoln."

Peppin chuckled. "Pretty damn smart of me I'd say."

Fort Stanton
Sunday, July 15th

"Telegram from Santa Fe, Colonel."

Dudley held out his hand. "Thank you, Sergeant." Could this be the long-awaited response to Marshal Ledger's request? He opened the fold. His brow furrowed as he read. Governor Axtell was asking for troops, all right, but not martial law. He asked for troops to help Sheriff George Peppin put down a civil disturbance in Lincoln. What happened to Ty? He guessed he'd find out when he got to Lincoln.

"Sergeant Caleb!"

"Sir?" He appeared in the door.

"Notify C Company and A Battery. We ride to Lincoln in the morning."

Lincoln

July 15th

Slanting sun greeted Evans and his men as they rode into town. They jogged up the street toward the Torreon when the opening shots in the battle for Lincoln erupted from the Tunstall store. Evans wheeled his horse off the street for the close cover of the tower. Peppin and his deputies returned fire from the tower. The sheriff climbed down to meet Evans.

"Anybody hit?"

"No. What the hell's goin' on, George?"

"McSween and his men are forted up in the store and the McSween house. It's been quiet up to now, but it looks as though they mean to make a showdown of it."

"Good. The sooner we rid ourselves of that pack of lice the better. How many of them are there?"

"Ledger counted ten guns plus McSween. I'm guessin' his wife is in there too."

"Where's Ledger stand in all this?"

"At the moment, he don't. Now that the shootin's started, I expect he'll show up."

"And?"

Peppin scratched his white bush of chin whiskers. "He's pretty straight. He ran Scurlock and his bunch off the House once already. It don't much matter either way. What's one man gonna do? Besides, with the sheriff on the job, he's got a perfect excuse to sit this one out. Be the smart thing to do, considering the risk of lead poisoning and all."

"Where's Dolan?"

"He set himself up at the Wortley. You and your boys can get there if you circle around south of town."

"Much obliged. Mount up, boys."

Ledger and Roth hurried up the street toward the shooting as Evans and his men galloped out of town. Peppin stood beside the Torreon.

"What happened, George?"

"McSween men fired on those boys."

"Damn."

"What do you plan to do about it, Marshal?"

Ty measured the Dolan man. He wasn't about to tip his hand on his hopes for the army.

Peppin patted his vest pocket. "I got warrants for most of the men in there. You can stand aside and let me and my men handle it."

"You and your men hold your fire. Maybe I can talk them out peaceably."

"Suit yourself. Sounds like a fool's errand to me, but I got time. I'm waitin' for reinforcement before I force their hand."

Ty turned back toward the back of the store. Roth matched his stride.

"Dolan's callin' in reinforcements. This situation is gettin' worse by the minute. What are you fixin' to do?"

"Try to talk sense into McSween."

Pale blue early evening light lit the McSween backyard. Ty and Johnny hurried up the back step and knocked. Muffled footsteps sounded.

"Who's there?"

"Ty Ledger. I need to talk to McSween."

"I'll see if he's in. The door's covered. Touch it and you'll get a load of buckshot for your troubles."

More muffled sounds. The door cracked open. The Bonney kid waved them in at gunpoint. "Leave your hardware on the kitchen table."

They unbuckled their guns and followed the Kid into the parlor. The place looked like an armed camp. Big Jim French and Tom O'Folliard sat beside the front windows cleaning their guns. Jose Chavez and Eugenio Salazar were stationed at the west windows with a view of the Wortley up the street. The Kid led them into McSween's office.

The lawyer sat at his desk with his head in his hands wreathed in a halo of lamplight. A plainly worried Susan McSween stood beside him. He turned watery eyes to his visitors.

"Ty, Johnny, good of you to come."

"This isn't exactly a social call, Alex. Your boys at the store started shootin' at people on the street an hour ago. You and your men need to put up your guns and leave town before this situation gets out of control. Dolan and Peppin have you boxed in. Evans and his men arrived this afternoon and they are waiting for more. This pot's about to boil over and there's not much I can do about it."

"I don't expect you to join us, Ty. Dolan has got to be stopped and we are determined to do it."

"Determined to get yourself and a bunch of others killed is more like it. Susan, talk sense to him. At best you could fight this to a bloody draw. Who knows what Dolan has up his sleeve? Give him time to do things his way and you'll get massacred."

"Alex, Ty may be right. If the boys slip out the back way tonight, Dolan and his men won't know they're gone until morning."

"That won't settle anything, Susan. This has got to end. You've said so yourself. Running away won't solve a thing."

"Alex, you got me this badge. My job is to uphold the law. No one should understand that better than you. You need to listen to me and do what I say before someone gets hurt."

"You think Dolan's going to let us walk out of here? This won't be over until one side or the other wins. It's plain enough this will only be settled with guns."

"All right, I've done about all I can. If you won't see reason, you won't need a deputy marshal much longer." He plucked the badge off his shirt and tossed it on the desk. "There ain't likely to be much left when the smoke clears. Com'on, Johnny."

Back outside they climbed down to the river. Roth shook his head. "You tried."

"All we can do now is pray the governor comes through."

Chapter Thirty-Nine

A knock at the door interrupted the clatter of supper dishes. Lucy dried her hands on the dish towel as she went to the door. She opened it cautiously to Ty and Johnny. She swallowed her heart and flew into Ty's arms.

"I was so worried with all that shooting. What happened?"

"Some of Dolan's men showed up. McSween men threw lead on the welcome mat." She trembled. He held her tight.

"Oh, Ty, what's to become of this?"

"Nothing good I'm afraid."

She kissed him deep and needful with no concern for Roth standing there hat in hand.

"Lucy, are you going to leave those men standing outside all night?"

"No, of course not, come in." She led them into the parlor.

"Have you had supper?" Mrs. O'Hara called from the kitchen.

"No, ma'am," Roth answered.

"I'll fix up a couple of plates of what's left. It's not fancy, but filling."

"Much obliged."

"Ty, where's your badge?" Lucy fingered his chest.

"I gave it back to McSween. If he won't listen to reason, there's nothing I can do to help him."

"What will you do then?"

The question had we underneath it. "Johnny brought up something I need to talk to you about."

Roth sensed he was about to be in the way. "I'll see about helping Mrs. O'Hara with those plates." He disappeared down the hall to the kitchen.

She settled on the settee and made room for him.

"Chisum gave Johnny and Dawn land for a wedding present. Johnny wants to go into the cattle business, but he says he doesn't know anything about it. He wants me to come in as a partner. Chisum says he'll stake us to the cattle to get started."

"Why, that sounds wonderful."

"So would you be willing to move down to South Spring as my wife?"

Her eyes went liquid in the lamplight. "Ty Ledger, nothing could make me any happier."

Supper'd gone cold by the time they finished kissing.

Ty turned down the lamp in Mrs. O'Hara's parlor. Roth spread his blanket on the floor.

"When do you want to ride down to South Spring?"

Ledger thought. "Soon as we know if the governor comes through."

July 17th

The column churned the street into a dun dust cloud. Ty and Johnny stood on Mrs. O'Hara's porch. Dudley passed at the head of a column of fours. The troop looked to be company strength, followed by a mule-drawn caisson towing a howitzer. Ty smiled.

"Look at that, Johnny. The governor came through." He felt the strain of two tense days lift like a weight from his chest. "Com'on." They started up the street after the troopers.

Peppin stepped out of the Torreon and raised his hand. Dudley called a halt, the command echoing down the column.

"Colonel, Sheriff George Peppin."

Dudley stepped down. He peeled the gauntlet from his right hand and extended it.

"Lieutenant Colonel Nathan Dudley at your service, sir."

"Glad to have your help."

"What's the situation?"

"Gunmen are holed up in the Tunstall store up yonder and the house next door. They've fired on citizens using the street."

Ty arrived, trailing Roth. "Nate, glad you're here. I wasn't sure the governor would act on my request."

"He didn't, Ty. My orders are to support Sheriff Peppin here."

Ty couldn't believe his ears. "You've been ordered to take Dolan's side?"

Dudley shrugged.

"I don't know anything about that. My orders are to assist Sheriff Peppin in putting down a civil disturbance in Lincoln. Now, Sheriff, I've got a company of troops and light artillery battery. How would you like them deployed?"

Peppin smiled. "We'll start with the store. If we can flush the men in there, the others may give up."

"Very good. Captain Purington!"

"Sir?"

"Have your men dismount and deploy across the street from that building." He pointed to the store. "Bring up the howitzer."

"Yes, sir." The captain saluted and turned to his command.

Dudley deployed his troops in the field across the street from the McSween house and store south of a small home owned by the Slurigos family who promptly decamped when the shooting started. Ledger followed Dudley, desperate to make him see reason. Roth followed his friend, determined to prevent him from doing anything foolish. Dudley positioned the howitzer in the center of his line with lines of fire to both the house and the store.

Peppin left his men in the Torreon and crossed the street to

303

Wilson's jacal on Dudley's east flank. The arrival of the troops gave Evans and his men cover to occupy the Slurigos' house. Dolan left the Wortley with them to join Peppin. With the troops deployed, Dudley reported to Peppin.

"My men are in position, Sheriff. How do you want to proceed?"

"Let's see if starin' down a cannon muzzle will get them to surrender."

"And if they won't?"

"I'm goin' over to the Torreon. If they won't surrender, my men will rush the store with your covering fire."

"At your service, Sheriff."

Ty couldn't believe his ears. "Nate, you can't do this! Artillery against civilians?"

"Sorry, Ty, I have my orders. Sheriff Peppin is in charge."

"You can't do this. If you fire on them, it's murder. Give them the chance to give up."

Dudley turned to Peppin.

Peppin looked past Dudley. He arched an eyebrow at Dolan. Dolan gave no quarter.

"Deploy the gun and prepare to fire."

Dudley withdrew to see to his troops. Ty cut his eyes from Peppin to Dolan. He started to reach for his gun. Roth grabbed his hand.

"It ain't worth it, Ty. You done all you could. Let's get out of here." Roth led him by the arm down the street toward the O'Hara house where Lucy stood on the porch waiting nervously. Peppin crossed over to the Torreon and gathered his men in the base of the tower.

"Yo the store! You've got two minutes to come out with your hands up or we're comin' in to get you."

★　★　★　★　★

Scurlock turned to his men. Threat thick as fog hung from one to the next. Bowdre backed away from the door. Middleton blinked.

"Shit, Doc, they's got a cannon out there."

Scurlock jerked his head toward the back door. "Go to hell, Peppin!"

"Get ready, boys. Colonel, you may fire when ready."

Dudley relayed the command to his battery officer.

"Fire!" The howitzer bucked, belching a great cloud of powder smoke. The concussion rattled windows. The door to the store disappeared in splinters and shattered glass. A volley of rifle fire shredded the storefront.

Peppin and his men rushed the back of the store. Scurlock and his men had their horses ready to mount. Peppin's men fired. Scurlock and Bowdre returned fire, allowing Middleton, Brown and Coe to escape to cover in the trees on the bluff leading to the river. They opened fire, forcing Peppin and his men to take cover until Scurlock and Bowdre joined them. Scurlock led the way through the trees down to the river. The Dolan men rushed to the tree line, firing at the Regulators disappearing down the bluff through the trees.

"Hold your fire. All we're gettin' for good ammunition is sawdust. You boys cover the back of the store. It'll be dark soon. I don't want any of 'em sneakin' back in. Keep an eye on the back of McSween's house too."

CHAPTER FORTY

July 18ᵗʰ

McSween sat in his office dimly lit by early morning. He hadn't slept. A two-day crust of beard shaded his cheeks and chin. His eyes were red-rimmed and sunken with worry. The concussion of the big gun shook the house. He thought it had been fired at them. Thankfully the men in the store escaped. How had Dolan turned the army against them? Santa Fe could be the only answer. They were doomed. He felt a presence in the office door. Big Jim French filled the frame.

"I don't mean to disturb you, Mr. McSween, but I'm worried."

"So am I, Jim, so am I."

"I spent these last months lookin' out for Mrs. McSween. I take it for my job now. We got to do somethin' to get her out of here. Them boys turn that big gun on this house, we don't want her hurt."

"You're right, Jim. Thank you for being so thoughtful. I should have thought of it myself. Soon as she's up and dressed I'll ask for a cease-fire to let her pass."

The big man nodded and returned to his post.

The sun was up when Susan came downstairs ready to face the new day. She'd slept fitfully. She looked pale and drawn by the strain. She made a pot of coffee and passed among the men handing out cups and pouring. She found Alex in his office.

"Did you sleep at all, dear?"

He shook his head and accepted the cup gratefully. "I'm glad you're up. I want you to pack a bag for yourself."

"Whatever for?"

"I'm going to ask for a cease-fire to allow you to leave."

"I'll do no such thing. I'll leave when you do."

"There will be no discussion, Susan. I don't want you in this house if they fire that cannon again."

"But what about you?"

"The men and I will look after ourselves. If we have to make a run for it like the others, I'd feel better knowing that you're safe." He took her in his arms and held her. Tears wet his shirtfront.

"Give it up, Alex. It's not worth it. It's not worth dying for."

"I can't give it up. Not yet, anyway."

Dudley and Peppin stood at the caisson, discussing their options. Dolan stood nearby, listening so he would know how to instruct Peppin. Dudley's attention flicked over Peppin's shoulder.

"Wait, what's this?"

Peppin followed his gaze. A white flag waved from the door of the McSween house. He turned to a scowling Jimmy Dolan.

"Looks like they mean to surrender," Dudley said.

"I'd be surprised."

Someone called across the street. "Colonel Dudley, may we talk?"

"Don't give the bastards nothin'."

"Let's see what they have to say, Sheriff. There are lives at stake here." He stepped out to the middle of the street. "Who am I speaking with?"

"Alexander McSween."

"What's on you mind, Mr. McSween?"

"Why is the army engaged in an assault on private citizens,

protecting their property?"

"We've been ordered to support Sheriff Peppin in putting down a civil disturbance."

"Sheriff Peppin does not represent Lincoln County. He's taken the side of the Dolan faction in this matter. If the army has a part in this, it should be to declare martial law and treat both sides accordingly until a court settles the dispute."

The man had a point. Martial law might actually avoid bloodshed just as Ledger had suggested. Then again, he had his orders. "That's not how the governor sees it."

"Governor Axtell is no better than Jimmy Dolan himself."

Dudley considered the argument. Part of him suspected McSween might be telling the truth. He didn't like the position in which he found himself, soldiers often didn't. In this case, he didn't give orders, he took them.

"You may hold that opinion if you wish, Mr. McSween, but the governor has the authority to call out the army. He has done so. I have my orders and you would be best advised to surrender peacefully."

"Your presence here and the governor's actions are a perversion of justice."

"If that is your final position, Mr. McSween, we have nothing further to discuss."

"There is one more thing, Colonel. My wife is here. Will you grant her safe passage before . . ." He paused to chose his words with care. "Before any further action is taken?"

"You may send her out, sir. I will personally escort her to safety."

"Thank you, Colonel."

Susan McSween stepped onto the porch carrying a small valise. She crossed the street to Dudley and met his eye level. "Colonel, please, can't you see this assault on my home is illegal and unjust."

"Ma'am, I can't speak for justice. That is for a court to decide. I can tell you the actions taken against your husband and his men are lawfully authorized. I have my orders. If you have any influence in the matter, I suggest you advise he and his men to lay down their arms."

"I have already made that plea. I'm sure you have your orders, but you still have the opportunity to prevent further violence and bloodshed."

"I know it may seem so, but whatever happens here is up to your husband."

She marched through the ranks of the troops, back erect, eyes straight ahead.

Dolan watched her go. "That was very humanitarian of you, Colonel."

"She and her husband seem to think you have an undue amount of influence with the governor."

"The allegation is little more than the deranged raving of unstable people who threaten the public safety."

"Is it? Governor Axtell chose to ignore Marshal Ledger's request for imposition of martial law. His request was an honorable one. It might have averted this entire incident. Instead we are called in to take your side in this dispute or rather should I say Sheriff Peppin's. I wonder who made that request of the governor."

Dolan smiled. "Now, Sheriff, how do you plan to bring this matter to a conclusion?"

Peppin scratched his chin. "Same as the store I reckon. Give 'em a chance to surrender and then have the colonel here punch a hole in the place with his gun there."

Dudley was stuck with his orders. Underneath, he had doubts. "Give it a day, Sheriff. I think they're sweating in there. Sending the woman out was a sign. Time is on our side. Waiting grinds on a man. It gives him a chance to look for a way out."

Dolan scowled. "Let's get this over with, Sheriff. Get on with it."

"Colonel?"

"I won't fire that gun until I'm convinced there's no other way. As of now, I'm not convinced. Good day, gentlemen."

McSween closed himself in his office, wrestling with his private demons. How many men would die? Would he die? All the blood shed and lives lost for what, Tunstall's business empire, to avenge his death? Was the money worth it? He could easily pack up and leave. There were other towns, other places with other law practices. Places where the law stood for something. Dolan stood for corruption that reached all the way to the governor's office. It needed to be exposed before it could be rooted out. That was something worth doing. Was it worth dying for?

Susan made her way to Mrs. O'Hara's. Her carefully constructed composure dissolved into uncontrolled weeping at the sight of Lucy. Ty and Johnny left the parlor to the women.

The day wore on. Sweat dampened a man's shirt in the day's heat. Up the street the guns remained silent. Roth sat at the kitchen table. Ty paced.

"I can't stand it, Johnny. I got to find out what's goin' on up there."

"My gut says stay away. No good can come of messin' in that business."

"I gotta know."

"I'll go along against my better judgment if you promise you won't try any one-man heroics."

Walking up the street toward the massed troops, Roth spotted Dudley sitting on the porch at the Wilson jacal. He relaxed a little. "Look there. The colonel's takin' his leisure. Don't look like a showdown's comin' anytime soon."

"Com'on, Nate will tell us what's goin' on." They crunched up the walk.

"Ty, Johnny." He looked around the porch for another chair. "I guess you'll have to pull up a step. Have a seat."

They settled onto the porch step.

"What's goin' on, Nate?"

"We're giving McSween and his men time to sweat a little. Maybe they'll see reason. I hope so. They're in a damn tight spot. I talked to McSween this morning. He had the same idea as you, about declaring martial law. I think he'd have abided by that."

"Then why not do it?"

"I don't have the authority. Like it or not, Peppin has official jurisdiction. My orders are to support him."

"He dances to Dolan's tune."

"I see that. I expect it was Dolan who asked the governor to order us in here. Funny he took that request and not yours."

"Nothin' funny about it. The Santa Fe Ring, the House, they're all in cahoots."

"That's the feeling I get."

"Then, damn it, man, do something about it."

"I'm doing what I can. I told them I wouldn't fire on the house until I'm convinced there is no other way to resolve the dispute. I'm buying time. I hope McSween uses it to come to his senses and surrender."

"He'd be signin' his own death warrant without your protection."

"You're talking martial law again. I have other orders."

CHAPTER FORTY-ONE

July 19th

The day dawned hot and sunny. Dolan, Peppin and Evans gathered at the Slurigos' house. Dolan paced, plainly impatient.

"Dudley still bent on playing his waiting game?"

Peppin nodded.

"Bullshit. I've had enough. George, you tell that son of a bitch McSween they've got one last chance to lay down their guns and surrender."

"Dudley won't use the cannon."

"We've got guns. Use 'em."

Peppin bobbed his head obediently.

Evans edged closer. "If that don't get 'em, I got a way to flush 'em without Dudley's gun."

Dolan arched a brow in question.

"Wait until dark and burn 'em out."

Dolan nodded.

"McSween!" Peppin shouted across the street. "You and your men are under arrest for the murder of Sheriff William Brady and others."

"We got warrants for John Tunstall's killers."

"I don't care what you think you got, throw down your guns and come out with your hands up."

No answer.

"Suit yourself."

Tom O'Folliard crouched beside the front window. "Now, what're they doin'?"

The Kid peeked through a crack in the door. "Looks like they got some kind of flag, a black flag. What's that about."

"No quarter," McSween said. "They aim to kill us all."

The Slurigos' house exploded in muzzle flashes and powder smoke. A volley of lead lashed the house shattering windows, chewing the walls and biting wood splinters in window frames, doors and furnishings. The Kid fired through the partially open door.

"They need better aim than that."

O'Folliard broke out the lower glass pane at his window with his gun barrel. "So far it's just the Dolan men shootin'. The army ain't joined in."

French levered the action of his Winchester, pouring return fire into the powder smoke.

"Damn it!" Dudley cursed the first volley. He thought he had Peppin under control. Now he'd have to do something, but what? He dashed off the jacal porch and double-timed for his troops. From what he could tell the fight was between the McSween and Dolan men. Maybe that's the way it should be. As he reached the center of his line near the howitzer placement, he heard Peppin call from the Slurigos' house.

"You may fire when ready, Colonel!"

The gunnery officer snapped to attention. "Prepared to fire, sir."

Dudley thought a moment. "At ease, Lieutenant, await my order. Captain Purington, prepare to fire in volley."

"Prepare to fire!"

The front rank knelt, rifles shouldered and cocked.

"Fire when ready."

"Fire!"

The rank erupted in a deafening charge and blue smoke. A sheet of bullets ripped the house. Men dove to the floor to get under the deadly rain whining through the room. The second rank stepped forward in line. A second cloud exploded before the first cleared away. The relentless pounding continued for thirty minutes before the shooting fell silent.

"Had enough, McSween?"

McSween never moved from the back corner of the office where he sat crouched in a ball.

"Peppin, it's Billy Bonney. Careful that dog don't pee on your shoe, old man."

The Dolan men poured another ten minutes of sustained fire into the house.

The afternoon dragged into a flaming sunset. The walls of the McSween house were riddled with bullet holes. Broken glass littered the floor. Shards of china and porcelain lay where each shattered piece had fallen. Bullets scarred and splintered finely crafted furniture and polished wood finishes. The remnants of a once-genteel life laid waste in the onslaught of all-out war.

McSween stirred in the corner. He looked around as though waking from a bad dream.

"It will be dark soon. Is there a whole lamp left to be found?"

"No light," the Kid said. "Light a lamp and them boys over there have a target."

"What do we do about food?"

"Jim, see what you can find in the kitchen before it gets dark."

The big man moved away from his post and disappeared in the shadows.

Evans and Bob Olinger circled the back of the store. Evans showed himself to the guards. A whispered exchange passed them on. Olinger carried a heavy can of coal oil. They paused in the shadows to watch and listen. The house was dark with no sign of a guard. Evans drew his gun, motioning Olinger to stay under cover. He stepped into the starlit yard. Nothing moved. Could they have left the back door unguarded? He approached the back porch. Nothing. He waved Olinger out of the shadows to the side of the porch. From there they could pour without risking the sound of climbing the stair.

Black liquid, silvered in starlight, spilled under the door. The slosh of the can sounded like a roaring rapids in the stillness. It raised no alarm. Olinger emptied the can. Inside, the black flood soaked the plank floor. He stepped back. Now it seemed the only thing that might give them away was the smell. Evans snapped a lucifer. He tossed it onto the spillway. They ran as an orange carpet of flame spread across the kitchen floor.

Jose Chavez smelled it first from the window closest to the kitchen. Then he saw it.

"Fire!" He ran to the kitchen. Flame pooled across the floor, slowly climbing the walls and blocking the door. He fell back from the heat. French bounded up behind him, silhouetted in the firelight. A shot rang out. The big man cursed, grabbed his arm and dove out of sight.

Chavez crawled to his side. "How bad is it, Jim?"

"No more'n a scratch. Do somethin' about that fire."

Billy and Big Jim grabbed the blankets they'd slept on and beat their way across the floor to the kitchen pump. Jim pumped furiously as the Kid doused the floor and door frame with buckets of water. As they worked, flames crept up the walls, climbing relentlessly toward the floor above. Billy set down the bucket to the realization, time would run out. Roasted or bullet-riddled, either way it made for poor choices.

Time passed. Heat and smoke grew in intensity. Flames lapped the floor above. It spread across the second floor, shedding a thin sheet of smoke through the ceiling to the rooms below. From the floorboards on the second floor, it was a short climb to the bare roof timbers above. Embers fell like heavy rain. Fire burned through the ceiling in McSween's office. A rafter crashed to the floor in a shower of sparks.

McSween sat balled in a corner hiding behind his knees. Salazar and Chavez waited white-eyed at their windows. French and O'Folliard turned to the Kid, their faces red masks in the glow of firelight.

"What are we gonna do, Billy?" Big Jim asked.

"How the hell should I know?" *Why the hell should I know?* Somebody had to. Another timber crashed through the floor above. It was up to him. "Mr. McSween, me, Tom, Big Jim and Jose are gonna make a break for the corral. Eugenio will stay with you. Soon as we draw fire, you sneak out the back. Get down to the river. If we get through, we'll find you. If'n we don't, find your way out of town."

McSween stared vacantly. Salazar nodded. He understood.

"OK, boys, let's don't waste no more time. That roof's gonna come down any minute." He led the way through the smoky kitchen to the smoldering back door. The starlit yard looked quiet. Quiet didn't start fires. He drew his gun. "They're out there sure as hell."

The boys drew their guns. They broke from the back of the house, dark figures silhouetted in firelight ran for the corral beyond the store. Dolan men fired from the shadows. Muzzle flashes and powder smoke targets bloomed in the night. Billy and the boys fired on the run. They reached the corral. "I'll hold 'em, boys. Get them horses saddled."

Another timber crashed into the parlor behind them. Flames licked at the front door, cutting off any escape there. "Mr. Mc-Sween, we must go." Salazar pulled his patron toward the kitchen by the arm. The sound of gunfire in the darkness outside roused him. McSween straightened up, strangely alert and led the way to the door.

"We're coming out!"

One of the Dolan men, young Bob Beckwith, stepped out of the shadows, thinking McSween had decided to surrender. "Come out with your hands up."

McSween led Salazar into the yard.

"With your hands up," Beckwith said.

"Surrender? Never!"

Shots erupted in the darkness behind the store and from behind the tree line at the back of the house. McSween's body jerked, hit by one bullet after another. Beckwith died in the crossfire. Salazar fell with multiple wounds.

Ledger and Roth ran out to Mrs. O'Hara's porch at the sound of gunshots. The McSween house gave the night sky an unmistakable orange glow.

"I've got a bad feelin' about this," Ty said.

Lucy and a shaken Susan McSween followed them to the door.

"What happened?" Lucy asked.

"Best you two stay here. Me and Johnny will have a look."

Evans crossed the street to the Slurigos' house. Dolan and Peppin waited on the porch.

"It's over. Some of 'em got away, but McSween's dead. That should be the end of it."

317

"Tell the boys I'm in the cantina," Dolan said. "The drinks are on me."

Men silhouetted in harsh orange firelight drifted toward the cantina and the growing sound of a raucous celebration. The door to the Tunstall store stood open. Men inside took what they wanted. Roth stopped a man with a whiskey bottle on his way to the store.

"What's goin' on?"

"McSween's dead. The others run off."

"I was afraid of that," Ty said. "We'll have to tell Susan."

Across the street from the store, Dudley's troops withdrew from their line to a campsite south of town. Ty found the colonel in the yard of the Wilson jacal. Dudley read Ledger's disappointment.

"Sorry for the way things turned out, Ty."

"Sorry. Sorry don't make it right. They were wrong on both sides. You could see that as plain as me. Why didn't you stop it?"

"I did what I could to prevent it. In the end, I had my orders."

"Your orders were wrong."

"Soldiers don't make that decision."

Ty clenched his jaw, seeing Dudley as if for the first time. "Soldiers don't make that decision. Men do." He turned on his heel and started back to Mrs. O'Hara's and another widow.

CHAPTER FORTY-TWO

July 20th

The Kid rode north with French, O'Folliard and Chavez. They had no way to know the fate of McSween and the others, but the shooting behind them said the escape had not come to a peaceful end. Likely they'd lost the battle to Dolan and the army.

The Kid called a halt in the gray light of dawn near a slow running creek. The horses needed water and rest. He had a hunch and made no attempt to conceal their presence.

"You think they'll come after us?" O'Folliard asked.

"They might."

"Maybe we ought to hide out for a spell."

"Yeah, but not yet."

French eyed their back trail. "So what are we gonna do, Billy?"

"Rest the horses and ride upstream."

The sun passed overhead early in its afternoon decent. The creek bed crawled along, climbing a narrow draw. The Kid let the roan pick his way through the rocks trailed by men dozing in their saddles. His eyes flicked back and forth across the rock walls beneath the wide brim of his sombrero. He watched and waited, wondering how far they had to go.

"Hold it right there and nobody move." The command had a hard steel edge. Men snapped awake, reaching for their guns and belatedly thinking better of it.

"Cut the shit, Doc. It's me, Billy."

Scurlock showed himself in the rocks above. "I thought you was, but I couldn't be sure." Middleton, Bowdre, Brown and Coe hid in the rocks on both sides of the draw.

"Where we camped?"

"There's a blind turn up yonder. We're camped in some caves just beyond. We'll meet you there pretty quick. John, you and George keep an eye on their back trail. The Kid here probably left enough trouble behind him to turn out one hell of a posse."

Billy smiled that crooked smile of his and rode on. A half mile up the draw the creek disappeared in a blind curve. Around the curve it opened onto sandy banks. A grassy bottom climbed a gentle slope to the west dotted with willow and white oak. Horses were picketed there with graze and water. Across the stream two caves gouged the east wall of the draw. The larger one sheltered the campsite. Billy stepped down on the creek bank.

"Home sweet home. Com'on, boys, pull down your gear and picket the horses."

Sitting around the campfire that night at the mouth of the cave, Billy recounted the burning of the McSween house and their escape for Doc and his men.

"What happened to McSween?" Doc asked.

The Kid shrugged. "We heard shots. If it came to gunplay, who knows what happened. One thing's sure, Dolan won the fight."

"We was licked when the army threw in with them."

Middleton turned to Doc with the faces around the fire. "So what do we do now?"

"I expect it's over. McSween's dead or ruined. I don't see Chisum fightin' the army. Hell, I don't fancy facing cannon again, either. The pay ain't that good. I'm ridin' out in the morning before Dolan and his boys decide to come after us."

Middleton, Coe and Brown nodded agreement.

"What about you, Jim?"

"I been lookin' after Mrs. McSween for some time now. I reckon she still needs lookin' after, at least for a spell."

"You're crazy if you go back to Lincoln," Doc said.

"Maybe so. Then again, if the war's over, why should anyone care?"

"What about you three?" He looked from O'Folliard to Bowdre to Bonney.

The Kid shrugged. "We'll figure somethin' out." The other two nodded.

A sad departure and hopeful beginning made for a bittersweet ride down to South Spring. They stayed in Lincoln long enough to see Susan through her husband's funeral. Lucy's departure made room for her at Mrs. O'Hara's while she decided her future.

Ty fought the feeling he'd failed to prevent the disaster in Lincoln. Lucy and Roth wouldn't allow his misery. She was on her way to a new life with the man she loved. Roth had newfound confidence the cattle business would bring them success. South Spring didn't feel like home, but it would.

EPILOGUE

Las Vegas, New Mexico
Christmas Eve, 2011
Rick gently closed Lucy's journal, careful of the cracking yellowed pages. The war ended. Great-great-grandpa Ty and Great-great-grandma Lucy found each other amid the violence, bloodshed, politics and greed historians call the Lincoln County War. At least that made for something of a happy ending. Of course, that wasn't the end of the story. The war launched the outlaw career of young William Bonney otherwise known as Billy the Kid. In a way, that brought the saga full circle for Rick. For him, it all started with Great-great-grandpa Ty's account of the Kid's death. In an odd historical twist Ty and Lucy's stories followed from that. But such is often the discovery of history. One chapter leads to another without necessarily falling in chronological order. In the end, his great-great-grandparents' legacy was one of high adventure, courage and love a great-great-grandson could take pride in. Rick smiled and switched off the desk lamp.

AUTHOR'S NOTE

The Lincoln County War is an enormously complex story. The business dealings, disputes and political maneuverings among the principals are enough to leave an MBA, a lawyer and a CPA all scratching their heads. The author has taken creative license in simplifying these aspects of the story while adhering to the basic events and motivations of the characters. The story is further complicated by the number of individuals and factions who became involved over the course of the hostilities. At the height of the conflict the McSween and Dolan factions swelled to significant numbers of supporters on both sides. The author has chosen to limit the number of characters presented to the most notable. Researching historical events invariably uncovers inconsistencies. By various accounts, for example, the cousins George and Frank Coe may have (1.) been confused for one another by some narratives; (2.) changed sides during the conflict; or (3.) fought on opposite sides. For purposes of this story the author has chosen the third interpretation. Where there is any conflict between historical fact and the author's interpretation, it is the author's intent to present a fictional account for the enjoyment of the reader.

ABOUT THE AUTHOR

Paul Colt's critically acclaimed historical fiction crackles with authenticity. His analytical insight, investigative research and genuine horse sense bring history to life. His characters walk off the pages of history into the reader's imagination in a style that blends Jeff Shaara's historical dramatizations with Robert B. Parker's gritty dialogue.

Paul's first book, *Grasshoppers in Summer,* received Finalist recognition in the Western Writers of America 2009 Spur Awards. *Boots and Saddles: A Call to Glory* received the Marilyn Brown Novel Award, presented by Utah Valley University.

To learn more visit Facebook @paulcoltauthor.